WHIR OF GOLD
Sinclair Ross

Whir *of* Gold

*Sinclair
Ross*

THE UNIVERSITY OF ALBERTA PRESS

This edition published by
The University of Alberta Press
Ring House 2
Edmonton, Alberta T6G 2E1

Printed in Canada 5 4 3 2 1
This edition copyright © The University of Alberta Press 2001
Text copyright © Sinclair Ross 1970, 2001
Introduction copyright © Nat Hardy 2001
A volume in (cuRRents), a Canadian literature series. Jonathan Hart,
series editor.

NATIONAL LIBRARY OF CANADA
CATALOGUING IN PUBLICATION DATA

Ross, Sinclair, 1908–
    Whir of gold
    ISBN 0–88864–355–1

    I. Title.
PS8535.O79W5 2001   C813'.54   C2001–910890–7
PR9199.3.R599W5 2001

Printed and bound in Canada by Kromar Printing Ltd., Winnipeg, Manitoba.
∞ Printed on acid-free paper.
Proofreading by Kate Hole.
The Press acknowledges the assistance of John O'Connor in the preparation
of this edition.

The University of Alberta Press gratefully acknowledges the support
received for its program from the Canada Council for the Arts. The Press
also acknowledges the financial support of the Government of Canada
through the Book Publishing Industry Development Program for its
publishing activities.

INTRODUCTION

Nat Hardy

SINCLAIR ROSS'S *Whir of Gold* is an engaging, carefully crafted novel of alienation and survival—the dark tale of an out-of-work jazz musician who migrates to the big city in search of fame and fortune. It is, as Ross writes, "the story of a raw youth from the prairie practising his clarinet among the cows and the chickens and then going wrong in the city." Through Ross's embittered narrator, Sonny McAlpine, we are offered a brutally honest portrayal of a down-and-out, self-hating musician struggling to pursue his lofty ambitions. In his quest for notoriety and affluence, Sonny abandons the Presbyterian dustbowl of Saskatchewan for the bacchanalian indulgences of Montreal. Sonny's distracted internal monologue, narrated by a bitter, jaded man suffering from anxiety, depression, and rejection, offers a musical montage of passion and betrayal. To use Ross's phrase, it's "Jazz and blues in exchange for the other."

Told in an apprehensive voice that vacillates between past and present, urban and rural, Sonny's first-person narrative offers an augury of innocence (in rural Saskatchewan) and an augury of experience (in urban Montreal) that is structurally similar to Blake's *Songs of Innocence and Experience*. For Sonny, the prairie past represents a golden age, a safe mental haven from the troubling present in Montreal. As a cipher of his own past, Sonny is haunted by his childhood. Although of Scots-Presbyterian stock, the McAlpine clan is not the run-of-the-mill Saskatchewan farm family. While his parents and siblings work hard on the farm, Sonny practises the piano and rides his horse Isabel. In his salad days, young Sonny was not only musical but a kind of horsewhisperer to an almost mythic horse who had, as rumour has it, killed men. Undaunted, Sonny bonds with the beast; against his parents' will, he enters a race with the horse and wins. This triumph is vital to his development, as the earnings go towards his flourishing musical education.

As Sonny attempts to block out his ongoing failings in Montreal, Isabel provides a summoning catalyst for Sonny's early successes. Of all of Sonny's reminiscent imaginings, therefore, the horse figures most prominently:

> Back on the prairie, riding Isabel and out for hawks and rabbits with my .22, I had been so sure where I was going, what I would find .... And now a room on Ste Famille Street. If you could only wipe the glass and see: blob-faced foetus of a dream run out before its time that never had a chance, or the first gasp for breath, the pain and choke and rawness of beginning.

With success in the distant past, however, Sonny has no horse or any sense of victory in the city; he has only the memory and direction he once had, and lives the dreaded "blob-faced foetus of a dream run out before its time."

While his fond and rebellious memories take him back to his youth, the euphoria is temporary: life in the city rudely wakens him to the present. Other characters from the past also haunt and help Sonny persevere in the face of adversity. Sonny recalls the memory of his mother, who ensures that her farmer son is classically trained on the piano; of her Sonny says, "instead of putting her into her coffin, they had her buried inside me." Sonny's music teacher, Dorothy Whittle, figures prominently as well, as it is Dorothy who assures Sonny that he "can do the impossible" and become a professional musician. Memories aside, however, Sonny's bad luck in the city and lack of self-confidence force him into self-doubt: "Whose life was I living anyway? All the way from Saskatchewan to make the big-time—no puffed up frog in a little Main Street puddle for Sonny—and still hitched to a horse-and-buggy mind."

Through his desperate retrievals of the past Sonny becomes further estranged from his acquaintances and his new environment, an alienation that rapidly advances his spiral into further misadventure and failure. In juxtaposing his glorious past with his grim present, Sonny's own "fearful symmetry" reinforces his hopelessness. The cold, bleak winter in Montreal pressures Sonny to rethink and ultimately reject the possibility of success.

Ross resurrects Sonny McAlpine from an earlier story, "The Outlaw," in a fashion similar to William Faulkner's characters from Yoknapatawpha County or Margaret Laurence's characters from Manawaka. In *Whir of Gold*, however, the former prairie *enfant terrible*, the rebel child with the spirited horse and pronounced talent for music, is all grown up. As he searches for work in Montreal, it is clear that Sonny has outgrown not only his breeches but his tolerance for the farm and being "Scotch-Presbyterian stock." Indeed, by the time Sonny reaches Quebec, he has faced a wealth of adversity from both city and the country. No stranger to alienation, Sonny fashions himself a bastard prodigal son of jazz, reared "in a community of practical, callous-handed farmers" who are more interested in threshing machines than jazz clarinets—Sonny's father and siblings included. Sonny has no option but to head to Canada's own Big Easy, Montreal. But as Sonny soon discovers, while there might be gold and glory in the hills of Mount Royal, down in the gutters of Ste Famille Street there is little more than pyrite and broken dreams. Sonny learns rapidly and painfully that opportunity and success are fleeting or, to use Ross's metaphor, simply "whirring," utterly illusive.

Whir of Gold records the tragic descent of a paradoxical protagonist whose character wavers between frontier maverick and willing victim, serious musician and frustrated slacker, kept man and criminal. Self-pitying without the saccharine melancholy one might expect, Sonny reluctantly resigns himself to what seems his unjust lot. Indeed, as the novel opens, Sonny is deep within the winter of his discontent: he's broke and in poor health, and his clarinet is in hock. Sonny fills his days with sleeping, doing odd apartment jobs, serenading his landlady with hymns for free rent, and even playing the odd funeral—not gigs to interest any serious musician. Saddled with a worthless agent and a series of disinterested club-owners who want saxophone players, not clarinetists, Sonny is pushed to his limits and continually threatens to return to Saskatchewan, frustrated by his own failings. He lacks the necessary determination and direction to prevail in his unwelcoming new environment. The notoriety he once enjoyed in Saskatchewan is absent in Montreal; as an unknown and undiscovered talent, Sonny complains, "Sagging and souring, homeless, bruised—I wanted to go back to being a big frog in my little puddle again, to be known, needed, talked about." The longing for the prairie past, which offers emotional stability (albeit temporary) and a much-needed sense of self-worth, resonates throughout the novel.

With his defeatism continually fuelled by rejection, Sonny's growing pessimism soon dampens any sense of hope. Sonny becomes an archetypal artist over a few months, alienated and struggling to survive in an unforgiving bohemian city. Impermanence and fatalism are the wellsprings of his angst as he moves from rural musician to tortured soul. A cynic of the first order, Sonny becomes the prophet of his own doom. Bemoaning the bleakness of his situation, Sonny reflects, "Just shovel snow and keep things clean up here, my future was assured." His barbed sarcasm and disparaging tone are indicative of the ennui that is his life.

Although *Whir of Gold* is very much Sonny's story, the tale concerns a motley trio of outsiders. Sonny, his live-in girlfriend Mad, and his shady friend Charlie are all bona fide *étrangers*, to use Camus' infamous term, uniquely foreign to Montreal. Sonny is a musical "lunk from Saskatchewan"; Mad, former stripper and star of *Watch Sheila Shake*, hails from Nova Scotia; and Charlie is an enigma, whose origins are ambivalent (we know only that he is a petty criminal of sorts, a racketeer, peddler, or pimp). The combination of the will to survive and the temptations of the metropolitan milieu corrupts these rural intruders enough to forsake most, if not all, of their rustic pretensions. As each character negotiates the cultural rifts between rural and urban, Anglophone and Francophone, vice and virtue, such divisions not only unify the three outsiders but are the forces that inevitably tear the trio apart.

Music is an integral element of the novel. As George Bernard Shaw writes in *Man and Superman*, "Music is the brandy of the damned." Music is Sonny's vice: addictive and consuming, it is his most indulgent passion. Indeed, music is, as Sonny says, part of "the major-minor diatonic forthrightness" of the story. At times, Sonny's narrative even resonates with a Beat cadence, a melodic jazz phrasing with a melancholic lyricism. While Sonny is the trained musician of the novel, Mad too has a sonorous air about her, as Sonny affirms:

> she kept repeating the names in a bouncy, sing-song voice, fitting them experimentally to the rhythm of our step. "Sonny and Mad—sort of like they were *meant* to go together. Sure, crazy names and big crazy me! Sonny and Mad, Sonny and Mad—"

In spite of Mad's be-bopping merriment at the beginning of the novel, however, Sonny's despondency obliterates any possibility of romantic optimism. In counterpoint to Mad's naïveté, Sonny's demeanour overwhelms the narrative with his own poignant lament—Sonny's ballad of regret. Despite the musical will to jazz, this book is dominated by the blues. Measure for measure, *Whir of Gold* can also, in musical terms, be considered an elegy, in that it laments a career never launched.

As the harmony of ambition descends into a plaintive drone in Montreal, the trauma of failure takes a physical and emotional toll on Sonny. Despite his hard-nosed exterior, Sonny is a frail character who is sick throughout the novel, largely owing to his mental state, his insufficient diet, and the squalor of the run-down boarding house. Depression, anxiety, and ultimately the women in Sonny's life worsen his deteriorating physical health. Although Sonny has outgrown Saskatchewan, he has not outgrown his dependence on women: as he did in his youth, the mature Sonny requires their nurturing presence. Sonny depends on women for help—on his landlady, Mrs. Painter, for free rent; on his lover, Mad, for money, sex, and goodwill—which further damages his sense of self-worth.

Because he cannot find a job, Sonny is unable to feed and clothe himself in the urban world, and this inability to be self-reliant proves unbearable. The women in his life, as Charlie insinuates, have reduced Sonny to a weak and dependent shell of a man. Female patronage exacts a high emotional price: Sonny perceives women's kindness as threatening, indeed castrating. As Ross's portrait of the artist as a jaded young man, Sonny McAlpine's story also narrates a tale of figurative emasculation at the hands of women. Haunted by his Presbyterian upbringing and his keen sense of frontier self-reliance, Sonny suffers the shame of being a kept man: "Living off a woman—it was the sound of it I didn't like." In the past, Sonny has solved his failed relationships and domestic problems with women by abandoning them. This destructive tradition continues as Sonny is convinced his is "a future in which [Mad] couldn't possibly be involved."

In keeping with its dark themes, the novel's romantic elements are dysfunctional and short-lived. The fatalistic, skid-row romance of Sonny and Mad is doomed from the onset. Both are broke when they meet in a bar, and they live together in domestic squalor—a grim reality that only adds to Sonny's growing depression. Mad inspires Sonny's "little throb of virility," but little more. Both are untethered; Sonny has thoughts of returning to Saskatchewan, and Mad is prepared to move to Toronto.

Mad is the novel's *ingénue*. Compassionate, generous, yet fatalistic, she recognizes that romance, too, is only temporarily "whirring" about, not lasting. Like Sonny, Mad has her own sense of romantic fatalism, as her own gloomy apothegm suggests: "When it's time it's time." In their short time together, Mad grasps for any fleeting affection she can wrest from Sonny. Sonny's narrative reveals his utter uninterest in Mad; the depth of Sonny's affection is explicitly carnal. During his first sexual encounter with Mad, for example, Sonny relives his adolescent "scratchy half-hour in the hay" with a fifteen-year-old girl. Although a redemptive temptress, Mad is not without her charms. She is, as Sonny confesses, "A big lump of a woman who would never grow up and never grow bad, not if she lived a hundred years, not if she slept with a hundred right ones."

After endearing herself to Sonny, Mad moves into his apartment. Although he resents her, Mad is Sonny's saving grace. This "harlot with a heart of gold" not only tries to get Sonny's clarinet out of the pawnshop but also tends him when he is sick and later wounded. Inevitably, however, this quixotic paramour is little more than Sonny's "bitch," a sentiment reinforced not only by Sonny but also by his disfigured landlady, Mrs. Painter, who considers Mad a "slut." At Charlie's prompting, Sonny comes to find Mad overprotective. As Sonny sees it, Mad is a woman whose "blazing protection [is] like a bitch when a stranger tries to touch her pups." Despite her "martyrlike endurance," Mad proves to be little more than "another piece of tail," and her virtue ultimately remains unrewarded as Sonny envisions her as both Madonna and, by the story's conclusion, abandoned whore.

Mad fears not Sonny's interactions with women but his relationship with Charlie, to the point of homophobia. Although Sonny is not represented as a gay character, certain episodes arguably contain a tempered homosocial subtext, fuelled by Sonny's failed relationships with women and what Charlie refers to as Sonny's effeminate and submissive nature. Charlie, of course, is also the character who describes his own brother in phallic dimensions as "over six feet and prick to the skull."

Charlie, described by Sonny as "to the pinball-manner-born," is without question the novel's most liminal character. Indeed, both Mad and Sonny are intimidated by the untold mysteries of Charlie's bold persona. Like Sonny, Charlie is something of a paradox: a man who lives high yet shares the same run-down boarding house. In an attempt to break away from his threatening patronesses, Sonny eventually succumbs to Charlie's offers. As Charlie "rub[s] [Sonny's] subconscious nose in the rancid smell of failure," he shames Sonny into a jewellery heist.

Although there are many instances in the narrative that reveal the daunting power of Charlie's character, the moment when Sonny describes Charlie's face relates the depths of Sonny's anxieties: "Something about the eyes—the queer cold way they had of coming forward in their sockets, the flat stare ... he had them fixed on me as a snake fixes on its prey." The combination of "queer," "snake," and "prey" quite deliberately fashions Charlie into something of a homoerotic beast, a phallic hunter who has Sonny in his cross-hairs. Considering Sonny's final rejection of Mad and the odd homosocial tensions between the two men (particularly in the bar scene in which Charlie lashes Sonny with a whirling chain, "like an extension of his finger, tongue or sting"), the masochism is more blatant than latent. Indeed, some thirty years after the book was first published, there may be, as Keath Fraser's *As For Me and My Body* suggests, a need for a "reconsideration of Ross's work in light of his homosexuality and personal sexual history." Marilyn Rose agrees, suggesting that Ross's work "invites revisionary thinking, particularly in light of the now-public knowledge of Ross's homosexuality." The veiled homosexual references in Ross's fiction solicit new possibilities of interpretive strategies, queer or otherwise. Yet despite the queer edge to Sonny and Charlie's characters, the homoeroticism remains ambiguous.

Ambiguous or not, the sexual subtext of the exchange between the two men as they prepare for the robbery in the second half of the novel is unquestionably loaded:

[Charlie] "And there'll be a place for you, too. God knows why—just because I'm so goddammed soft and you're so goddammed helpless. Or maybe instinct."
[Sonny] You mean you've smelled me out?"
[Charlie] "Could be—like the queers say it takes one to know one."

Perhaps Mad's homophobia is understandable when she is threatened by Charlie's increasing influence over Sonny. For Mad, part of Charlie's mystery is his sexuality. And, as Sonny understands, Charlie's inclusive reference to "queers" is analogous to their own venture: they are partners in crime. This sexually charged exchange is highly symbolic as it both cements their bond and provides the trust necessary for robbery.

Although he apparently brings women to his room, Mad senses in Charlie a homosexual streak. "You don't mean," asks Mad, "he's one of those fellows that don't like girls?" To force her point, an anxious Mad warns Sonny about the perils of homosexuality in the city of sin:

Oh, Sonny—don't you *ever.* If you knew some of the things that go on in this town—back home they'd string you up for even thinking about them ... But even so— maybe if you were hungry and liquored up a little. That's the way they work, you know, taking advantage. You and that tooter of yours, wanting a job and no luck. Clubs and places like that are just full of them.

As Mad intimates, for these displaced outsiders Montreal seems somewhat of a Sodom-on-the-St. Lawrence where anything goes. What was explicitly taboo in the country is more culturally acceptable in the city. Mad fears that as Charlie tempts Sonny into a life of crime, Sonny can easily fall into a life of homosexuality. Naïve Sonny enters into a pact with Charlie and robs the jeweller. In a matter of tense minutes, however, Sonny is betrayed and departs not only empty-handed but with a hot bullet inside of him.

Sonny and Charlie prove misfit criminals. Sonny escapes from the scene in a snowstorm, bleeding and on the run from the police. The narrative scenes of Sonny's paranoid escape are intensely visceral and captivating: "I staggered, clutched a lamp standard; then for a long time stood watching the blood creep out from my shoe and eat its way into the snow." Not only do Sonny's footprints leave a revealing track in the snow, but the telltale blood provides an indisputable trail of evidence. As a weak and terrified Sonny finally returns home to "lie low," he embarks on a truly precarious recovery.

The flesh wound develops into a lethal infection. With no earnings from the heist, Sonny is once again defeated, once again sick, and once again dependent on the help of nurse Mad and a good-natured physician. Part journey, part rite of passage, Sonny completes a pivotal cycle in Montreal. From dependence to a brief, failed independence, back to dependence, Sonny remains raconteur of his own futility. In the end, the hopeless defeatist is resigned to his fate. Thus with Charlie and Mad finally out of his miserable life, we imagine Sonny—like Sisyphus—absurdly happy.

SINCLAIR ROSS PRODUCED FOUR NOVELS—*As For Me and My House* (1941), *The Well* (1958), *Whir of Gold* (1970), and *Sawbones Memorial* (1974)—in addition to eighteen short stories, collected in *The Lamp at Noon and Other Short Stories* (1968). Ross's *oeuvre*, with all of its human anguish and suffering, has a profound edge. As Margaret Laurence observed in a letter to Adele Wiseman, Ross's stories "reveal a prairie ethic that is positively frightening—the man has to prove absolutely strong in his own eyes; the woman has to endure all, silently. Impossible standards, and so people break down." For all the beauty of the physical landscape, the prairie culture is sublime. But, as Sonny discovers, the city is no less so.

In many ways, Ross's writings form a prototype for modern Canadian prairie fiction. As Robert Kroetsch mentions in his Afterword to *As For Me and My House*, it is possible that Ross's character Mrs. Bentley "writes the beginning of contemporary Canadian fiction." Transcending the literary achievements made by R.J.C. Stead's *Grain* (1925), Martha Ostenso's *Wild Geese* (1925), and Frederick Philip Grove's *Settlers of the Marsh* (1925), Ross moves beyond the hardships of the pioneers and focusses his attention on the social, sexual, and emotional implications of the Dirty Thirties. Unlike many of his forebears, Ross took the liberty of placing his rural characters in urban environments during a particularly uninviting time. As his body of fiction continues to testify, Ross captured the West—its people, idiom, and manifold struggles—offering a bleak if poignant impression of the rural life. Intimately familiar with rural Saskatchewan and the scope of the prairie experience, Ross also wrote compellingly out of his lived experience in the city, particularly Montreal.

Although he spent part of his childhood in Indian Head, Saskatchewan (where a literary shrine dedicated to Ross now stands), Ross worked as a bank clerk in a variety of small Saskatchewan towns before he was transferred to Winnipeg in 1933. After a four-year stint in England, serving with the Canadian Army during World War Two, Ross was transferred to Montreal in 1946 where he worked until he retired in 1968. Not a particularly prolific writer, Ross supplemented his writing career with a day job—the economic reality of many Canadian writers. Like contemporary Canadian poet Al Purdy, who also had no university training, Ross was a self-taught, well-read writer. Also like Purdy, Ross shared an attraction to the past and carefully crafted his vision of the Canadian experience in tight, engaging fiction. As *Whir of Gold* affirms, Ross was a patient craftsman who was meticulous with his spare and lucid prose. Banker by day and novelist by night, Ross forged *Whir of Gold* over some twenty years—indeed, the novel was not completed until his retirement in Greece.

It is astonishing that Ross was shunned by the Canadian literary establishment, despite the fact that *As For Me and My House* is considered a Canadian classic. As David Stouck notes, Ross was never awarded a Canada Council grant, never won a Governor General's Award, was never made a Companion of the Order of Canada, and did not receive an honorary degree from a Canadian university. Whether owing to his inferior education (by the standards of the university-educated literary elite), his occupation, or possibly even his homosexuality (although apparently closeted), Ross's dismissal by the Canadian literary establishment remains a mystery. Despite his inability to impress the *literati* with his art, Ross wielded a sphere of influence over literary critics, other prairie writers, and readers. Indeed, it was *As For Me and My House*, as James King notes, that secured Margaret Laurence's "destiny as a writer": "I saw, reading it, that a writer could write out of a background similar to my own," wrote Laurence; "You didn't need to live in London or New York." When Laurence wrote the Introduction to *The Lamp at Noon and Other Stories* (1968), she reaffirmed the profound influence Ross had on herself and other prairie writers. Indeed, the next generation of prairie writers—including Robert Kroetsch, Guy Vanderhaeghe, and Lorna Crozier, among others—has sung the various praises of Ross as an influence on their work.

Like most writers who do not suffer from hubris, Ross was his own best critic. Upon reflection, he later described *Whir of Gold* as "a shaky novel with some fairly good things in it." A harsh, albeit somewhat redeeming self-criticism, it is in keeping with the high demands Ross typically placed on himself. Although many critics still consider the much-celebrated *As For Me and My House* Ross's magnum opus, *Whir of Gold* is a masterful *tour de force* on its own terms. If anything, it affirms Ross's status as a major figure in prairie fiction: he is a writer whose work demands both critical attention and reappraisal in this new century.

Whir of Gold provides a rich repository of prairie innocence and urban experience that reaches from Saskatchewan to Quebec. As Laurence wrote three years prior to the novel's original release, "... within the era and the idiom, [Ross] has portrayed an entire people, their spiritual goals, their vulnerabilities. He really doesn't have to worry about whether he does anything more. He's done it."

Whir
of
Gold

I

"SONNY AND MAD—craziest names you ever heard of but they got a swing. Listen now—sort of go together. Sonny and Mad, Sonny and Mad—" As we walked back to my room on Ste Famille Street, she kept repeating the names in a bouncy, sing-song voice, fitting them experimentally to the rhythm of our step. "Sonny and Mad—sort of like they were *meant* to go together. Sure, crazy names and big crazy me! Sonny and Mad, Sonny and Mad—"

Sometimes I used to say why not? Why all the fight? At least till spring and I found a job. "Just *enjoy* it, Sonny. Stop worrying so much about things and let yourself go. Spring's coming—all kinds of jobs. Somebody like you—pretty soon they just got to wake up and realize how good you are."

She enjoyed it. Thirty-one, experienced, weathered in the street, and every time as if it was the first. As if I were performing miracles, conducting an experiment in rapture. Delight with a twitch of fear in it, steeling herself for what was coming next. "Talk about knowing a right one when I see him—oh Sonny, if ever I was a virgin I'm sure not going to be one now."

Why not? For the winter anyway—sit tight and practise, let her carry on. Get some meat on my bones, get my cough cleared up. Two or three months—by May the resorts would be opening up north in the Laurentians.

And she was asking for it. There had been no promises, no lies. I had spelled out exactly what she could expect. So take her at her word—relax, enjoy. Steaks and bed and plenty of time for the clarinet. Wake up, Saskatchewan! You've got it made.

There were even times when I wished my mother out of the way. Lie down and turn over, I'd say. Stop showing your hands.

She had been a help at first, an ally, the hands pointing the way I knew I ought to go. "Make something of yourself, Sonny. Don't go soft—don't come down to their level. All these years it's what I've lived and worked for."

The hands again, knuckly, creased, with jagged nails. "Just the thought that you'd be different, wouldn't end up like the rest of them—it's what's kept me going. Work hard and keep away from the drink. When the time comes, find a good girl and settle down. Promise me! I won't mind then— I'll go easy."

My father and my two elder brothers were "the rest of them." It was their waywardness that had shamed her, and their cloddish lives that mine, with its banner high for the things of mind and spirit, was to redeem.

My father was a tireless, wind-whipped, dour man, and for roughly three hundred and sixty days of the year a sober one. He went to town regularly, often two or three times a week, but only on special occasions—when the crops were in, when it was harvested; sometimes when there had been a row and a long spell of reproving silence—would he yield to his thirst, slip into the bootlegger's for an hour or two and come out singing.

That was the humiliation: not that he drank—who didn't?— but that he sang. Hymns—"There Is a Happy Land" and "He Leadeth Me"—in a deep, honking baritone as dry and gritty as Saskatchewan itself. Up and down a deserted and embarrassed little Main Street, from doorway to doorway as if he were seeking converts, meekly yielding to every right-about thrust—the garage, the grocery and hardware stores, the Chinese restaurant—then weaving on again, head back, full-throated, like a dog baying at the moon. *"There is a calm, a sure retreat, 'Tis found beneath the Mercy Seat"*—thus coupling besottedness with blasphemy.

Once there was even reference to it from the pulpit: "The sad spectacle recently witnessed in our streets which we can only hope will serve as a warning,"—that was *him*—"and the even sadder spectacle of the child drawn into the orbit of such depravity"—that was *me*, sent along to keep an eye on him.

There was someone, inevitably, who thought my mother ought to know what the minister had said, and when she heard she wept. A controlled, dry-eyed, often harsh woman, she stood erect for a moment, a white-knuckled hand at her throat, then carefully put on the kettle for a cup of tea. "That I should live to see the day! The man I loved and trusted—an example in the very House of God!" The voice as white as the knuckles. The silly words redeemed by two small awkward tears.

As to my brothers, Tom sired a bastard and then set things right by marrying the girl—only shamelessly she wore a white dress and veil which nothing, of course, could set right; and Allen sired another on a married woman and then went on happily playing horseshoes with her husband every Sunday afternoon. Everybody knew. Three times while the husband was in hospital with a broken shoulder he was seen slipping out of the house at six o'clock in the morning and, as final proof, there were the McAlpine eyes and nose. "*Grandmother* McAlpine—spitting image. Fancy horseshoes they were playing that summer!"

The horseshoes, the singing, and the veil—until sometimes, turning from the sight of the ruined hands, I would pace and mutter, "If you were only here to get an eyeful of your white-haired Sonny now!"

Contradiction: she was there. Like a fly in the ear, too deep for match or pin. As if, instead of putting her into her coffin, they had buried her inside me.

It was because of her, in fact, that I met Mad. Objecting to Charlie—Charlie and his offer of a dirty job—that was what finally drove me out.

I had two dollars, two bottles of beer, a loaf of bread, and some hamburger and I planned staying in. I had been asleep most of the afternoon. My clarinet was in hock and it was Saturday, and Saturday when you're broke and not going up town sleep's the best way to put in the time. When I woke up the street lights were on and it was snowing. The window was the kind that splits down the middle and opens in like doors, with a deep, cold sill that was good for keeping things like beer and butter, and out past the beer bottles I could see the big flakes spinning and tumbling through the branches of the tree and I lay still awhile, not thinking much, just watching the snow and wishing I had a handful because my throat was sore.

It was a big tree but my room was three flights up and the top branches came only a little higher than the window. A big, sturdy, very self-possessed tree; I often watched and listened to it. We were on good terms: a relationship. It was the only living thing in Montreal that winter I could under-stand and talk to, that knew about me. Sometimes, coming up the front steps, I would lean over and touch a branch; or stop a few seconds and stand rubbing face and hands against the bark. The same as at home when I had troubles to talk over I would slip into the stable and rub noses with Isabel.

Half an hour or so—remembering the rough clean feel of the bark on my skin and not minding too much about staying in. All planned: I would get up after a while and fry some of the hamburger and make coffee. Taking my time, so there wouldn't be too long to wait for the first bottle of beer. Which I would drink slowly, small sips, making it last till nine. An interval, maybe another cup of coffee—then the second bottle at about half-past ten. An hour and a half—taken thriftily it would last that long—and then Saturday night would be over. And Sunday you stay in and have a lazy day anyway; don't feel out of things, don't mind; and then Monday I would still have my two dollars and perhaps, if I went back to see the old man in the pawnshop, I could make a deal to swap the clar-inet for my watch.

All planned—vaguely pleased with myself for having so much character and will, for controlling the urge to go uptown and spend the two dollars in a bar—and then I heard Charlie come in.

He knocked; I lay still. A light knock, as if he thought I might be asleep and didn't want to wake me. Three times—then the sound of his own door opening and closing and the creak of the springs as he bounced onto the bed.

But he was there. Before the evening was over I would have to go to the bathroom two or three times, and if I didn't use the gas-ring in the hall I would have to eat my hamburger raw. He would hear me and come out. He would stand eyeing the hamburger a minute, then say why don't we go out and eat somewhere? Saturday night—a good meal and a couple of drinks—

All the while shaking his head incredulously, his pitying look, as if I were a half-wit who liked living in a slum and cooking on a gas-ring. It didn't matter that he lived in the same slum, his room next to mine and not even half the size. He had the edge on me, always got his licks in first. The kind of lick that never roused an impulse to retaliate, cut him down to size, but only to explain and justify. Licks that rubbed in Main Street and confirmed all my country fears.

He had a way of doing it: neat, the nerve every time. Assured, insolent, a slick, cocky air—to-the-pinball-manner-born; wise to the lowdown, wise to pretentious hicks like me. I could never slam the door. His opinion was important. Write him off as a small-time crook and a minute later I was fidgeting to present myself again. Hopeful that this time the light would be right, that I would find the right words.

Besides, complicating things, there was the concern. The exasperation was always big-brotherly. "Brighten up, for Christ's sake, and listen. It's for your own good. Somebody's got to tell you." Hard not to believe it was genuine.

"Get it down now when it's hot and suck a couple of these things and then if you don't shut up and go to sleep I'll ram this goddam pillow down your throat."

It was our introduction, two or three nights after he moved in. My cough had been keeping him awake and he had gone first to the drug store—something to sniff, some kind of candy for my throat—then down to the basement to ask Mrs. Painter to make me a hot drink of rye and lemon. "Other people want to sleep even if you don't. Everything comes through—the wall's like paper."

Just a front, though; not nearly so tough as he liked to let on. From the sticks, as he never missed a chance to remind me, but I could see through that one. Which meant, probably, that the licks weren't quite what they sounded either. In any case, that was the way I liked to think of him. Reassuring: it let me go on believing in the basic goodness of my fellow man; easier than turning the coin over. In the dark of Ste Famille Street, a tough guy with a heart of gold made a good whistling tune.

Not fooled by the bullying, and not fooled either by the seven-dollar-a-week room. A hideout: just laying low till the heat cooled off. Easy for him to sneer at the gas-ring and the poverty-stricken derelicts who used it: he ate in restaurants. Not greasy spoons, either. Twice he had dragged me along—literally dragged, for my mother had also sized him up for what he was and thought I shouldn't—and we had had T-bone steaks and double scotches. (Oh yes, like a good Westerner she too had faith in basic human goodness; still, where her Sonny was concerned, there were certain types at which she thought it wise to draw the line.)

So that Saturday, instead of eating my hamburger and settling down to drink my beer, I lay quiet until about nine o'clock, pretending to be out, and then went uptown. Because he would curl his nose at the sight of the old frying pan and invite me out again; because I would want to go; because at the bottom of the glass there would be the offer of a dirty job.

So far he hadn't got round to details. Sensing it coming—*she* always knew—I would laugh, look blank, talk earnestly about *my* kind of job.

"You'll never make it in this town—not your way. Even if it turns out you're good. You've got to know somebody, sleep with somebody, *buy* somebody—"

It was the attack that made it hard to distrust him—the sting. I would recoil, smarting, hating, then think what a fool I was. For if there was a dirty job, if he really wanted to work me into something, wouldn't he have a smoother come-on?

"Ever stop to think how many others there are just like you? Better? Young men with horns—and saxophones and guitars and clarinets—all headed for the big time?"

"I'm not sure yet. If it turns out you're right, then I'll just have to head back home. Get another band going."

"And won't that be the big day! The starch out, picking up the pieces. Ever think how you'll hate them? How they'll hate you?"

"So what do I do? Stay on and shovel snow for Mrs. Painter?"

"Stay on and smarten up. Make yourself useful to somebody—then, like I say, go out and buy a band. Find a spot you like and make it worth somebody's while to put you in."

"That's going to take an awful lot of cash, Charlie—know any good rackets?" A laugh, a feeler. "How about protection? I'm a fair size—think I could scare them into paying up?"

"I daresay you could be brought along." The eyes coming forward a little in their sockets, shrewd, estimating; the smile encouraging. "That big-raw-wholesome-kid-from-the-West look—just give it a shine. Nobody'd ever take it for a front."

One shoulder hunched, one corner of the mouth pulled down. "Lots going on—you'd be surprised. Right here in Montreal I used to know somebody—trumpet and peddling ...."

Watching to see if I was following—the way I used to walk in front of Isabel shaking a tin of oats to bring her from the pasture to her stall. "Big blue eyes, big honest smile .... First just for some of the boys where he played—then one thing leading to another .... Now I hear he's got a club of his own somewhere."

"That's the last thing I'd want." Suspicious now, shying. I hadn't left my puddle in Saskatchewan to get mixed up with pedlars. "Just a *band* of my own. The one I had wasn't bad. I could do worse than go back to it—even with the starch out."

Maybe dope, maybe girls. All I knew about the underside of a big city was the magazine and movie versions; and still a little raw, with a tendency to gape, I was quick to sniff out something tough and dirty. I kept away from Charlie but I spent a good deal of time thinking about him, building him up. Living next door to a racketeer or pedlar—a pimp, even—relieved the drabness, added drama. If I had to go back to my Saskatchewan puddle I'd at least have some stories.

Girls because, once or twice a week, he brought one to his room. And every time the voice was wrong. Sour, wrangling, exasperated—as if warning her that she, too, might get a goddam pillow down her throat. Payment might give him the right; still, it wasn't the voice for the occasion. So probably, instead of paying, he was collecting. It went on. You read about it in every paper. Down on the Lower Main, you saw it in every club and cafe. Why not, then? They had to live somewhere. Why couldn't it be the man next door?

Sometimes I tried to draw him out, to encourage him to talk about himself and what he did; but then, afraid of involvement, Saskatchewan Main Street to the core, I would shy again the moment he showed signs of being ready to begin. Perhaps, without knowing it, I led him on.

"I hope we didn't keep *you* awake."

Only a few nights before, right after one of them had gone, he brought me in two inches of scotch. He hadn't dressed, just his trousers, and even in the display of skinny arms and knobby chest, ugly with a grizzle of reddish hair, there was aggression, a kind of smirk. Skinny and hairy, so what? *He* had just scored; how was I doing?

"Nicole from Chicoutimi—sometime I'll bring her in. I was telling her about you and she says she's never had a cowboy."

"And come to think of it, I've never had a professional." Standing up to him, my own man. Ignoring the glass as he set it on the table. "If she's your type you'd better hang on to her."

"Share the wealth—at my age twice is plenty. No, no—" A hand up, peremptory, as if we were in a bar and he was insisting on paying for the next drink. "Just leave everything to me—maybe this Saturday."

"A fine husky specimen like you—you'll make it three times easy." Snotty; intact. I hadn't had the advantages of a good, Presbyterian upbringing for nothing. A drink or a meal now and then was one thing; a woman was another. "You'd better take the drink with you too. It'll help put you in shape again."

He left the scotch and I drank it the moment he was gone; and this time, instead of a dirty offer at the bottom of the glass, there was a dirty taste. Because I had listened to him, let itch and interest show. Because I would listen again—the next time might consent.

Saturday, he had said, *and today was Saturday*. For then I would be one of them—on the other side—and whenever it was time he would move in on me, and whatever he wanted he would take. I was sure of that. Somehow, as I lay there in the half-dark, watching the snow through the branches, the two were linked—as if part of me had already secretly responded, as if a deal were being made behind my back.

Uneasy; a long way from home. I had exaggerated and built him up before, but there had always been a fence between us. We had watched and sniffed each other through the wire. A whiff of something shady, sly—but nothing to do with me. No danger: he was on his side and I was on mine. Part of the scenery: in a place like Montreal you saw all kinds. Now, though, the fence was down and he was moving closer.

Two dollars and a pound of hamburger—what was going to happen Monday morning?

So to escape him I went uptown. A no-good bum with his ambitions snagged at fly-level, waiting for a free half hour with one that he had already used? Not quite—not yet. He came out of his room when he heard me starting down the stairs and I called back I had fallen asleep and had to run now—somebody was waiting. All quiet in his room, no sign of Nicole; somebody was waiting for me anyway. A stand; a little spurt of will and decision; the illusion that I was walking out on him.

2

IT WAS STILL SNOWING and the sky hung pink and woolly just above the trees. Mild and windless, as if we had jumped to March. The big flakes burst in my face soggily— the slap of wet mouths—and as I walked along, slowing at each tree to reach up and touch a branch or rub my hand against the bark, I forgot Charlie and felt good again.

It was a decrepit street, with run-down, old, stones houses and uncurtained basement rooms; but all along, both sides, the trees were fine. The way they stretched up black and wet and strong, not minding. A life of their own; creaking and reminiscing in the snowy night like country trees.

But less than five minutes and I was at Sherbrooke Street, exposed and furtive in the bright, whirling light; and all the cars as they passed were watching me.

Nowhere to go. Not to a movie: Saturday night they put the prices up. Not to a tavern: sour, stale, smoky smells and old drunks mumbling back at the television—the last place. A snack bar for a sandwich—then what? Back to the room? Creeping up so Charlie wouldn't hear me, huddling down for the rest of the evening with a beer and an old magazine?

Saturday night—I wanted that. Music and people, a drink; talking, seeing, going somewhere; another drink. I hesitated a moment, mindless and blank with craving, then set off at a half-run down the hill to St. Catherine Street. In the crowds, nobody would notice my windbreaker and old pants. I wouldn't be a gangling six-foot-two.

But St. Catherine Street was eating. Other times you passed movie houses and invitations to winter in the Caribbean and stores selling shoes and cameras; but tonight, just because I hadn't had my hamburger, every window was a restaurant. Chickens turning on spits, steaks sizzling over charcoal, white-capped boys doing juggling turns with pizza and spaghetti. Up one side and down the other: finally a lunch counter for a sandwich and a cup of coffee. A sliver of tomato, a rag of lettuce—and now, after all the windows, it was the taste of meat I wanted, work for my teeth, something hot and strong. Meat and a drink. Two or three mouthfuls and I pushed the plate away. The girl who had served me—red hair, doll-nose, falsies. She'd given me that kind of sandwich because I didn't rate a better one. *Bitch!* I paid and stalked out without leaving a tip; and then, back on the street, bumped straight into Sonny McAlpine.

The one with the clarinet—in an uproar over a tomato sandwich and a ten cent tip .... How right you are, Charlie; down and out in mind as well as pocket.

Wanting a drink but holding out, just walking .... Right, maybe, about a lot of things. Time to smarten up, get wise to myself. From the sticks and broke—who was I to lay down the rules? A clean-cut, upright young man—wasn't that living it up a bit beyond my means?

Maybe a lucky break. A foot up, a helping hand. At least listen. Young man with a clarinet—young man on the make; you had to listen to everybody. Thumb my nose at him tonight, but remember Monday morning. Nicole from Chicoutimi—maybe she was what I needed too. And it was a big town. Nobody with an eye to the keyhole.

And then, blue and clean through the snowy light, there was the sound of music.

I remembered the place: only a few weeks before I had been there looking for a job. A doorman with a fancy blue and yellow monkey-suit getting greasy down the front; behind him, a steep, bashed-in looking stair. I remembered the stair and the misery in my throat as I came down, telling myself it was time to go back to the farm where I belonged. But now the piano came through the window with a cool slap and spangle and a raw, tender horn complained as if inconstancy were something new.

I stood listening a minute, playing with them, my name in lights again. The old Sonny and a little over. My blood had spangles in it too, and the night was snowing stars.

I went up. Windbreaker and an old sport shirt open at the throat and white streaks down my pants where I had tried cleaning them with the wrong cleaning fluid. The monkey-suit pushed towards me, hand out, and I smiled. A couple was coming down; I flattened myself against the wall to let them pass and smiled. And as I stamped the snow off my feet and ran a comb through my hair the world was waiting for me. A clean, brave, honest world, where men and clarinets alike received their due.

But at the top of the stair a bouncer glared and a waiter looked the other way. My nerve buckled. I stumbled in all windbreaker and feet again.

And just at that moment the stage show finished, and as the music and applause faded out there was the dead, turned-off sound of flat voices and scraping chairs that's like a winter morning, bleak and dim, when you first turn off the light. There was an empty table at the far side of the room and with music I would have strode to it, confident and easy; but instead, stranded, out-size, I had to stumble and shoulder my way through the gaping crowd alone.

For come from the farm and they do gape. You miss nobody and nobody misses you. Live in the city a hundred years and you'll never be convinced that they look without looking, neither see nor care. On the farm you count. There are so few of you—you feel known and watched. Afterwards you never quite come to terms with crowds and anonymity.

Now, though, after wincing under the eyes of people who weren't watching me, I sat five minutes sipping at a beer without noticing somebody who was.

Almost without noticing her. Naturally I knew she was there—only two tables away, with all that shape and yellow hair—but as I also knew what she was there for, I just took her in and looked away. Less than two dollars in my pocket—why work myself into a lather over something that would cost at least fifteen?

Looked away—tried to look away. The effort kept drawing me back. And each time she was waiting for me at the ready, flashing a big, come-up-and-see-me smile.

Between sips, curious and puzzled, I watched her. For how could she be so slow at catching on? My old windbreaker and the way I was spinning out a beer—how could a working broad not tumble to the signs?

And worth her price at that. A big, husky girl, not far off thirty, starting to plump out a little but still fresh and firm. A gash of lipstick and a showy fluff of hair, but bright, clear eyes, a soft, friendly mouth and a tough, no-nonsense chin. She'd been around, but she hadn't hardened or gone sour.

And then the hair again. Not fluffy at all when you looked a second time, but shining and smooth and silkily compact— something the way Isabel used to shine after I'd rubbed her down with buttermilk. Somehow, though, a fluffy look—so much of it, perhaps, and the way she laughed and tossed her head.

Why her interest, though, in me? What was on her mind? My long legs wouldn't stay out of sight under the table and I even caught her taking in the white streaks on my pants. Making good time, too, with the old fellow at her table. Bald and pink and jowly—hungry and at the same time scared. Not quite sure where he stood with her but working hard to put it across he could hold his own with the young ones. Winking and mugging and giving her a little knee. Play him a little longer and she had him for an easy twenty-five.

A vague smile of embarrassment, as if I had walked into the wrong room. Trying to look away, take an interest in someone else, but my eyes flicking back. Was I wrong? Was I the one who couldn't read the signs? Fresh and green from the country? Not a broad at all?

No—thirty was right. At least not far wrong. And an old hand at the game—she knew the score. Just the way she sat there with her drink, hitching her coat back off her shoulders—you knew she'd been through it a hundred times. The same as when somebody sits down to the piano or puts a trumpet to his lips—before he plays a note you've a fair idea what you're going to hear.

Finally, to help her get things straight, I stretched out one of my legs so she could see the streaks again; then, to get things even straighter, I brought out my money, counted it, slipped it back into my pocket and shrugged. But a few seconds later when I glanced up again she was still there. Plus a wink this time to button down the smile. I looked again, wondering if I might have seen her somewhere, spoken to her, and then, involuntarily, gave a vague smile in return. Invitation: the man she was with had just ordered two beers; picking up hers, with a wave and a smile and swing of her hips, she sailed over grandly and sat down with me.

"Hope you don't mind. A place like this if there's one thing you need it's company. Especially Saturday night."

Arrival, entrance: a faint smile of bestowal as she settled herself and hitched back her coat again. Just as if I had been sitting there all evening waiting for her, gnawing my nails for fear she wouldn't come.

"Can't stand seeing somebody like you drinking alone and looking so lonesome. Not when everybody else is having fun. And this town, if you ask me, is just about the *meanest* place."

"Who's lonesome?" I scowled at her, picked up my beer. "It's not hard finding company if you want it. For that matter, even if you don't."

She missed it. "Come on, drink up and have another. You don't need to put on an act with me. Lots of times *I've* been lonesome since I landed here."

"Look, Sister—"

"Name's Mad, if you don't mind—short for Madeleine. Kind of nice name, I always think, even if they did a pretty poor job picking it for me."

"Why? Not for blondes?"

"No—she was supposed to be some kind of saint. French maybe—a long way back. My old lady had a grandmother used to live up north somewhere with the Indians and nuns."

I met her eyes and laughed. "I know what you mean. At home once they called a colt Star that didn't have one."

"That was even worse, because they could *see*." She raised her glass gravely, then without touching it set it down again. "No, with me there was a fifty-fifty chance. Or maybe it was something about the way I looked and they figured it might help."

"No stars on me either, Mad—not even that fifty-fifty chance."

She hesitated, swirling the beer in her glass, veering from rejection, and I said quickly, "Your boy friend doesn't look exactly pleased about it either. Better not keep him waiting."

"Never saw him before—no friend of mine." She tossed her head disdainfully and fished for cigarettes. "Buying me a drink was his idea. Picking me up the same. I didn't promise anything."

"I'm only trying to be fair. You're just wasting your time."

The smile again, light-hearted and at the same time stubborn. "Having a good time's never wasting it. Now drink up like I say and we'll have another."

Cigarettes, lighter: formally. Fingers touching; smile suddenly self-conscious and prim. Then, with an airy little flourish of her cigarette, "You've got a name too, I suppose? ... Just the first one—"

"I've got a name but they always call me Sonny—"

"I like that—nice and friendly .... Sonny and Mad—"

"But right now I'm broke—I have about a dollar ten. Ever since you sat down I've been trying to tell you."

"That's all right—I'm broke too." She put her head back and laughed, as if poverty set everything right between us, then leaned towards me with a contented sigh. "Anyway, the old girl sure knows how to pick them. The minute you walked in—just one look and I knew."

"Knew what the minute I walked in?"

"Somebody comes along and he's the right one and somebody else just misses out." Voice and eyes slipped past me a moment, marvelling. "Looks all right—sometimes looks fine—and yet straight off you know. No thinking—fast—you just know."

"Sounds as if there's been a lot of right ones. None of them still around?"

She took a deep breath and brought out her compact. "Well, they sort of come and go and I'm never one for trying to spin things out. I mean, when you know it's over anyway."

"So it looks like you don't do such a good job picking them after all ... And I'll be another. You won't want to waste time spinning me out either."

"Oh no, Sonny—" She snapped the compact shut and leaned towards me again. "They're all all right while they *last*. I'm not complaining. And you never know—some day, maybe there'll be the one that'll last a little longer."

"Don't look at me. Must be the light—or maybe because I'm just getting over the 'flu."

"I know all right." She nodded, smiling serenely. "I always know. Sure, I've had them walk out and play dirty tricks on me, but they were always all right while they lasted. Somebody can steal your things and boot you downstairs and be just fine right up *until* then."

"Then it's not the beer, you're plain crazy. But never mind—" The smile was coming on strong again and I raised my hand. "You can pick them and we're not going to argue. I wish, though, you'd go back to your own table because beer's sixty cents in this place and I haven't enough for two."

"Talk about crazy—you think I came over scrounging beers? You get one and I'll get one—or, better still, let me get both." She winked, tapping her purse, and dropped her voice to a whisper. "Because I'm not *flat* broke—I still got five or six dollars and if I feel like it there's a job waiting for me Monday morning."

"If you go right now he probably won't mind. Tell him you used to know me. Met me once somewhere—at a dance—"

The smile again, pure bliss, pure mule, "I'd rather stretch out one beer with you, Sonny, then have a night on the town with an old fool like him. Drinks don't matter—not when you're with somebody that does."

I held up my hand, rubbing thumb and finger together. "Cash, though—that matters—and now's your chance to make a little more. Remember tomorrow's Sunday—things may be dull."

Blunt and crude because I was beginning to want her. Because without thinking about it I knew, a kind of self-protection, that driving her off quickly, offending her with a reminder that she was peddling herself, would be easier than starting to see her as a possibility. Easier than imagining her back in the room, filling it with her big, beery laugh and then—reality restored—climbing the splintery old stairs alone.

"Just trying to be honest with you; there it is." I brought out my coins and laid them on the table. "You can't afford me. He's going to start looking around for somebody else in a few minutes—to show you that he doesn't care."

"Who's worrying? I don't care either, so let's just have fun."

But this time the laugh, even though it was as big and bouncy as ever, didn't quite come off. A narrowing of the eyes, the upper lip drawn in—just enough to let me know that I'd hit home.

"Slip me fifty cents—" Now I was sorry and anxious to make it up to her—"so I'll have something for a tip."

"But then *you* won't have anything!" The hurt look vanished in a blaze of concern. She dipped swiftly into her purse for a dollar bill, crumpled it small, and pushed it towards me. "Go *on*—just between ourselves—what difference does it make?"

Enough to make me rear up on my rickety legs of independence and push back the bill. It was the familiarity I didn't like, the lowering of the voice, as if we had already reached the what's-mine-is-yours stage. "Just fifty cents—sorry to have to ask."

She made the exchange quickly, submissively, and before she could gather herself for another protest I beckoned to the waiter. It was between shows: the band began to play for dancing. The horn was good and without intending to, listening, I shut her out. The beer came. She was silent a moment, twirling her glass, then said cautiously, "If I did something wrong, Sonny, I didn't mean to. You look so blue again—so *sore*—"

I came back amicably and touched glasses with her. "It's just the band—don't give it a thought. I was listening to the horn."

He wavered on a high note, weakened, soured, and measuring my clarinet against him I gave a cluck of satisfaction.

"I bet you're like me, Sonny. I bet you like something with a good beat. The dances we used to have back home in Nova Scotia—two and three a week sometimes. Real whoopety-up ones."

I frowned and stubbed without answering, and seeing that the whoopety-up ones weren't going over very well, taking it on herself, she said, "Go ahead then—say it's me you're sore at. I was just trying to cheer you up but it doesn't matter. I'm not used to being handled careful. No sense pretending it's the horn."

"Somebody else's horn—why not? Why can't I get sore at it?"

Puzzled: head tilted as if I were the price tag on something in a window.

"That's what I do—when I do it. Not horn—clarinet."

She took it in slowly. Then, with a half-gesture of sympathy, her hand moved across the table. "You mean you were playing here? And got let out?"

"Not exactly—you can't get let out till you get started."

Quicker this time. "That's Montreal for you—got to have pull for everything. A fellow I once was sort of friendly with that played the drums, couldn't get anywhere, just like you. And he'd played all kinds of places—California, Chicago—"

He didn't appeal to me. I didn't want him on my side. "Pull helps," I said curtly. "Having the goods helps more."

"Oh, you've got the goods all right—goods to burn. Something about you—the way you talk. Easiest thing in the world to tell."

"I don't know about the goods, Mad. Right now I haven't even got my clarinet."

"Hocked it?"

Instant: this was something she could understand. "I know—once I lost a coat like that. A *fur* coat—cost a couple of hundred dollars and all they'd give me was a measly twenty-five. Just enough to stand off the old landlady for a couple of weeks, but do you think I could ever get ahead that much and get it back?"

"Fifteen more than I got for my clarinet."

"And here you are buying drinks and spending money on me. And looking so thin—like you're not getting very good meals."

She reached for my hand and I yielded it to her, letting her mother it with little pats and pinches. A broke Sonny, a scared Sonny—wanting someone to come out of the crowd and see him, talk to him, make a sign.

"As a matter of fact this is the *worst* town to get anywhere. All those French—most of the time you don't even know what they're talking about, let alone thinking."

Wanting her too, now—her and the little throb of virility that at least for a moment or two wipes out insignificance and gives a lord-of-creation hoist to your self-esteem.

"I've still got five dollars, Sonny. You can have that."

I brought my head up. "Is that what a right one looks like? You think I'd take it?"

"I know—it hurts because you're the kind that would be a real good spender if you had it. You like to treat a girl right."

I touched glasses with her again. "I'm afraid the record wouldn't stand looking into too closely, but Saturday night's no time to argue."

Her face lit. She took my hand again. "That's right. Saturday night and just the two of us alone in Montreal, what difference which one's spending? Nobody cares. You know I passed out once right in the street—pneumonia—bad—thought it was just a cold—" The words stumbled in a sudden urgency to make me see the need to hurry, snatch—"and when I got out of hospital even my room was gone. They'd stuffed my things into cardboard boxes and put them in the basement. And they'd got wet."

She broke off a moment while her eyes went on with the hurt of it. "You're young, Sonny. You don't know yet how much nobody cares. What I mean—a couple of people like us all alone, what's the harm in being friendly, making the best of things?" Again she broke off, swirling the beer in her glass nervously. "You lose people so easy—the ones that make a difference. Big town like this, you never see them again, never get another chance."

And then, abruptly, with a laugh and another toss of her hair, "But that's me, pushing in where I got no right, making a big fool of myself. Scrapper—just like my old man. Five-foot-six and with a couple of drinks he'd take on anybody, twice his size. And when he went down he went down swinging."

"It's a good way if you've got to go down. But sometimes isn't it just a waste of good scrapping? Better, maybe, if you take on somebody your own size—"

Prompt and pat, all lined up and waiting: variation on a tune I had been whistling for the past six or seven years. The *real* big-time—Bach and Beethoven—not a chance. Like reaching for the moon. Well, then—why not something closer? A clarinet, say, and a good little band—

"The trouble keeping to your own size, Sonny, it's some-times not much fun. Sure, if I was smart like you say I'd string along with old Baldy—and then Monday morning I could turn over and have a good sleep. But then where would you be? See what I mean—what I'd have missed by being smart?"

Our eyes met. She flushed and fumbled in her purse again. "I know— where'll you be anyway? It takes two. I can't put a rope on you."

"Got a place where we can go?"

A little stab of a glance, then the cigarette again. "Well, where I stay she's getting sort of strict—one of the girls has been making trouble—but I know where we can get a room. Four dollars—so we'll be all right."

"I've got a room—and a couple of beers. I mean if you're crazy enough to want it that way—just for the night—and no use promising to make it up to you later on."

She looked at me again, wetting her lips, and I added quickly, "Because next week if I don't find a job I'm clearing out. Toronto—I know somebody—just looking for a ride—"

Right. She couldn't put a rope on me, but no harm making sure she didn't get a chance to try. For there was something in the eyes that might insist, refuse to understand—something childlike, unanswerable. A threat of devotion: better straight speaking now than rough handling later on.

"That's real nice of you, Sonny. And you don't have to promise anything. I'd like it fine just the way you say."

Shy now; the manner almost social; the eyes so moist and bright I was half afraid for a moment she might be going to cry. But instead, at once puzzled and triumphant, she put her head back and slapped the table. "Funniest thing—I just *knew* it would work out all right. You know how it is sometimes—you get a feeling—"

"Just so long as it's the right feeling—and you understand it's not going to work out for long—"

"I heard you the first time. You said your little piece real nice."

"Maybe if I don't leave town—I mean, now that we've got to know each other—"

"It's all right, Sonny. I'm asking for it." She looked bleak a moment—a cold, early-morning look through a dirty windowpane—then shook her head and bounced a laugh again. "Let's go—we've only got tonight so let's not sit here wasting time .... There's nothing worse than Saturday night alone—unless it's somebody that makes you *want* to be alone."

3

SHE WAS GOOD AT STAIRS. All the way up to the third floor, forty or forty-five steps, we creaked in unison.

How many times had she done it? How many visitors—right ones—had she smuggled up to her own room? I said nothing, made no sign. She climbed in careful step as if it were the proper thing to do in a strange house, like remaining standing until asked to sit down, or being pleasant to the children.

And yet she made me look at the stairs, the slivery wood showing through the holes in the linoleum, the blackened walls and broken plaster; put the smell of old drains in my nostrils. To that extent she had imposed herself. I imagined her judging me by the house I was living in and was apologetic.

But at each landing as I turned and waited for her she pressed against me with a round-eyed, conspiratorial wriggle. We might have been ten-year-olds, exploring a boarded-up house where someone had been murdered.

Inside the room at last, I stood motionless a minute, my hand still on the switch, wincing at the disorder, the litter of papers, the gobs of dirty socks; but with a sigh and another wiggle she said, "Sure glad I moved in fast on you, before anybody else had the chance."

"I wasn't expecting a visitor—sorry it's such a mess."

She glanced around and nodded. "It could do all right with a little looking after, but it's a nice big room. Straighten things round a little and you could have a dance."

A housewifely narrowing of the eyes: cleaning, tidying, rearranging. "What the landlady calls a housekeeping room," I explained. "There were two of us but the other fellow left. Now she says I'll maybe have to take a smaller one."

"I've had them like that too, pushing you around and giving orders, but now I've got a room with my girl friend Cora so it's more like home—sometimes. Little surprise I've been keeping for you—it's just over on Hutchison—so we're neighbours."

Too close: thinking fast and raising my own voice, I said, "You don't have to whisper. We're on the top here and she won't be up to check on things till the morning. You'll hear *her* all right when she gets started."

There was no danger. Old Mrs. Painter had sores on her legs and hadn't been out of the basement for a month. But no need to tell Mad: less chance of an argument in the morning; that much easier to see her on her way. No harm either, while I was at it, substituting bad temper for bad legs.

But in telling her she needn't whisper I was also thinking of Charlie. He was in—coming up the stairs I had seen the light under his door—and I wanted him to know I had a woman of my own with me, wasn't waiting for a turn with his.

"What about next door? No use *asking* for trouble."

"Just my neighbour Charlie, and he won't bother you."

"It's not *me*, Sonny. You're the one she'll take it out on."

She was still whispering—whispering as on the stairs she had climbed in careful step with me—and again I wondered how many furtive nights with a "right one" it had taken, how many houses where she didn't belong, to teach her control of the big voice and the whoopety-up laugh. Taking her coat and finding a hanger for it, I explained about the pipes. Something had gone wrong: there was no heat coming up in the back rooms, so everybody but Charlie and me had had to leave.

"How about you, Sonny? You warm enough?"

"Depends on the direction of the wind. Not bad."

"And your coat—I bet you hocked that too?"

The snow had finished and it was getting windier and colder—the damp, clammy Montreal cold that if you're from the prairie you feel more than a crisp thirty below—and walking along with her I had done my best to keep from shivering, to hold my head up and face straight into the wind as if I went without a coat because a windbreaker was all I needed. But she had noticed. There was reproach in her voice—a rueful, mother-touch, as if I were a knee-high with wet feet—and to make an end of it I drew her towards me and began, hands and mouth, to explore.

"Say what you like, though, weather like this you need a good warm coat—" She resisted, backed away, not quite ready yet to begin what she had come for. "On the way up you must have coughed a dozen times—besides sneaking in a lot of little sniffles too—"

I drew her to me again, and as my hand went down she buckled and wriggled away. "The light, Sonny—put out the light." The voice was breathless, empathic. "Start carrying on like that, it's time. Put it out first, and then."

"Why? A night like this you think somebody's sitting in the tree?"

"Doesn't matter—just behave until you do."

"What's wrong with seeing? Turning into a nice girl on me now you're here?"

She stared back a moment, uneasy, not quite sure what I meant, then seized my arm and pressed her face against it. "No, Sonny, but we don't know each other yet. And somebody like you, so different—I just mean the first time it's always better in the dark."

Not quite the dark. The street lamp threw a bright, clean rectangle on the ceiling and the beer bottles on the window caught a little of the light and bent it in on us in amber rays. She undressed quickly, silent and hard-breathing. Watching as I slipped out of my own clothes, I could see the faint whiteness of her arms like frantic semaphores.

"Sonny—you there?"

The voice taut, huskily eager. And as the floor creaked and the blurred whiteness of her body came towards me I stood contracted, raw, almost as if it were something hazardous and unknown again—a first step in sin.

"There you are—you were so still I thought you were trying to hide on me." And then, her voice shooting up to a little squeal as her hands discovered me, "Oh Sonny—you mean that's all *you*!"

Almost like the first time, late at night in the loft with Millie Dickson. Trembling and clumsy, yet insistent; the insistence of a fifteen-year-old who, in a community of practical, callous-handed farmers, takes music lessons. Hands soft and cared for—suspect. Everything to be proved. A backward fifteen-year-old, moreover, off-balance with a streak of precocity; dreamer and fool enough to expect a revelation, something to ransack life, then illumine and restore it—a break-through, a shattering of the glass, something to compensate for wheat and windy bleakness.

A demure, very proper little girl who had probably never so much as watched a bull and cow; somehow, though, I had got her up there. That kind of insistence. Hand in hand into the pitch-dark barn, furtive as if we were there to steal something; sleepy little whinnies from the horses, wondering if there were to be oats; the dog tangling with our legs in whining welcome; along the feed-alley and up the stairs into the high, vaulted stillness of the loft.

Not quite dark that time either, not quite still. A thin shaft of moonlight through the little window high in the gable; sparrows somewhere, chirping in a flurry of unease at our intrusion.

"What did you want to come up here for?" she asked, standing wooden, arms rigid at her sides; and masterfully, for all my clumsy ignorance, I forced her down into the hay and showed her.

Letdown. Reluctantly, unwilling to admit it was over, that that was all, we stood up and adjusted our clothing, then sat down again.

Silent a while, her pale profile just visible in the darkness. Then, to assure her she hadn't disappointed me, I put my face against her breast and pressed her into the hay again. "I'm sorry—I thought you'd like it better. Girls are supposed to like it but you didn't help."

"I was scared—and I thought it would be different."

Instead of saying that I had expected it to be different, too, I lay still awhile, listening to her heartbeat, trying to work up appropriate feelings of achievement and virility. At last she stirred and I said, "I think I could do it better now—so you'd like it."

"You mean now—*again?*"

"Well, it's what we came for, isn't it?"

And less because of desire than unwillingness to admit that what had happened was in fact consummation, I insisted again. And this time it at least lasted longer and I at least knew what I was doing. Instead of groping awkwardness there was experimental detachment and control. An important experience: to be lived all the way and recorded carefully—some day, perhaps, to be discussed with the other boys. And afterwards, helping her down the stairs and cuffing away the dog, I did feel mature—initiated, adequate. As we stepped outside she began inexplicably to cry, and assuring her there would never be anyone else in my life I promised to marry her, even if it meant selling Isabel, the day I was seventeen.

The last of Millie. We were neighbours and there was no lack of opportunity, but I never so much as danced with her or held her hand again. For I had taken her wanting a revelation and had got instead a scratchy half hour in the hay. And I never quite forgave her for it, always bore her a secret grudge.

No revelations with Mad, either; just experience and expertise; just uninhibited enthusiasm, uncomplicated delight. Even when we had finished and were lying back quiet and settled, shoulder to shoulder, I could feel little tremors running through her body as if the delight at its peak had spilled over and left pools behind that only now were trickling away.

"Sure was lucky meeting you, Sonny. If you knew how close I was to walking out of that place. Another five minutes and I'd have never known."

The wind was stronger now, whining and slapping the tree against the house, and we lay listening to it in silence a while, staring at the window and the soft glow of the beer bottles and the thin, swift streaks of snow beyond. "Safe and warm like this," she said presently, reaching for my hand and snuggling closer, "makes you wish you could stop the clock so it'd never be morning. You ever feel crazy things like that, Sonny?"

"Ten at the latest—sorry. The old lady's going to be up and I've got to keep on the right side of her." And then, a little more gently, "I don't pay rent here, so I can't afford to get thrown out."

"Oh no—I'm not trying to muscle in." She raised herself on an elbow, leaned over and put her lips on my forehead. "It's just being so lucky—straight from the sticks and not exactly amounting to much, and if I was one of those fancy movie stars with a couple of million stashed away I couldn't be having it better."

Meaning every word of it. Her lips dry and gentle on my forehead again, then a big, soft sigh as she lay back on the pillow.

"You're crazy, you know." My eyes fixed on the window, I linked fingers with her. "Why don't you get serious and find a real right one? A little older, maybe—steady job. A couple of days, like as not, and I'll have left town."

"What makes a right one, Sonny, isn't how long or often. Sure, you'll go. I'm no fool—we Maritimers got good heads. But once is worth it. Something to remember—something good."

Then, raising herself again and peering down at me, "Funny—some ways you're so much like Bill—and yet you're not the same at all. Same mouth, maybe—same turn. But even allowing you're a little older and been around more—"

"I'm supposed to know Bill?"

"Back when I was sixteen. Just one look—straight crazy. My old man couldn't hold me."

The brush of her lips again. "Stranger in town—had an uncle with a bad back and he'd come up to help him with his boat. Supposed to be from Halifax but I found out afterwards he'd told other people it was Saint John."

A brief pause and the faint sound of swallowing, as if all over again she was trying to understand and come to terms with such deception. "Couldn't get a word out of the old man. Sore because he'd been counting on a lot of work out of him—said it was me ought to be run out of town for leading a good boy on. But it was my old man scared him off. Marry her, he said, or I'll fix you so you never marry anybody else, and he skipped town, not even coming round to say good-bye."

She settled back on the pillow reminiscently. "And the baby came too soon and didn't live so we'd have been all right anyway—only naturally he had no way to know about that. I skipped town too, everybody saying what a disgrace and my old lady taking it so hard, but mostly hoping I'd catch up with him some day."

Halifax for a year, then Montreal. Always in restaurants—"thinking he'd come in for a meal some day and there I'd be." Walking the streets, waiting at the station when the Halifax train was due, seeing him for sure just half a block ahead and sending everybody flying—

"Four or five years like that and then I started getting over him. More or less. I mean I've still sort of always got my eye peeled, but when I stop and think I know he'd be such a lot different anyway."

"And somebody who looks like Bill, that's what you call a right one?"

"Doesn't matter so much how he *looks*—just so long as he brings it back. A little of it."

"And you want it back? It was worth it?"

"Just a little, just enough to keep me going."

"The way you tell it all you got out of Bill was trouble and a few pieces of tail—and if I'm typical of your right ones that's still all you're getting. Why don't you try for something better? You've got the looks."

"But there was something, Sonny—something happening that you just didn't believe could happen—"

She tossed her head on the pillow a moment, then lay abruptly still. "Afterwards—well, I just couldn't settle for anything less."

"Somebody who had his fun and then walked out—less than that?"

A twitch of impatience; the sound of swallowing again. "I wanted him so much and then I got him—that was it. I went uptown one day and there he was. Real. Something about the way he looked at me like he'd been waiting too."

She left me a moment, then with a stumble of words, catching up, tried to explain, "I'd been wanting him from away back, years, ever since I was as little as twelve. Crazy kids—seeing movies and lying awake at night thinking about them .... Till first thing you've made up somebody for yourself, somebody that's going to be the one. You don't actually believe you'll ever find him and at the same time you do .... And then you see he did come—just like he was supposed to be—just as good."

Her voice quickened, glowed, still filled with the wonder of it. "I used to meet him up the shore a piece—rocks and an old boat and a nice little place in the sand—and I'd be there first and watch him coming, straight out of the sun when it was starting to set and all the light on him. I don't know how to tell it—sort of like a dream coming true. Crazy as crazy, but coming true."

She broke off a moment, came back insistent. "I mean if there's no more of that then there's nothing more. Money and things—wouldn't make any difference, wouldn't count. Cora talks like you. Watch it, she says, or some day you'll come to and crack—maybe turn into an old lush—"

Crazy as crazy was right and I shied uneasily. "Look—we forgot the beer."

"Oh no, Sonny—we don't need beer *too*. Save it for tomorrow."

The voice of country thrift and common sense. I laughed, reassured, and said, "I'd hate to be your little boy. 'You've had a cone, so keep your peanuts for tomorrow.'"

"How about two cones?" She laughed with me, then said seriously, "I can take a drink or I can leave it. No difference—unless it's somebody I'm just trying to play along with. Then a slug of something helps. But I don't need help with you, Sonny. Nothing at all—just more."

She patted my thigh approvingly, as if I were a horse that had just won a race. "Besides, tomorrow's going to be a long day for you. Broke and no place to go, you'll need your beer."

"Don't worry about tomorrow." A reflex, a slap: I didn't like being reminded. "If I want a beer I can always get it from Charlie."

"And who's this Charlie?" Her voice had a sudden edge. I could feel her body sharpen with the question. "A while ago when we came in—the way you said it didn't matter if he heard us—like you *wanted* him to hear—"

Sharp—sharper than I expected. "Just what I said—there's nobody else up here, and he's not likely to run down and tell Mrs. Painter."

He seemed unimportant now, diminished. All the menace was gone. A small-time crook with a dirty, small-time record—at the worst. I had been imagining things: alone too much, too much time to brood and worry. My own mind was starting to go sick. And the impulse to stand up to him, defeat him, show him I was independent and could sleep with a woman of my own—that seemed childish now, out of proportion, like taking a stick to a fly.

"Just the same, there was something funny about the way you said it." Her voice narrowed and she hitched on to one shoulder. She didn't let go of things easily. "You don't mean he's one of those fellows that don't like girls?"

"He brings one up every so often. What I hear through the wall sounds normal enough."

But just the thought of it had roused such combative, protective energy that my answer bounced off unheard. "Oh, Sonny—don't you *ever*. If you knew some of the things that go on in this town—back home they'd string you up for even thinking about them."

"You sound as if you had your doubts about me?"

This time she heard and laughed. "You, Sonny? I'd just like to see what you'd do if anybody came along and tried."

She lay silent a moment, enjoying the havoc, then took a fresh grip of my hand. "But even so—maybe if you were hungry and liquored up a little. That's the way they work, you know, taking advantage. You and that tooter of yours, wanting a job and no luck. Clubs and places like that are just full of them."

"That's right—that tooter of mine."

"I mean, sometimes when you want something a lot there's nothing you won't do for it. Some people, that is—I don't mean you."

She nestled down contentedly, her hair soft and faintly sparking on my shoulder. "No, Sonny—not you. It'd take an awful lot of liquor."

Silence for a while. The light spearing at us through the bottles on the windowsill in golden slivers and the house creaking faintly with the wind.

If you could only know: see a here-and-now for what it was, how it fitted in, its place in the terrain of your existence: a slough-bottom on the prairie—as little as that—or a dip to a lost valley, descent of no return.

Back on the prairie, riding Isabel and out for hawks and rabbits with my .22, I had been so sure where I was going, what I would find .... And now a room on Ste Famille Street. If you could only wipe the glass and see: blob-faced foetus of a dream run out before its time that never had a chance, or the first gasp for breath, the pain and choke and rawness of beginning.

"You're going to go places, Sonny. Don't you worry."

It was as if she had been listening in and wanted to reassure me. "Somebody setting out to play in a band or sing—he's always got it hard. Stories and movies—you see it every time. And when it comes to getting the breaks—" Her fingers tightened: sympathy to belligerence—"this town if you ask me's just about the worst. All those French—speak good intelligent English and you get nowhere. Sticking together—that's them. Giving themselves all the breaks."

I didn't answer, didn't approve, just as I hadn't approved her drummer from Chicago. Since coming to Montreal I had sometimes cursed the bloody Frenchmen too. More than once, waiting for a chance to speak to someone, hoping for a try-out, I had nursed along a sense of slight until my lip was raw. But now—just because, ironically, the staunchness in her voice had stirred a bit of the old pride—I was above whining and griping and putting the blame on the Frenchmen. A flicker of belief—strength to take my failure neat, to remind myself I had been given the brush-off by the Jews and Greeks and English, too. To raise my head an inch or two and see I was in the wrong company now.

And then quickly, almost an apology, I turned and closed on her again.

It was expected. A cluck and purr of appreciation as she received me; and then, staunchly again, "You're going to go places all right. Handle that tooter of yours just half as good—"

4

WHEN I WOKE, a few minutes past nine, she was already up and working.

Just as I opened my eyes she came into the room, her hands full of wash, and closed the door with a bunt of her hip. A slam—harder than she had intended—and with a quick crouch, guilty, caught, she glanced at the bed to see if I had wakened.

I was in time. My eyes open just enough to make out her blurred outline, I stirred a little and went on breathing evenly. She stood frozen a few seconds, poised, alert, then put the wash on the table and passed a hand across her forehead.

Her face was flushed and glistening. The roots of her hair along her forehead were dark with perspiration; a loose wisp hung over one eye. And in the unsparing morning light her dress—blue silk, tight over the hips, with ruffles and beads— looked cheap and loud.

But she had stood it fine. Soap and water, no make-up, a quick comb through her hair—she had come through. In a way she looked even better than the night before; for the dress now, in this light, was no longer part of her but only something put on, slipped into, that she could just as easily shed again. Like coloured paper round a pot of healthy, pink geraniums.

She even looked triumphant. She had done it, brought it off—washed my socks and shorts without wakening me.

Slipping out of bed early, probably to go to the bathroom, she had looked around at the disorder, the litter of dirty clothes, and said to herself, *Why not! Slick things up a little, then clear out. Ten o'clock, he said, and he wasn't fooling. And now it's time .... When he wakes up he'll say, Well, what do you know! Mad for Madeleine—quite a girl. Well, that's the way it goes.*

She had brought it off. *Sweep the floor for him, clean up some of the mess*—probably with as little as that it had begun. Then, daringly, she had listened at the door, peered out to make sure the coast was clear and scurried along to the bathroom with the dirty dishes. Success! Back safely, she had looked at the shorts and socks and said again, *Why not!*

For the floor was swept, the dishes washed, the litter of cigarette butts and papers cleared from the table and dresser. Everything neat, in piles. And now as I watched she put up the clothesline—a bit of string that the previous tenant had left dangling from a nail and that had only to be tied to another nail on the next wall. No pins: she looped things over. All the time glancing at the bed to be sure I was still asleep. A furtiveness that was genuine. Not pretending, not trying to get caught. Nothing on her mind but to surprise me; clean things up, leave me a little more comfortable than when she came.

Sonny the Rat. I had played it so safe, taken such pains, even as I climbed into bed and spread her legs, to make sure she didn't over stay. And now, in return, that look of triumph. No strings—just to let me know she had had a fine time.

But there were a few bad minutes to come. She finished hanging the socks, looked round the room to see what else she could do, then faced it. What it meant to close the door on herself and disappear: until this moment the game of getting the job done without waking me had held it off. Faced it—asked herself what difference it was going to make to *her* whether or not I said she was quite a girl. One thing to imagine my surprise at finding her gone, what I would feel, how I would remember her; another to put on her coat and go.

But she was game. She stood motionless a moment, eyes wide and fixed like flies on pins, impaled by the realization that still another of the right ones wasn't working out, then with a twitch of her hips tiptoed quickly to the closet for her coat and slipped it on.

Another glance towards the bed, wavering, resolution close to breaking-point; fussing with her hair a minute in front of the dresser mirror, applying lipstick; and then, almost defiantly, as if she could feel herself being watched, another twitch of the hips, exaggerated this time, crude, forlorn.

And in fact she was being watched: the hard, cold, January eye of her own common sense, her thirty-year-old aware-ness, drilling it in that none of us was working out, that she was only getting older. A critical, dubious eye. What she had always lived by—the bouncy, Mad-can-take-it essence of her—was at stake. A defiant bump and grind right now was necessary.

I sat up and said, "Hi! Where do you think you're going?"

She jumped like a rabbit when your aim is a little off and you just graze its spot of tail. Her face as she spun round was white, set in the grimace of making-up, down-drawn eyes and puckered lips; the splash of lipstick, raw and bright against the pallor, gave her a hard, bedizened look, like you see them sometimes, old and ravaged, watching from a doorway; and the dress, a glimpse of ruffles through her open coat, suddenly matched again.

But in almost the same instant the miracle began and the ageing that had set in was halted, then reversed. The eyes lit, the mouth softened. The pallor cracked like a shell, dissolved like a skiff of ice; and with a little flush she was restored and young again.

"I was just going—honest I was." Still holding the lipstick, she motioned vaguely towards the door. "What a scare you gave me sitting up like that. I thought you'd be out for a couple of hours."

"Nice job—I've been watching. The place hasn't had such a going over since I moved in."

Pleased, with a shy, self-conscious shrug, she glanced around. "The right soap and a little more time I'd have everything shining."

"Shining enough—where are you off to? Not talking to me any more?"

"Well, that's me, you know." She put the lipstick away and stood snapping and unsnapping her purse. "Like I told you last night, no sense trying to spin things out. When it's time it's time."

Jauntily, with an effort to make the movement match the independence of her words, she threw her coat back off her shoulders and reaching in under the tail gave a tug at her dress where it was wrinkling over the hips. Then we looked at each other, she still fussing with the wrinkles, I with my knees nearly up to my chin and my hands locked around them. Embarrassment; silence. To break it at last, snatching at the first words that came, I said, "I wish you'd take that damned dress off—all those frills and beads—"

"My *dress?* You serious?" The words a little plop of astonishment; the hand fussing with the wrinkles arrested like a hand in a movie when something goes wrong with the projector. "It's a *good* dress, Sonny—real good. What don't you like about it? Blondes are supposed to look good in blue."

"Sure it's a good dress—you look fine. Pay no attention."

"Sonny—" She advanced a step and peered down at me cautiously. "When you said take it off just now you didn't mean *again* did you?"

It wasn't what I had meant but I lay back and laughed. "Well, Sunday and broke—can you think of a better way to spend the time?"

She teetered on her toes a moment, silent, delight stuck in her throat like a fish bone; then, with a swift, eel-like twist she was out of her coat and saying, "All right, but not till you turn *round.* I told you before—no watching."

I hadn't much more than turned when she bounced onto the bed and rolled over me so that, without turning back, I lay facing her. A big happy laugh at my surprise, another bounce, and then abruptly still. Expectant, confident, like a little girl as she falls asleep on Christmas Eve. And as I raised myself and began to explore her again I was relieved; exposed in the candid, winter-morning light, she looked resilient and young. The old tramp with defeat in her face was gone: a trick of the eyes, an illusion. Relieved because an old one— free at that—would have been another turn of the knife, would have confirmed the rating: derelict and failure.

She lay with her eyes closed, passive, receptive, and at intervals, teasing, I stroked her with my fingertips, sometimes just a nail, moving from breast to chin to thigh haphazardly, so that she would not predict the touch and each time would respond with a little contraction, a flicker of skin. Important: only young skin would flicker. Old would be toneless, slack.

And then, perhaps still uneasy, fearing that if there had been one trick of vision there might be another—that this might be illusion and the old, bedizened look reality after all—I said and did things to make her open her eyes and look up at me. The smile, I remembered, had been young; the eyes even younger. And again I was reassured. The eyes danced; the smile bubbled into laughter. I closed on her and it was good again.

Even better—as I had never had it before. No revelation this time either, but a strange sense of being one. For I could see her now, catch glimpses of the eyes, shining and blind, and it was as if I too were something coming true, coming towards her, incredible and unknown, with a swing of light around my shoulders. A swan, a bull, a shower of gold.

I wanted it to last, to stretch pleasure like a curtain and shut out the day and week ahead; but making it last is for the ageing and the jaded, for mortals, and I gave myself without restraint or calculation. Largess befitting the rank to which she had raised me, a reckless fling as if I were born to it and need never stint myself or think about tomorrow; then lying back exhausted with an empty purse. The curtain fell. The glass behind it was as cracked and dirty as I feared.

"Sure glad you woke up before I got away. A couple of minutes more and just think what I'd have missed."

My turn to be game. I squeezed her hand and without looking at her rubbed my cheek against her shoulder.

"Sonny, you know something?"

The voice wary, reconnoitring. "I'm just lying here thinking I've still got five dollars."

"Good. Hang on to them."

"But I mean, since you've caught me anyway—"

"Some catch. I ought to hang you on a hook and get my picture taken."

"Some day we will. *Mad the Tuna—five hundred and ninety-five pounds*. I'll get my hair done .... Now keep the way you are, no looking—"

There was the sound of hard breathing for a minute, the swish and rustle of clothes. Still facing away from her, I said, "Better leave me your number. One of these days maybe I can take you out. We'll do the town."

"I was thinking about it myself—a couple of drinks and so on. Right now, though—"

"I'm sorry about last night—telling you to get out first thing this morning. But you know how it is—some of the people you run into—"

"That was just being smart. A town like this you can't trust anybody. All those French—"

She was dressed now and making up again in front of the mirror. "Worse even than the Greeks and don't think some of *them* haven't got funny ideas what a girl's made for. Right now though I'm thinking since you caught me anyway we might as well have breakfast. Bacon and eggs and nice hot cup of coffee—"

I explained there was just hamburger and stale bread. "Better run along yourself for breakfast—I'll turn over and have another sleep." But no—she meant bacon and eggs and she meant them *here*.

"I've been looking around and you've got lots of things—dishes, coffee pot, frying pan. Like you said last night, it's a housekeeping room."

"But just hamburger. We'll go out for bacon and eggs the next time."

"Don't lie there making excuses—there's a place over on Milton stays open Sundays. Groceries and everything—just around the corner—"

"Just soft drinks and magazines—I've been there."

"I've been there too—magazines *and* groceries." She took three one-dollar bills from her purse and thrust them at me, then threw my pants on the bed.

"A dozen eggs and a pound of bacon. Cream, oranges, cigarettes—here, better take four. And some kind of paper with the funnies. There's enough coffee and while you're away I'll get it boiling."

A swing to her words: she had taken over. I hesitated a moment, trying as I pulled on my pants to maintain a front of pride and independence; and then, famished at the thought of bacon and eggs, let her shoo me out.

It was cold. I ran. Better to do exactly as she said than to see myself, to think.

And breakfast, half an hour later, was well worth the run. She presided easily, with expansive, housewifely ease. Two grease-spattered gas-rings, a few old plates and cups and saucers, knives and forks that looked as if a dog had tried its teeth on them—she had taken them in her stride, brought off a meal as she had brought off the washing and sweeping. A meal and a feeling of well-being and homeliness. She was meant for the part and she revelled in it.

Yet at the end, when we were smoking and taking our time over a second cup of coffee, there was a kind of constraint in her voice, something taut, guarded, as if she too were holding up a curtain.

Time now, but I delayed. Shrinking from the bright Mad-can-take-it smile that would flash on as she picked her way among the ruins—that was part of it; but also because, like a bystander, sympathetic but uninvolved, I was secretly *for* her, hoping she would get what she wanted just because she wanted it so badly; and most of all because I was curious to know more.

Did they really come like that? Harlot with a heart of gold—in Montreal? Or was it all just a front, a come-on? The clean socks and swept floor—an act? As she worked had she known or suspected I was watching? At the last minute would she have dropped something, knocked over a chair?

Talk about catches, though—

"I'll be hocking it tomorrow, so if you'd like to stay till I can straighten up with you—" I tapped my watch, then leaned back and tried to blow a nonchalant smoke ring. "I ought to be able to raise fifteen, maybe twenty—"

"There's no straightening up, Sonny. You didn't, what you might say, knock me on the head and sling me over your shoulder."

"The groceries—I just mean if you've got nothing planned and *want* to stay—"

"Sure, I *want* to stay, but what about your landlady?"

"How's she going to know?"

"She'll see me, that's how she'll know. Or *smell* me. When there's another woman round a woman always knows."

"She's got a bad leg—maybe two—didn't I tell you? She hasn't made it up this far for the last month."

She sat still a moment, remembering all over her face what I had told her last night. Then, alert and concerned, "Just the same I wouldn't trust her. There's never yet been a landlady with legs *that* bad."

I explained it was how I had the room: there had been two of us for a while, somebody I had played with in Toronto; then he cleared out and she said if I was broke I could stay on and work for the room. "Encouragement—shovelling snow, sweeping the stairs. She thinks I'm an upright, God-fearing young man."

A little nod. "And she knows all right. That's one thing about them, they get pretty quick at sizing you up, seeing what's there."

"Maybe .... But in fact it was my old man got the room for me. Ever hear a hymn called 'There Is a Happy Land'?"

"Sure I've heard it—where do you think I come from? We used to sing it back home in church."

"He used to sing it too when he tied on a few—one of his favourites. It started running through my mind here one night and I tried it on the clarinet—straight first, then variations, fooling around, seeing what I could do—"

"*Far, far away*—something about *angels bright as the day*—no place for me."

She began to hum it, tapping on the table, and I went on quickly, "Anyway, she recognized it and sent word would I come down and play something for an old friend who had just lost her husband. The funeral service had been terrible—all new-fangled tunes. She wasn't satisfied and she was sure the dear departed wasn't either, so while she blew her nose and drank tea and munched fruit cake I played 'Safe in the Arms of Jesus' and after a while—a message having come through that all was well now—she dried her eyes and blessed me and in return Mrs. Painter said the room was mine as long as I needed it. Just shovel snow and keep things clean up here, my future was assured."

She blinked and patted the front of her dress uneasily. She hadn't quite understood what I was saying but she had sensed irreverence. Sensed, too, perhaps, something false. For I had given almost as many variations to the story as I had to the hymn. Arrangements for the free room, for instance, had already been made, and "Safe in the Arms of Jesus" had been practically a command performance. And I, too—glad of the chance—had drunk tea and munched fruit cake.

"So if you think you can make out for another night—"

"Understand, though, it's on account of you I'm staying—nothing to do with your watch." She reached for my cup and drained the old black coffee pot authoritatively. "Matter of fact, I think you're crazy. The things I've lost that way—I could set up storekeeping. I mean since you're sure of your room and it's just a case of eating—"

"Eating and a haircut and a new shirt—and soles on my shoes—and rubbers. At that I might get by—but there's my clarinet."

She cocked her head and eyed me narrowly. "You mean you hocked your clarinet and now—to get it out—you're going to hock your watch."

"I've got to practise."

"So why hock it in the first place? Why not the watch first and *then* the clarinet?"

"At the time it seemed a good idea. It just hasn't worked out."

(You'll get it back because you won't be able to live without it. You'll go after it the way you used to go after things ten years ago. Nothing'll stop you—nothing. And once under way—just like a stalled car—give it a push and then you've got to run to catch it. That was what I had believed, been sure of—what the old Sonny would have done. But the ruse had failed. The legs hadn't even twitched. Days on end, instead of responding, Sonny had just lain staring at the ceiling, thinking about a drink.)

"A spell of bad luck—you don't have to tell me what it's like." Bewilderment, then commiseration. She didn't know what I was talking about but she understood how I felt. "Plenty of times I've gone looking for a job .... The way they look you over, like there's only two things you're any good for."

"That's two up on me." It was a long time since I had had anyone to talk to and the sympathy drew like a poultice. "The size of me and the size of my clarinet—I'd be better off with a tuba .... And getting your tie straight and your face set right—remembering to look cheerful, sure of yourself, wondering if it mightn't have been better to forget the tie and not look such a square."

She tried to follow, then spread her hands. "Your watch, though—it's good to hang on to something like that, just for the feeling. Something to fall back on—supposing the worse comes to the worst—"

"That's what I'm doing—falling back on it."

"If you could just get a little loan to help you through—you don't know anybody? Like the old girl downstairs?"

"If I need it ... I think I'll take it in, though—get it over with."

I spoke curtly, with an involuntary movement of my head again towards Charlie's room—another reflex, an upstart thrust of the old arrogance to let her see I wasn't completely destitute, completely dependent on handouts from her—and she pounced, "That fellow Charlie! Then there *is* something!"

Off balance a moment: I hadn't expected it. "Charlie seems to bother you. Can't I have my reasons for *not* wanting to borrow from him? You don't go round putting a touch on people just because you happen to know them."

"What reasons?" All along she had been careful with me, almost deferential, ready at the first sign of irritation to retreat; but now, blazing protection like a bitch when a stranger tries to touch her pups, she squared up to me. "There's something funny going on—he's willing to lend and you're scared to take. I knew last night, soon as you started talking about him."

I stared back, hostile a moment, then shrugged. "Not scared exactly. For that matter I don't even know if he *would* come across. I just don't want to get mixed up with him—staying clear."

"Clear of what? What's he been trying to talk you into?"

I shrugged again, stood up and sat down. "Sounds like he might have a job for me—maybe looking for a partner. Or maybe I'm just imagining it."

"Something tricky's coming sure. Just the way you tell it—the look on your face."

"But I'm not telling it. There's nothing yet to tell."

"There will be. And you know, too." She raised herself off the chair and then sat down heavily, like someone plumping a cushion. "Montreal for you—every time. A nice, clean decent boy like you and you can't even rent a room without running into trouble."

"Let's forget Charlie—there's no trouble." Scowling, suddenly irritated by the look and tone, I snapped it at her. "And I'm not a nice, clean, decent boy and if Charlie thinks I'd make a partner it's ten to one because he's been looking me over—and come up with the answers. And anyway, I can handle him."

She watched dubiously a moment, and at the same time with a kind of indulgence, as if she had her own ideas about the right way to handle me. Then, quietly, "A lot of times when they look you over, Sonny, they come up with the wrong answers—wrong ideas what you're good for. And if you're not sure yourself—I just mean it can get you into some funny places. Like me once—somebody took a look and figured I'd make a stripper."

5

WHAT DO YOU DO when you're not in bed with her?

"No, better go shave now," she said quickly when I picked up the paper, as if sensing the problem, understanding that absences were to be made the most of. "You can have a read when I'm gone, because if I'm going to stay I've got to run over home .... Pick up some things and change. It's a good dress even if you don't like it."

She turned to the mirror for confirmation, patting her breasts and smoothing the wrinkles over her hips again. "Too good to go slopping around getting spots on it."

When she was gone I lay looking through the paper and wishing she would forget to come back. The room seemed big and still without her—abandoned, like a house after the departure of too many guests, and at the same time restored. The faint sputter of a snowplow brought a feeling of seclusion. The old walls creaked and muttered in the wind as if it were Saskatchewan, and the branches made busy little scratching sounds like sparrow feet; but here it was sealed-off and secure, a cell of coffee smells and warmth in the heart of the January cold.

Half an hour: simultaneously I began to hope and feel uneasy. Probably gone for good. She'd done her best, a good night and a good breakfast, and still it wasn't enough. In a hurry to get rid of her. I had let it show.

An hour and it was the other way round. What was there to come back for? Didn't Maritimers have good heads?

"I thought it was a line," she was probably telling Cora, "but it turns out he *is* broke. If you saw where he's living—sweeping the stairs to pay the rent. Big chump me! Anyway, I fried him bacon and eggs for breakfast and told him what a wheel he was in bed—"

But she just laughed back at me, pouring me another cup of coffee, going into another bump and grind. Again and again I ran her through my mind, the way an expert, looking for a foul, might run the film of a race that had ended in disaster, and each time every word and look and gesture came out true. Big chump was right, but she would never say it. The pickings had been fine. One of the right ones—I'd given her the time of her life.

She burst in with a bulging shopping bag and more triumph. This time, pork chops and a radio. "She's got *three*, will you, and if you knew the time I had to bring her round. All right, she says at last, but just for a week and remember if I don't get it back it's forty-nine ninety-five. What she paid for it five years ago—*actually remembers*."

"Sound like Cora's got a head on her shoulders. Another Maritimer?"

"Cape Breton—the worst. Got in a jam one night when I was making out not bad and I stood her fifty dollars bail. A good ten years ago—never got over it. Her, the way she's made, it'd lay her up a week to stand anybody fifty cents." She paused a moment, then added fairly, "Except me, of course—since. But I don't take advantage. I get behind a little with the rent sometimes but I always catch up. And she knows."

The cold had brought a flush to her cheeks that made her hair double yellow and her eyes double blue: the blossomy, overdone blue and yellow of a girl on a chocolate box. "And here's a couple of tins of soup—good for your lunch. Something hot on your stomach's what you need to fight that cold."

I didn't like it. We had been poor farmers with a rattle-trap Ford truck and patched overalls and a perpetual mortgage, but we had never accepted handouts of soup and pork chops. I seized one of the tins, intending to put it back in her bag; and then, because she was beaming—the look of a successful forager, returning from an expedition into enemy territory with a whole pig on her back—I patted the tin instead and said, "Nice work—we'll have to send you out again."

But she had caught it. Her voice rose defensively. "What's some soup and a couple of pork chops to Cora? Besides, it isn't as if we're not going pay her back."

I still didn't like it. Montreal didn't make us a team, didn't wipe out differences. Not by a long shot. There were still lights for Sonny. I hadn't come from Saskatchewan just to sleep with Mad and eat Cora's pork chops.

She hadn't meant it that way. I met her smile again, sunny, guileless—its triumph clouded just a little because there were only two pork chops—and wondered what was at stake, why I was fighting her so hard.

"*Owns* her house—almost. Nine rooms and never an empty. A couple of diamond rings—real sparklers—and if you saw the hands on her, all knuckle and skin. Just like she's getting herself inside."

She went to the closet and brought a plate for the pork chops, stood a moment looking at them critically, then picked up her coat from the bed where she had tossed it and fished out two tins of peas. "Who's it this time, she says, Sonny Who? and I up and tell her a couple of nights with Sonny's worth more than she'll ever have—for all her scratching and skimping."

She was breathing hard and her eyes were bright. Cora, I guessed, had gone down swinging too.

"No idea what I'm talking about. Nothing but experience—all the wrong kind. Sometimes I feel like walking out on her only then if I was ever up against it I couldn't go back. Like I say, real Cape Breton—hangs on to a grudge like a dollar. And in this town you never know what's waiting round the corner."

Then, slapping her hands together, dusting off Cora, she carried the radio to the dresser, knelt down, and plugged it in. A dance band, sleek and crisp: she watched me carefully a moment, to see if I was satisfied. "Maybe you'd like another station—something slow and serious? A lot of people do on Sunday."

"You're worrying about *me* because it's Sunday? After last night?"

"Well, it's sometimes hard to tell. I don't suppose you'd have learned to play hymns like 'Happy Land' unless you sort of liked them."

"In a way—not exactly .... And a long time ago; doesn't make much difference now."

"I know what you mean—a lot of things don't make much difference now." She gave a small, comprehending nod, her eyes fixed on the radio. "Back home, believe it or not, I used to sing in the choir myself. 'Hoink-hoink'—one of those—but the preacher figured it was a good way to keep us out of trouble."

"Safer in the choir than the bushes?"

"Running the streets, my old lady used to call it. Still, he got some of the boys going too, so we didn't do too bad—sort of a meeting place .... But that was all. It never *meant* anything to me, not like church is supposed to."

She turned and faced me, her eyes still perplexed by the failure. "Up in the choir instead of listening to the preacher I'd be away off, wondering about my hair or trying to catch somebody's eye. Not a word of it getting through. Same as after Bill came and I was going to have my baby and he started acting mean—"

Voices and eyes circled away from me, picking their way back alone. "I figured it would be a good time to do a little praying—that was what the preacher was always telling us to do, pray when you're in trouble, and this was trouble sure enough, up the stump and nobody to marry me—but I guess I didn't do it right because instead of acting friendly again he just picked up and disappeared."

She walked to the window and looked out a moment, then came back to the radio. "And in a way it's too bad, because for somebody like me praying and so on would be just the thing. All by myself, I mean, and not exactly what you'd call well-educated."

A commercial jingle began and she played back and forth on the dial, then halted a moment, suspended between stations. "Like a girl I know can't eat eggs. One of them that used to be at Cora's—and being so fast and easy to cook she's always saying what a shame. A girl living alone in a room with a hot-plate—a couple of nice fried eggs in the morning would be just the thing."

6

THAT EVENING, a few minutes after the pork chops, Charlie knocked.

"Thought you might like a drink—I heard the voices." He stood motionless a minute, just inside the door, smiling and appraising, then nodded towards his own room. "Tired of talking to myself and it's too cold to go out. Better bring a chair—there's only one. I'll sit on the bed."

The smile had a kind of wry, boyish appeal; the voice was insistent, with a drawl like a whip in slow motion. We went. I said to myself it looks like a long evening, listening to the radio; and later, explaining her consent, Mad said she just wanted to look him over and find out what was on his mind; but we went because he had decided.

"Rye or gin? Gin of course for the lady. I've got some left from last night." It was sometimes a pleasant drawl, as if he were imitating or making fun of someone; and you went along with it indulgently, as you would with the affections of a youngster. "I had a visitor too last night, but I just kept her half an hour."

Ice cubes—obviously for us—so he must have gone down early and had Mrs. Painter freeze them. Why? Why make a drink such an occasion? Not to impress Mad: the look of appraisal as he stood in the doorway had also been one of confirmation. Already sized up and dismissed: just an easy lay. One corner of his mouth amusement, the other contempt. But she had brought a radio, was apparently staying on a while. If there was a little cash as well, she might prove a nuisance. Interference—so he was out scouting. He had his own plans for me. The drink was to determine what size ammunition would be needed.

"Just a beer for me." Rejection—involuntary—for I would have preferred rye. "We've been drinking beer since last night. I'd better not change."

Charlie was a sandy, thin man with a double-take face that ran the gamut of age. Sometimes you caught the callow, awkward look of an adolescent—wanting approval, watching for signs of it; sometimes the craftiness of an old man, isolated in suspicion and defeat. In years, he was about forty. The lips were red and full, almost a pout: a late raspberry on a dry stalk; and the eyes peered cautiously from deep, dirty-finger sockets. A spoiled, ill-tempered little boy, trying to scare you with a skull.

His clothes were good, too young. He wore them with an air—"sharp"—that most of the time was convincing. Beside him, I always felt a lout.

"I've seen you drink hard stuff and like it. Don't you know you ought to cultivate your expensive tastes? And then the need to satisfy them will speed you on your way to fame and fortune."

It was his way of talking, mock-pompous with a sneer, as if he wanted to let you know not only that he had been to school and learned the big words but also that he despised them—almost as if some of the poolroom boys were at his shoulder, listening in, and the sneer was to prove gang loyalty.

"It's just that beer doesn't provide much incentive." He smiled from me to Mad, seeming to regret the turn the conversation had taken. "Even an old rubby down on the Main usually gets two or three glasses a day."

Crowded into the shabby little room—Mad and I sat side by side, our backs to the dresser mirror, Charlie solemnly playing host, the windowsill his bar—I felt like a child's drawing of a Sunday afternoon visitor, stolid, angular, too-big. "There are other incentives," I said flatly, as if the words had been written for me. "I can get along without the hard stuff."

"Spoken like a real pioneer—somebody who knows where he's going and how he's going to get there." He poured a beer and stood over me a moment. "Seriously, how are you making out? Anything in the way of a job yet?"

I shrugged, and drank without looking at him. A taste of gall. My back was to the mirror but I could see myself.

"How can he? He hasn't even got his clarinet." Mad to the defence, the quick turn of her head making her hair seem to bristle. "Even the weather—walking around a day like this you'd freeze."

"Somebody determined, though—spirit of the frontier, sweat of the brow—"

I rallied a little, thinking it was just his words that had fooled me. A small-time crook was supposed to talk like one—movie-style, in grunts and monosyllables, out of the corner of his mouth. And I, country-style, had upgraded him because he was fluent; had shown him, unconsciously, a kind of respect.

"It's not a very good time right now for jobs, January and February. And of course there aren't many jobs I'm much good at."

I stretched my legs cautiously and watched him. Façade— what we'd call out west a false front. And behind it a scared little man in his hideout, talking tough and cocky as an alternative to biting his nails. *His* way of whistling in the dark. "Apart from the clarinet—and it's still a question whether I'm much good even at that—at least in Montreal— I can drive a tractor and ride a horse and at a pinch milk a cow. Any offers?"

"Shouldn't be too much trouble getting you fitted in. We'll have to have a little talk one of these days."

"By the look of this room you'd do better trying to fit yourself in somewhere. Just leave Sonny alone—he's going to come along fine."

For a second or two his eyes made me wonder if he might be sick as well as scared. Sick, even dangerous: the blank, bird-hard glare was like a concentrate of tantrum. Get in his way at the wrong moment and you might be sorry. But recovering quickly, the smile slightly weary, the drawl sly, he continued, "Speaking of rooms, we'll maybe all have to move. Mrs. Painter tells me she's going to sell—they're going to pull the house down. Where'll you go, Sonny? Nice little set-up you've got here. Double room, house-keeping privileges, linen and cutlery, friendly cockroaches—"

"I saw a couple this morning, Sonny, but I didn't want to tell you." She turned, lowering her voice, and touched my hand with her glass. "Nobody seems to mind here—just another crunch—but coming from the country same as me I said to myself he won't like it. Even supposing you've seen some already—no sense rubbing it in."

"All the things you've got in common!" Raising his glass to the light, he smiled. "Sooner or later, I suppose, you just had to find each other. *Like draws to like*—how does it go?"

"We didn't find each other—I found *him*."

A spring to her voice. This was something she wanted to talk about, even if it meant talking to Charlie. "For a good half-hour he wouldn't even speak hardly—just dirty looks and sulky."

She broke off, catching herself, and as if to make up for her lapse into such a friendly tone, stood up and let her eyes travel around the room. Sagging bed, fly-specked calendar, dirt-grey floor with a bit of threadbare rug; the inventory was complete and scathing. And then, with apparent irrelevance as she sat down again, "You know Sonny, it's not nearly as good as yours."

She spoke slowly, letting the weight of her preference sink in. "There you were last night, making such a fuss about letting me see where you're living, and here's Charlie with a room not half the size to say nothing of the bed. And pouring the drinks like the mayor himself, and just look at the fancy shoes!"

Poor Mad—With all her years of schooling in the street, this was her deadliest, her bitchiest worst. With a clink of ice she added, "All the rooms I've seen in Montreal I'd say this was just about the worst."

And yet it pinched a nerve. "The room I live in doesn't matter. And I'm not shacking up with a bag so the size of the bed doesn't either."

Out of control a moment, his mouth working as if there were a bit in it and a rough hand on the reins. And then to me, with a snort of laughter, "Jesus, Sonny—ashamed to let her see where you're living—that's pretty small-time isn't it? Sure have your fun—all along I've been telling you—but you've got to see it for what it's worth."

"There's nothing small-time about Sonny and it's a big mistake to go round judging other people by yourself." A sudden swing to her words, as if she were up again and striding. "Just wait till he gets started—he'll show you who's a small-timer!"

The swiftest of glances: contempt, then exclusion. "Seriously, Sonny, what are you going to do? You're starting to worry me."

It was as if we had walked into another room, just the two of us and the door closed. "No fun, no contacts—you're eating yourself out." The voice warm and big-brotherly again, the concern like an arm around my shoulder. "Supposing something does turn up—you haven't even got your clarinet."

"There's all kinds of things he's going to do." Still striding, Mad was far from excluded. "You don't keep somebody like him down—just because he's had the 'flu and a run of bad luck."

"That's what I mean—" Seeming to realize that there was no way to keep her down either he rolled with the punches. "It's not a question of keeping him down—but helping him up. I mean—"

Mad or Charlie—that was what he meant. Which?

"You heard Mad; all kinds of things I'm going to do." Sullen a moment, then defiant. "If it comes to it, I can always write home."

Meaning it: realist. As a youngster on the farm I had planned escape and built fine futures for myself, but always with restraint—almost a sense of propriety—careful never to overdo it and run wild. The farmer in me: you hoped for a sixty-bushel to the acre crop, even when the rain was holding off, and experience told you that with luck you'd harvest twenty-five. You knew your land, though, and never hoped for a *hundred* and sixty.

"They can always sell a couple of steers. I'll get my bus fare anyway."

"And you'd go?" He said it in a small, wondering voice, shaking his head in disappointment. "Settle for three square meals a day and your country dances—I wouldn't have thought you could."

"In the spring there'll be lots of jobs," Mad came down on him again, "and long before that anyway he's going to be blowing that horn of his so they'll hear it right down in the Maritimes."

"Good—that's what I wanted hear." Again, without turning his head, he rolled with her. "Only in the meantime, until the sound carries that far—"

"What's it to you anyway? Checking up and asking questions like you had the right. Just leave him alone. Supposing we started checking up on *you* and what you're doing. Funny things we'd maybe find."

"I had a job for a couple of weeks on a beer truck, heaving bottles." Embarrassed for her, I spoke quickly, trying to work in a laugh. "And I suppose I can always find another. Nobody starves."

"Nobody gets far either heaving bottles. And your lip—don't you have to practise, keep in shape?" Closing in a little, crowding me towards the door marked Charlie.

"I said I'd heave bottles if I have to. Any job—or go home."

"You're not going home, Sonny, and we'll do better than a beer truck for you." Expansive again, he waved his glass, then reached over and patted my shoulder. "A car's more comfortable—why not? Big shiny new one—squeeze in half a dozen blondes. Maybe sooner than you think. First step start thinking big—"

"No, first step start thinking about my lip; you were right a minute ago." I stood up abruptly and made a sign to Mad. "Just as soon as I get my clarinet—maybe a couple of days. The walls are thin so you'll be hearing me."

"Nothing like a friend in need. Glad things are starting to work out for you." With a little bow he handed me the chair I had brought, then opened the door and stood smiling. Our visit had lasted only ten or fifteen minutes, but he made no effort to detain us. Easier than he had expected: small shot would do. "Bedtime service *and* your clarinet. Forget Saskatchewan. One of these days you'll be striking out for new frontiers in Nova Scotia."

7

"WHO IS HE? What do you suppose he's after?" Face to face with him she had spoken up harsh and fearless, but now, hunched forward, she was whispering as if he were still within hearing.

"Just Charlie—just there. You know as much as I do."

"Sure he hasn't got something on you? Sure sure? Doesn't matter what—you can trust me. Maybe I could help."

"Sure sure—not a thing."

"The way he talks—like it was his business what you're going to do. Nosing in—and you not talking back."

I looked at her and nodded. Who? Where from? Why the interest? For in the country, farm or town, you always know. No one's just there. There's always a source, a why and where-fore. Charlie would probably have made me uneasy in any case, but there was an extra twinge, a second shadow, just because he was unaccounted for, because I couldn't place him.

"Holing up in there if you ask me. Lying low till it blows over."

"Till what blows over?" I had thought it too—put it to myself in the same words—but I spoke aggressively, to rout her. A kind of snobbery: not wanting to admit our minds ran parallel.

"Whatever it is he's done. Lie low and wait—that's the smart ones."

"So what do I do? Call the cops and tell them there's a man in a seven-dollar-a-week room drinking rye and gin?"

"Don't tell the cops, tell *him*. Next time he knocks—you're busy, you don't like his company." She straightened and gave a toss to her hair as if she were doing the telling. "All the same—*yellow*—streaky like a snake's back. Stand up and talk straight and that's the last of them. Soon as they see."

"The trouble is I get tired sometimes of my own company." I went to the window and stood staring out a moment, then sat down on the bed. "For the last few weeks I've been holing up here too."

"He's got a sly look—sly and mean. Take it from me, when he stands you a drink, it's not *just* a drink."

I told her again how it started: my cough, his trip to the drugstore, the hot drink of rye and lemon. Patiently, companionably—as if I had acknowledged a danger and were accepting her to share it with me. "Three nights he brought the drink—then he saw me at the gas-ring frying hamburger and took me out for a steak."

"And now you feel you *owe* it to him to be friendly."

She nodded, trying hard to be fair. "It's just the way he talks—and *looks*—and you being from Saskatchewan and not knowing how they do things."

She brought an orange, sat down beside me on the bed and peeled it gravely. We ate in silence, leaf by leaf. Then, wiping her fingers on her handkerchief and passing it to me, she nodded again towards Charlie's room. "Creeping up on you—waiting for his chance. You know it, too. Every time you talk about him, all over your face."

"Doesn't make sense—just look at me. I'm not worth creeping up on."

"Shaky and scruffy—he knows what he wants all right. Somebody like you comes along it's only natural."

I stood up and our eyes met. She waved a fistful of orange peel. "Somebody to lean on—he doesn't like holing up in there alone."

I started to answer but her voice rose, a slight tone of warning. "There's more than one way you can lean, Sonny.

Shaky, like I say—not so sure—and in this town they play tough."

"So my job's to protect him? Bodyguard?"

"Once down on the Main I saw somebody getting beaten up. In a club—two of them taking turns, and the waiters all keeping busy at the other end, not seeing a thing." She sat with her brows wrinkled, her fingers opening and closing on the orange peel, not understanding but sure she was right. "Everything so still you could *hear* the slugging—and when they'd finished he was hanging over a chair with the blood running out of his mouth like something ready for a butcher shop .... There was another girl, fixing her face and not seeing a thing either, so that's what I did, too—lipstick to the ears—and then when everybody started drinking again got going fast."

"And what's that got to do with Charlie? Or me?"

"Just to show you how they play—too tough for him." She stood up and put the orange peel on the table, then carefully, her whole body thinking, sat down again. "Tough and dirty—he'd never hold his own .... I don't mean he wouldn't play dirty too, but he's got ideas about himself. It wouldn't suit him to *think* he was playing dirty .... Know what I mean? What he's looking for?"

"No—and I thought you just finished telling me they were all yellow?"

"Tough and yellow both. Tough when they got something on you, or fighting among themselves who's to get most."

"And supposing he does have a job for me—" I shrugged dismissively and took a cigarette. "I can't turn him down? Saying 'Hello' means I've got to play along?"

"He's smarter, Sonny. He's been around."

I looked at her and it was like pretending something to the sky. "All right—let's say he is holing up. I've thought about it too—and it would explain everything. Keeping out of sight, nothing to do, nobody to talk to—it's only natural he comes in and talks to me."

"Makes sense—sure, at least back home it would make sense. Here, everybody's got an angle. Maybe in the first place he just came in to talk—"

"And finding me a lunk from Saskatchewan, decided he could use me?"

She ignored this, her eyes like a hand on my forehead, as if I were feverish, not quite responsible. "What he really wants— he hasn't said yet? Nothing to make you think?"

"Just that he could cut me in on something. Feeling me out maybe— watching to see if I'd jump for it."

"Something coming up all right." She nodded vigorously, tamping it in. "Something dirty. If you're smart you won't start counting on your cut."

"What do you think I'd be good at? Mugging somebody? Peddling?" I was edgy and tired, ready to let fly and tell her to shut up and get out; and at the same time I wanted to keep her talking. For Charlie had penetrated, settled in to hatch like a tick or larva under the skin, and the little lump needed scratching. "Or maybe driving for one of the bosses? Can you see me?"

"Maybe he can. They play funny games and they're all tied in."

Nodding and tamping again. Genuinely concerned and at the same time, like an old country gossip, enjoying herself as she piled it on. "It's not like back home, you know, where somebody steals something or gets in a fight and knocks somebody's eye out, or takes somebody's wife in the bushes. Not just bad and natural but bad and snakey—bad and mean."

"Montreal has a few more of them, that's all." Dismissive again, tolerant. I'd had enough, but I was determined not to quarrel. "They pull snakey tricks out where I come from, too."

She angered suddenly. "You stand there talking god-almighty wise and smooth and you don't *know* what you're talking about. You haven't been *in* anything yet. Nice fellow Charlie— just wants somebody to talk to! Keep it pretty and clean! You don't look at him straight because you're too god-dammed *scared* to look."

Our eyes held steady for a moment, hostile. And then, exploding again, but this time more in bewilderment than anger, "All the people in Montreal and you've got to get mixed up with *him*. It's so crazy, Sonny—somebody like you that's got everything to lose—"

She turned and gave a little dip to her head. "I *know*, Sonny. I've had my run-ins. A couple of them worked me over once—just like him. Same funny eyes—brings it all back. Talk about your bands and clubs—ever been down to some of the places on the Main?"

Her mouth hardened, drooped. She looked haggard and old again. "I was in an act once, stripping. Sheila, they called me—*Watch Sheila Shake*. Sounded fine the way they told it but they didn't tell it all. Just a couple of weeks and there was a raid—took us all in and was I ever glad."

A speck of something on her skirt in urgent need of scratching. For a moment, the sound of scratching. Then, softly, looking up again, "All kinds of things I could tell you. Like somebody you think you know and then all at once he changes on you. Right in front of your eyes—a face you've never seen before."

She sat on motionless a minute, eyes fixed on the wall, hands limp and heavy on her knees, then with a laugh and another toss of her hair stood up. "There—big-mouthed me! I wasn't going to tell you but I guess it doesn't matter anyway. Now how about a nice hot cup of coffee and a fried-egg sandwich?"

8

SHE WOKE ME AT SEVEN with more coffee.

"Bacon and eggs in the pan all ready and there's soup for later on. And a dollar, so if you feel like it you can go out for a sandwich. I'll be home around six."

I stared up bleary and disgruntled, vaguely troubled by the word "home." Her hair was done, her lips touched up. A look of competence, decision. "I've got to hurry, so drink your coffee while it's hot, and listen."

As she talked she slipped her shoes on, then her coat. "I lay thinking about it last night and I'm going to stay. A while—a couple of days maybe—we'll see how things go. I didn't say move in, so you don't need to be scared."

Her voice was quick and thin. Even in my bleary state I could see that the look of decision had been clapped on like a mask. Beneath it there was uneasiness, a doubt.

"Because you're not doing so well, you know .... Coughing terrible again last night—a couple of times I thought you'd bring the bed down." As she talked she kept darting glances at me, afraid of faltering or forgetting her lines. "No job, no tooter—and that fellow Charlie just waiting for his chance—"

She stood straight a moment, head back, coat half-buttoned, then sat down beside me on the bed. "I mean I want to. It's for me, not you."

A little pause while she bent to do something with her shoe. "Like I say, just for a day or two. Or longer, depending on you. I'll come home and get you a nice supper and wash your shirt and rub liniment on your chest—just like everything was real."

It was real. She laughed, pretending to make fun of herself, as if we were playing games, but her face was shining. "Those knees of yours—we just got to get some good meals into you, put a little beef on your bones. The digs you were giving me last night, I wouldn't be surprised if I'm all black and blue."

She stood up and looked towards the window. "So it'll be good for both of us. Me for you and you for me. Sort of an arrangement. Sensible."

Her hand came out, hesitantly, and touched my cheek. "I've got to run now. Have a nice easy day, and I wouldn't be surprised if we have steak for supper."

"But it's still dark—where are you going at this time?"

"Better if I don't run into anybody. It's all quiet, except a while ago somebody was working at the furnace. Around suppertime's all right—everybody has visitors."

"But I told you—she never leaves the basement—never up this far."

"I've got to go to work anyway, it's Monday. I don't start till ten, but the bus takes an hour and I've got some things to do at my own place."

She glanced at the mirror, stood busy with her gloves. "By the way, the door downstairs—seems to be open all day but when you came in Saturday night you had a key—"

"It's open till about eleven—sometimes all night. Nobody here's got anything to steal."

"And your door?"

"I'll be here."

"You say that nice, Sonny—like you'd be waiting .... Your coffee, before it gets cold."

With a flurry and a swish she was gone. A silent commotion, a hushed bang—careful not to disturb anyone on the way out.

I drank the coffee and went to the bathroom, stood a moment looking out the window at the grey, windy morning and then, instead of thinking things through as I told myself I should—about her and us, what was happening—slipped back into bed, drowsily at peace and guiltily comfortable. I slept most mornings until eight or half-past but now her departure, into the dark and the cold, made another hour a luxury—a reprieve from the day ahead that deserved to be enjoyed, made the most of, not wasted in more sleep.

A reprieve, though, that wasn't quite my due: the same as when I was a youngster I would waken to the sound of the alarm clock in the next room and then, curling back into the blankets, lie thinking guiltily of my father and brothers who, with all their other work, had to attend to Isabel.

My mother was like a rock: who ever heard of a boy his age getting up at such an hour just to feed and water a horse? What if it is *his* horse? He needs ten hours sleep. He's got to grow.

While my father made contemptuous noises and said he had always got up and done his share when *he* was a boy.

A matter of principle and discipline, though, not mean-ness, which made me feel all the guiltier. For she was mine—not so much a gift as a response, a moment of understanding—and the wonder of it always hung over me. A dull, work-bent, blindly practical man, and yet he had paid out hard-earned money for her. The most impractical of horses—there was even the story that she had thrown and killed a man; nothing on the credit side but a blaze of speed, a halo of outlaw light-ning. At the sale that day as I stood at his side and they led her out, poised, dramatic, radiant, some of the desire that over-whelmed me must have leaped from my face and melted him.

"Anyway, she's a bargain," he defended himself at the supper table. "And I can always sell her again and get back what I paid. But first I want to see what a little good hard work will do."

We still had horses—about half and half, my brothers keeping to the tractor—and it was his intention to work her on the land a month or two, just till she was tamed enough to make me a serviceable saddle horse. But less than a week and he let her keep her stall. She was too hard on his nerves, he said, straining ahead and pulling twice her share. She was too hard on his self-respect, actually, the slender limbs, the imperious head.

For she was a very lovely reprobate. Twenty years of struggle with the land had made him a determined, often hard man, but he couldn't bring himself to break her spirit with the plow.

One horse and all horses—somehow representative. Chargers, mustangs, Arabians, standing beside her in the stall, I knew and rode them all. In the neigh and eyes and forelock there was history. Battle and carnage, trumpets and glory—she understood and carried me triumphantly.

She was coal-black, gleaming, queenly. Her mane had a ripple and her neck an arch. And somehow, softly and mysteriously, she was always burning. The reflection on her glossy hide, sun or lantern, seemed the glow of some secret passion. There were moments when you felt the whole stable charged with her, as if she were the priestess of her kind, in communion with her deity.

For all that, though, she was a very dangerous horse, and dutifully my parents kept reminding me. "We've got troubles enough without broken bones and doctor bills. You hear now—not till you're sixteen." Facts didn't lie, they pointed out. She had killed a man, and a record was a record.

That was the trouble—a record was a record—and now, as I lay remembering, my own crept up on me.

Mad was right: not doing well at all. Well over a year now since I started out and not so much as a toehold. Ontario, the Laurentians—a week in one place, two in the next—all little jobs, no future. Nothing good enough for Sonny. A shot of scotch or rye to pull the switch and put the lights on. Another shot to keep them on. And now Ste Famille Street and the blonde from Nova Scotia—bacon and eggs for a good night's servicing ....

I got up and dressed and shaved and ate the bacon and eggs and then, my belly full, started fiddling with the lights again. Not bad: I was still Sonny McAlpine. I still had purpose, identity. Things had gone wrong but only because of miscalculation, unlucky breaks. At the worst, cocksureness, too big an opinion of myself. A Main Street head. Within myself, though, I was still intact. Damage temporary. Still a long way from the point of no return.

But the dollar she had left—and my hand so ready, unconcerned. A flash of panic as I caught myself, a sudden lost feeling, as if a lever had been pulled, a trap sprung .... An alien in a ugly, through-the-mirror world, no longer in control.

The dollar, the tin of soup, the radio: in sudden defiance I put the clarinet to my lips. Top form: notes silver-clean through the squalor—both the world and I restored. Where to? Roads in all directions. I had only to choose.

Briefly, though, and then reality bore down. Even uglier and more insistent than before, as if angered that I had tried to rub it out. Determined on a showdown, once and for all to put me in my place.

I smoked and paced, made the bed and washed the dishes—panic still there. And nothing now to allay it but the clarinet—the real one. No other way to hold myself together, go on sanely. I sat on the bed a minute, my knuckles in my eyes, then slammed out to see Mrs. Painter in the basement.

"Just fifteen dollars—"

She had always been there, but I had resisted. Already under an obligation to her, I shrank from being scowled at, lectured, perhaps refused. But going back to the pawnbroker, asking him to accept the watch in place of the clarinet, protesting, giving him my word—that would be humiliation, too. For it was one thing to talk to Mad about the exchange as if I had only to suggest it and another to remember the old man's indifference, the contemptuous, take-it-or-leave-it mouth and eyes .... And now I needed the clarinet, urgently, *today*—and she was only the stairs away—

"Just fifteen dollars and you can keep my watch. I only took ten on the clarinet but there'll be something to pay .... Look—my name's on it—so I'll want it back—"

"Sure it's for the clarinet? Or to pay off your fancy lady friend?"

She was a big, block-faced woman with the stance of a pyramid. Squat-necked, cold-eyed; iron grey hair drawn up on the top her head in a tight little knot like a handle on a bell.

"It's these old legs or I'd have been up and chased you both out. Like a couple of stovepipes—getting worse. The size of me and never a minute to rest."

"I'm sorry, but everything's all right up there—nothing to come up for—"

"Why don't you find yourself a good girl and get married? It's not so bad—I could do with a man right now to see the furnace and keep people like you in your place."

"I'll help with the furnace—any time. I told you—"

"Some help you'd be—smoke us out or blow up the boiler. Too old and tricky—nobody's got the knack but me. I keep saying I'll put in a new furnace—for oil—but it'd be such a lot simpler just to sell."

She stood a few seconds clicking it over, enterprise and profit versus comfort and convenience, then let her voice rise angrily. "The whole top floor bringing me in only seven dollars. That talky little man next to you. And as if it's not enough having the big one free you're starting to bring home women. And the nerve to ask me to pay!"

"There's nothing to pay—it's for the clarinet."

"So you can start in again and drive everybody crazy. The last couple of weeks we've had peace."

"I didn't know—nobody complained."

"It wouldn't be so bad if you'd play *tunes*—it's that skittering around and the way you keep up at it—"

"Look—it's got my name—so I'm not going to run off without it—"

"Never mind the watch—just keep things clean up there and shovel the snow. Around at the side and at the back—you're only doing the front steps. And no more fancy ladies."

I had intercepted her in the half-dark, cement-floored passageway that led from the rooms where she lived to the furnace room; and now she stood massive and motionless, seeming to wait for me to go, as if the matter of the fifteen dollars and my clarinet had been disposed of. The silence hung between us awkward a moment; then she said stolidly, "Look in the furnace room for me and see if Tommy's there. The cat—he sometimes slips out—and these old legs of mine I've got to think of every step."

Tommy yawned up sleepily from a bed of rags and sweaters. Fat and rheumy-eyed, he looked as if nothing less than a boot or a broom would make him slip six inches. When I closed the door on him and stepped back into the passageway she was still standing where I had left her. The same flat, all-seeing expression and the same bulldog set to her head; but her hand now, slightly extended towards me, held the money. Our eyes met a second: I guessed it had been in her stocking and she hadn't wanted me to see her swollen legs .... Or the size of the roll, not quite trusting me.

"So long as it *is* for the clarinet. I hate to see your making such a fool of yourself."

"You've got it wrong—she's the fool. How you knew, though—who told you?"

She had been waiting for it. Her face relaxed slightly, as if acknowledging a tribute. "It's my house. It's my job to know."

She paused a moment, letting it sink in. "Old Miss Crombie underneath you—she gets taken short a lot and goes up to your floor if the bathroom on hers is busy. And she says it was clean for once—so she could sit down and feel comfortable. And she knew besides because there was the smell."

I nodded. "That's what she said—you'd know by the smell."

"The stuff they plaster on their faces—all their tricks. But I figured it's something anyway to have the bathroom clean so I didn't come up after her. Although I would have only for my legs. I couldn't even go to church last night. I just sat here and prayed for you."

I smoothed the bills without looking at her. "Thanks for thinking of me—and I'm going to get my clarinet now so maybe you got through."

"Mind, though—next time I'll maybe not be in the mood for praying. And if I come up and catch you—" She broke off a moment, fists clenched, eyes dilated, as we went hurtling down the stairs. "Because I run a clean house—clean bathrooms, clean people. It's a fair warning."

9

DOWN THE HILL TO CRAIG STREET I didn't mind the wind. Thinking of my clarinet, I didn't even feel my hands and ears. But on the way back, up Bleury, I buckled, shivering and coughing, and three or four times stopped in doorways to set down the case and rub my hands.

The clarinet itself was somehow small and dead. No glow, no leap—not mine. As if its surroundings in the shop had dried and dulled it; the clutter of lamps and drums and accordions, the shelves of old suitcases and toasters that had never been redeemed.

I had opened the case when the old man brought it for me from the back of the shop, and he had given a smirk that said I was worrying needlessly. Go ahead and look—you think it's valuable? You think anybody in his right mind would go to the trouble of making a switch?

It was to greet the clarinet that I had taken it from the case, to charge and restore myself, not to check on its identity; but when I lifted it there was no response, as if it lived on touch and been left alone too long. I rubbed it a little, turned it to the light: like a patina or tarnish the old man's smile persisted. Rubbed it again—only rubbed it in.

And now as I walked up the hill it was still listless in my hand, still sullen and reproachful. Not ready yet to forget either the neglect or the company— the lamps and accordions, the drums and roasting pans. I huddled in a doorway, watching cars and buses churning up the dirty snow, and wondered again what the company was doing to me.

A pair of us. All at once I saw myself, isolated in the here-and-now of Bleury Street on a January morning, like a specimen in a jar of alcohol. Without roads, either to or from; without gloves or overcoat; without lights. As Charlie no doubt saw me. As somebody in a welfare or relief office would see a "case."

There was still Mrs. Painter. For all her grumbling she was on my side. Say I left her both watch and clarinet—perhaps she would let me have my bus fare home.

Bluff: no intention of going home. Not now—not yet. It was almost as if I were standing apart, looking on, and the Sonny McAlpine making his way up Bleury Street was not the real one. As if I didn't believe him, didn't take his distress signals seriously.

And yet I was getting scared. The bad moments—when the real Sonny and the twisted image ran together, blurred—were coming faster now, and the bus fare home was just a nod to myself that I understood what was happening, as promise that something would be done.

In the room again I steadied. I sat quiet a few minutes, resting after my last, half-frozen spurt along Ste Famille Street, breathing carefully to control the tickle in my throat and hold off another fit of coughing. Alert, an almost wily calm, like something wild. Mindless, yet with a kind of poise and calculation.

For if my throat got worse it could mean the hospital. And "case" was right: they might wire my father, send me home. I didn't think about it. It was just there, like something to be swerved from on the road at night. I took off my shoes and got into bed, pulled the covers up and lay still for half an hour. Still and blank, in suspension, yet all the time relaxing carefully, with determination.

And then like a sleepwalker, still mindless but with purpose, all the rest blinkered out, I got up and heated the soup. The clammy, sucked-out feeling in my legs as I came up the hill

had been a warning; I wasn't hungry but I ate. For I was alone now and knew it. Nothing but my own resources, tag ends of will, like someone lost in a blizzard. As I walked up Bleury the unawareness
of the city had taken on a new dimension, grown colder.

I ate the soup and what was left of the bread, then stretched out again on the bed. Just as she had said, I needed beef on my bones—reserve, stamina ...

A matter of survival—more stamina and less squeamishness. It didn't bother me going to bed with her. Why all the fuss about her soup and pork chops? For someone like me she was a gift—a hen for a coyote. Silly hens that went wandering—wasn't that how coyotes lived?

A long, mindless blank. Then it was time to try the clarinet.

Not bad—better than I had expected—and for a minute or two the lights were blazing. But I caught myself—Bleury Street looking over my shoulder—and settled down soberly to work. Applause later: for the time being, better if I tried for competence.

Salutary. Dull. Instead of playing to show what I could do I practised carefully to remind myself of what I couldn't. Half an hour exactly—I had to think about my lip. Then I made coffee and smoked a cigarette.

After all, it wasn't as if I was trying to take advantage of Mad. On the contrary—she herself had said it—I was giving her the time of her life. My squeamishness was only word-deep. Living off a woman—it was the sound of it I didn't like. Not the taste of blood: the sight of a feather sticking to my chops.

I began to play again; then Charlie interrupted.

"Not bad—take it all back." He stood frowning a moment, severe, then came forward and patted my arm. "That's right—my apologies. I've been putting you down as a bag of prairie wind and big ideas. What do you mean you can't get a job? Never let anybody hear you?"

Enthusiasm, almost respect; Sonny warming to it fast. "I thought I told you, they all want saxophone or guitar or somebody who sings Western .... Although when they do listen they don't seem worried they're letting a future all-time-great slip through their hands."

"That's because you're not letting the right people hear you." He patted my arm again, drew back a few steps, and stood looking at me. "Meeting a lot of squirts and jo's. And some of the right people shouldn't be too hard to arrange."

"I've got my name with an agent—he hasn't managed it. Just looks cut up and says a clarinet is a problem."

"That could be arranged too—a good agent."

"He nearly pulled it a couple of times but then I couldn't speak French and they were afraid I wouldn't get along with the other boys. The spring, he says. Everybody says the spring."

"If he knew his job he'd send you where French doesn't matter. It's you that does—you and the clarinet."

Warmed to him, went on. All over again about my big prairie feet and getting flustered and losing my lip. Not looking the part—that was the first strike against me. Big hick with big ideas—he himself had said it. And the jobs that had come my way how I had walked out on them. Dead ends, no future; some pipsqueak little bastard getting snotty with me. Not used to it—never forgetting I had had a band of my own. And getting my nerve back with a drink and then another—

"No stripes, Sonny. All you need is someone to open doors for you—a few introductions."

Went on again, confiding. That I had a stubborn streak and wanted to open my own doors. That I could take responsibility for myself, and didn't put the blame on luck or lack of breaks.

"And here I was thinking you onward and upward boys had died out twenty years ago—even in Saskatchewan." The sneer was involuntary, faster than he was. What I deserved, the right response to such blather. "I just hope your girl friend knows how to take precautions. I don't think you should be allowed to breed."

And then, straddling a chair, his arms resting on the back, he watched me curiously. "Twenty-four, so you must have started young." A slight hitch forward, like a muzzle working its way into your hand in search of sugar. "A band of your own, you say—and over a year now since you left home—"

"Not so young—eighteen before I had my own clarinet." Autobiographical: nearly ten years at the piano—Bach and Beethoven—big ideas was right. Then the doubts, then the local band, the offer—

"What kind of doubts? I don't understand." Another hitch; the muzzle starting up my sleeve.

Foolishly: the proud streak and the practical—the realization I would never make it with the piano. Started too late—always a second-rater. So why—the farmer in me—keep on knocking myself out for nothing? And all the time this man in town with the clarinet.

"You don't have to worry about knocking yourself out." A little smile, encouraging, almost deferential. "Just steady up and think straight. Somebody to show you around and get you on your feet—that's all you need."

"Sounds easy—as if I just had to look him up in the phone book."

"Never mind the phone book, Sonny." The voice with a twang; the eyes like bits of chipped glass. "You're looking at your man right now."

I laughed uncomfortably, running a finger under my collar. "But you don't any more than come up to my chin, Charlie—isn't it going to be a job getting me on my feet? I mean the size of me—"

He flushed, then whitened—the same, flattened-out whiteness that sometimes for a second or two follows a blow. And somehow it seemed—a twitch of muscle, perhaps, a shake of the head—that the eyes retreated again, hostile, bitter, into the shelter of the sockets. "I suppose it's fair enough." He shrugged, felt for his cigarettes and held out the pack. "I've been judging you by your Saskatchewan slouch. You judge me by the seven-dollar-a-week room."

I took a cigarette and leaned towards him for a light. "We come in all sizes out West. Some of us are too short to slouch."

"You can have a slouch in your mind as well as your back. You, now—you learn to play a good clarinet and then you sit back waiting for something to happen. That's slouching."

"You'd hardly call it waiting. Big frog in a little puddle— and I walked out. We used to play in five towns—lined up weeks ahead—"

"Leaving a little puddle isn't what counts. It's making it in the big one."

"The point is I didn't just sit—"

"The point is you're sitting now." Barking, vicious—he hadn't liked it about just coming up to my chin. "No job, no contacts—nothing but your Nova Scotia blonde. Whining about your big feet—*I'm from Saskatchewan and nobody listens to me.* Jesus—you've got to *make* them listen—wise up to things, yourself, the town."

"Wise up to the fact, you mean, that I need a little push from Charlie?"

"Joke—still thinking about the seven-dollar-a-week room."

He inhaled a few times, silently; then, all-boy again, looked up and smiled. "Why not? You'll admit Montreal's getting along fine without you—giving you long, uninterrupted nights with Nova Scotia. The old stone wall—and I don't think you've got a very thick skull."

"Thick enough. It can hurt without cracking."

"A waste of time, though, apart from the punishment. You'll admit a push and a leg-up would be faster."

"Go on." I shrugged indulgently, at the same time curious and alert. With the sound of the clarinet still in my ears, I felt a match for him.

"Something I've been thinking about for years—you'd just be right." He flung himself on the bed suddenly and lay with his mouth slack and half-open, a spidery twist to his legs. "A club—my own. Not one of the scruffy little joints where you go—I mean for the right people, the big names— the kind they'll talk about."

He rolled his head with the words and then lay staring at the ceiling as if it were a screen and he was running a film off his little fantasy. "And that means a band, too—*your* band—

got it? *Sonny McAlpine and his clarinet*—sound fine. We'll work you over, knock off a few corners."

"Sounds fine is right, but first—before we start working on the corners—"

"You think I couldn't do it? You think I'm a bag of wind too?"

"I didn't say that. I'm just curious."

Still alert and probing, for you didn't just dismiss Charlie as a fool. Even now, smiling up raptly at the ceiling, seeing his own lights, he was on the prowl. There was a sniffing restlessness, a kick of will.

"I'm not sure, Sonny." He sat up with a jerk and swung his feet to the floor. "I could work you in on something— just right for you—but I've got to know. Be sure."

"Too vague. There's still a lot of the farmer in me: I look at the teeth before I buy."

"I've got to know first—somebody who'll be with me all the way."

"I'd have said you're the type that likes to work alone— just like you're holing up here alone .... So maybe it's because you've sized me up as a big enough country hick to make a good stooge."

"No, Sonny—a good enough clarinet player to make the grade."

Smiling again and pacing, pleased at the way he had picked up the words and thrown them back at me. A quick, sly glance at himself as he passed the mirror.

"But today was the first time you heard the clarinet—and you've been wanting to cut me in on something for the last two weeks."

A little chain had appeared, ten or twelve inches, wrapping and unwrapping itself around an upright finger like a toy propeller. Still pacing, without raising his eyes, he asked, "How are your nerves?"

"Average, I suppose. Depends on what's to be done."

"Say a thousand—could you use it? Fast and easy—we'll be back counting it inside an hour."

"Sounds like it might be a little holdup you've got on your mind, and it's not for me. I've got a clarinet."

"All the more reason. Give your clarinet a break." He halted, his fist closed on the chain, and faced me earnestly. "It won't be the first one, you know. You could say I got my papers when I was seventeen. Bigger ones, tougher ones—so many now I've lost track."

"*Stick 'em up—I've got you covered!*" I put my head back and laughed. Relief—it was the last thing to tempt me—and at the same time a vague feeling of letdown. For two weeks now, working in unknowns, my imagination had been building him up, involving him in such dirty deals and rackets that a holdup in comparison seemed practically clean. "No—the only gun I've ever had in my hands was a .22 for rabbits. As for nerve, I'd probably have to stop on the way to change my pants."

"I carry the gun—there's only one—and it's never loaded anyway. Just in case of accidents—one of my rules. Chances are I'd want you at the wheel."

I whistled and drew away. "Your mind's been working overtime. You don't even know if I can drive."

"You can drive all right. We'll make a good team." He stood looking me up and down a moment as if for verification and then, the chain whirling, began to pace again. "Not far from here—just like going for a beer. Think what you could do with a little cash right now—a thousand—maybe more—"

"I'm thinking—how to make a mess of my life in one easy lesson."

"The gun I carry's got a lot of notches, Sonny, even without bullets—" He held out his hand as if offering the gun for inspection, "and my life's not messed up."

There was a change now, a hardening. The teeth were slightly bared. The face was white and stiff like plaster. And the voice had a ring of competence, the assurance of someone who had been there. I said warily, my skin starting to prickle, "You're overestimating me. I wouldn't have the nerve to hold up old Mrs. Painter in the basement."

Warily, but with concern rather than uneasiness, as you would be wary with someone ill and raving, not quite responsible. "All those notches and no slip-ups—you've been lucky but you shouldn't push your luck. Better take it easy for a while."

"Not luck, Sonny, head." He drew back a step, erect, and smiled.

"Take it easy anyway. I want you in a good mood before I start practising again."

The impulse was almost protective. For a moment, understanding, I almost liked him. Notches on his gun and no one he could tell. And bursting to tell, the vanity throbbing like a boil. A mixed-up little man with an adolescent itch to shine. So ease the pressure, let him talk. "Speaking of nerve," I said respectfully, "you must have plenty."

"Enough Sonny. Enough for both of us."

"But isn't it a sort of crazy way to make a living? In the long run, I mean? Dangerous?"

He stared back flat and blank, like an affronted owl.

"Or is it the job itself—the satisfaction of getting away with it? Or for kicks—just because it is dangerous?"

"The job itself—that's part of it." The chain hung limp; the smile drooped. Condescension, acknowledgment of a deference that was his due. "Winning—like a game of pool— taking some slick little show-off bastard that thinks he's good. But kicks and danger—no. Because the way I work there's no danger."

"There must be times, though—things you don't expect. Say you walked into a bank and there was a policeman ...."

"What do you think? I'd ask for a dollar's worth of dimes and walk out again." Smiling at my half-wittedness.

"But supposing you didn't know—supposing he was plainclothes?"

"I would know."

Invulnerable. The smile like armour. I waited a moment for it to fade and then said, "You usually work alone?"

"Some jobs take two."

"Well, then—you might know but how could you be sure *he* would?"

"Just what I'm trying to tell you—it takes someone you can count on. Somebody's that not going to let you down. That's why I'm talking to you."

"Now you're letting me down." I laughed again and looked at the clarinet. "Because if you'd pick *me* for somebody to count on—well, it means I couldn't count on you."

"Don't worry about it—we'll make a good team. You've got lots of nerve—just waiting for somebody to bring it out."

"But Charlie—you don't go ahead and do just whatever you've got nerve to do." I hesitated, embarrassed at this sudden upcropping of Presbyterian conscience, at finding myself starting to sound like a preacher or my mother. "It's a holdup you're talking about—somebody else's money."

"And what about bringing home a whore for the weekend?" He took a step away, then whirled round, spitting the words in my face like a mouthful of tacks. "In your book that's all right? Broad-minded Sunday schools in Saskatchewan?"

"There's a difference .... First of all, I'm broke, so if she was a whore she wouldn't come for the weekend."

"People like you there's always a difference." His nose twitched, like a dog's sniffing the wind. He looked scornful and at the same time dejected, as if perhaps I wasn't the first prospect to fail him. "It's all a holdup anyway—money, body, brains. Do you think anybody's ever satisfied with what he's got a right to?"

The last words weakened, groped. Our eyes met and it seemed there was a break, almost an appeal to understand. The bristle was down, like a cat that spits at a rival, then turns and runs.

"I didn't ask for it this way either. I never planned a stopover on Ste Famille Street." A tired look, hunted, shifty; a glance in the direction of his room as if it were the final corner. "I just wanted them to play fair—half-fair. Just once—to *try* to see it my way—"

But the next instant, snarling, he snatched back the softness as if it were something breakable, he had almost let it fall. "Nice clean country boy—why don't you get your girl-friend to buy you a paper and read about the jobs the big boys pull. The politicians—see whose money they *worry* about. And the police—have a run-in with them sometime—they'll wise you up to the facts of life. Especially if you can't slip them something or afford a smart lawyer."

"And that's why you want me to join you—just to complete my education?"

He came close again, rapping with his knuckles on his chest, shoulders up to his ears. "You'd be surprised—I could maybe even teach you how to farm. *Right!* A *Reform* Farm, for incorrigibles. Nearly a year and then I ran. My old man stood up in court and said he had failed and was afraid to take responsibility for me. A stronger hand was needed. Nice husky little shake in his voice—'As God is my judge I don't know where I went wrong!' All cut up but taking it like a man ...."

And then his story. "When I was only sixteen—this dick—plain-clothes—dirty." A stutter of urgency—he had a listener and was under way. Picked up in a bar because he was under age. A crooked detective and a stolen car racket. Driving for them—caught. Everybody against him—even his own family—

A story he shouldn't have told. Hackneyed and touched-up, in the aggrieved tone of a victim. He floundered in it like a horse in a snow bank.

"What was I doing in a bar? Finding out about things. For myself—it's the only way." Callow for a moment, as if he was still sixteen, earnest and wide-eyed. "You've got to know the score if you're going to get anywhere. I was always like that. I always wanted answers and at home I never got them. Just cracks about not knowing so much when you're seventy."

"But that was a long time ago. And it's your life—what's good for you now."

The chain was whirling. He didn't hear me. "I wasn't incorrigible. I just wanted them to talk straight, stop playing it so phony. My sweet saintly mother, worrying more about the big wedding coming up than me .... My brother—same as you. I didn't any more than come up to his chin—over six feet and prick to the skull. The girl he was going to marry—what would her family say? So hush it up, get me out of town, send me to *school*—two years—and if you knew what went on, the way they did things—"

His eyes came forward, glassy. His face looked thin and sharp as if the skin had been put on wet and then let dry.

"But Charlie didn't play along. One year, not two. A week in the bushes till there was time for them to figure I'd got back to town. A *week*, Sonny—seven days! Blueberries and slough water—bugs and scum. Try a swig of it sometime and *then* talk."

He drew back a little, nodding at the memory, the lines around his mouth like old, corroded scars. "A week and then a gas station—forty-two dollars and fifty-five cents. A bit of stick I'd planed and painted in the toolshop ... Just seventeen—and I've been a couple of jobs ahead of them ever since."

Rang true, didn't ring true. A few grains of truth imbedded in it and a hard lump of hurt.

"Twenty years, you mean, you've been on the run?"

It caught him off guard, stripped him clean. For a second I saw twenty years of fear.

"You never think there might be an easier way? *Not* running? *Not* keeping a couple of jobs ahead?"

He recovered, smiled. "I'm thinking right now, Sonny. When you asked a minute ago did I always work alone I said some jobs take two. That was only half an answer. All the good ones do."

He brought out his cigarettes and stood tapping the pack slowly. "And isn't that all there is for us? More jobs, better jobs? I can't go back; *you* can't go back .... Working together, we could pull off some real ones."

I shivered, shook myself. "But why me? Twenty years—you must have met plenty who'd know how—who'd be right—"

"Plenty I'd trust like a rattlesnake. Plenty who'd squeal or double-cross."

"And you know me? You're sure what I'd do?"

"You might do something stupid but you'd never squeal. That sticks out even more than you think your feet do."

"Thanks, Charlie. But right now I'd better do some work—see how my lip's standing it."

"I don't *need* help on this one, Sonny—it's just such a good chance for you to learn. Easy—just the right size—"

He took a deep breath and held up both hands, fingers spread as if he were describing a water melon. "A little job I did out West a couple of years ago—your country. Nearly four thousand—*alone!*"

Another story: how he had dunked doughnuts with a cop the day after and filled him in on things down east—a paper and the headlines right in front of them.

"You mean you're pretty smooth?"

"Smooth enough—I'll take you places."

"That's what I'm afraid of—too smooth." I stood up and reached for my clarinet. "You'd probably talk your way around me too."

"Only for your own good. And you're wrong if you think I just want to use you."

"And you're wrong if you think I'd make a good partner. Maybe you don't know it yet but you're like a lot of other people in Montreal: a clarinet's not what you're looking for."

He watched me a moment with his lips puckered as if he were going to spit, then dipped a shoulder and came up with a forbearing smile. "There's a chance, though, an up-and-coming young clarinet might be looking for me. Nothing to lose—at least think it over."

"That's what I'll do, Charlie. Sounds like good advice."

IO

MAD ARRIVED AT SIX, laden with groceries and an ulti-
matum.

"Steaks, Sonny, look! Celery and tomatoes—all kinds of
things—an apple pie. But it's got to be a deal. Not a bite till
you sign up for a week."

A laugh and a toss of the yellow hair as if it were just a
crazy joke, but mouth and eyes with anxious corners.

I shrugged. "Why not? Except there's Mrs. Painter. She
knows."

"You mean trouble?"

"I got out of it this time. She thinks you've been and gone."

"I'll be careful. Rushing this morning I maybe banged the
door." She bit her lip, self-reproachful a moment, then rallied,
"But even supposing she does catch us. Wouldn't take ten
minutes to find another room. And look at this—"

With another toss of her hair she opened her purse and
held up some bills. "Best day I've ever had in tips—everybody
glad to see me back, and you bring me luck besides." She
beamed, waving the money as if trying to signal me from the
other side of town. "And I talked Harry into giving me twenty-
five on my pay, so there's plenty for your tooter too. First
thing in the morning, away you go and get it out of hock."

Her big moment—restoring what she had guessed I needed
most—but I dropped my eyes, embarrassed at her offer of the

money and at the same time reluctant to burst her little bubble, and then said dryly, "It's a clarinet, not a tooter. And who's Harry?"

She froze a moment, her mouth open. "Oh *no*, Sonny! I've worked for him off and on now a couple of years. An old Greek—hair in his ears. But now I wouldn't anyway, not while I'm living with you."

"You're not *living* with me, and I only asked who he was."

"Sure I'm living with you—as long as it lasts. Even if you say on your way right now—it'll have been two days anyway. Best two days of my life."

Meaning every word of it and at the same time hoping hard. No strings—giving out of sheer big-heartedness—and at the same time rolling the dice.

"Making it last, Mad, only makes it that much harder. If you bring steaks when I'm hungry I'm naturally going to eat them."

"But that's *why* I'm bringing them. You can stand another thirty pounds on—easy."

"I'm only trying to tell you—so when the time comes—"

"Won't even hear me going. In the meantime, every day I'm still around, well, it's sort of like living on velvet."

"Pretty scruffy velvet. Take another look."

"Suits me fine—some day I'll maybe make myself a dress. Just the right colour for my hair."

She laughed again, faltered, ran the bills through her fingers. "Anyway, you do now like I say—whatever it is you call it— and tomorrow when I come home we'll have 'The Red River Valley.' You know the one I mean—an old Western."

She broke off, humming a few bars. "We used to sing it back home too sometimes—about the poor half-breed girl and loving you so true."

I stepped aside and pointed to the bed. "I got it out this morning. That's why I went to see Mrs. Painter."

She had been holding out two ten-dollar bills and now, with a quick, consuming movement, like the jaws of a big insect at work on a small one, her fingers gathered them out of sight into the palm of her hand. Then, hand held tight against her breast, she took a step and peered down at the clarinet as if it were something living, possibly dangerous.

"We'll have 'Red River Valley' right after supper. You won't have to wait till tomorrow."

And to myself: this is the way she takes it when I don't need her twenty dollars. A sweet time we'll have when I tell her I don't need her.

"Sure looks a nice one, Sonny." Reaching down, she touched it carefully with the tip of her finger. "After supper I'll go at the nickel and see if I can give it a shine. And when you're not playing, it'd look sort of nice maybe hanging on the wall."

She straightened, bent again—not sure of me, asking herself if it was time to go now; and then, with decision—almost defiance, ready to risk the consequences, whatever they might be—she kicked off her shoes and began padding around the room, picking up things, tidying, pretending to grumble at the litter I had made.

But only a minute or two—lifting and laying, finding plates—and she was restored. Housewife; in charge. Movements quick, assured; voice managerial. "You're too big, Sonny. Up on the bed with you out of my way."

Good steaks. Like the bacon and eggs and pork chops, she brought them off with a sizzling flourish. And as we ate she presided, hungry herself, enjoying her steak, but keeping an eye on me. Glad I knew enough to like a steak red and juicy. Some of them in the restaurant no idea—making you cook the life out of it .... Go ahead—pick it up and suck the bone—just the two of us no sense worrying about fingers. Too bad she'd forgotten ketchup but it killed the taste of a good steak anyway. All right in the morning—bacon and eggs—perk you up—and the rest lost in munch and greasy fingers.

"Funniest thing at work today about my feet."

It was a little later, coffee and a cigarette, and with an elbow on the table she was cupping her chin wearily. "The size of me, and all at once so light. Just like when you're dancing—a nice tune and away you go, floating along right off the floor—"

I caught the smile and stubbed my cigarette self-consciously.

"Just knowing you'd be here—the difference something like that makes. Never happened before. Never so *much* difference."

A statement of fact, an appreciation. One of the right ones—I would understand. Sonny and Mad—why pretend? Why play games with each other? The little subtleties and stratagems of man with woman—not for the likes of us!

"By the way, how about Charlie? In again bothering you?"

I took another cigarette quickly and bent forward to light it from hers. "Just for a minute on the stairs. Just said hello."

"And the stairs is a good place to keep him. No meals, no drinks, no fancy offers. I told Harry today I'll be staying on steady a while, so we'll get along just fine."

"Well, so long as it's a good job."

"I've had worse. A couple of hours around noon you rush crazy. The rest of the day it's not so bad. Some kind of factory across the street. Trucks coming and going till five and then it's dead again. So I've always got good hours."

"That means a lot, good hours."

"And Harry always giving me the breaks—the best tables. Says I've got a way with the customers."

She smiled over my head, recalling encounters. "Taking and giving, if you know what I mean. Some of the truck drivers—letting them get fresh once in a while but just so far. Having their fun and little jokes—that's fine. Hands, though, you've got to draw the line."

"Sounds like a friendly little place."

"Up around forty-five or so, stiff in the knees and getting thin on top. The trick's to make them think they're still real killers with the girls and at the same time see they don't get fresh ideas. So you never have to slap them down."

Another smile; more encounters; and then solemnly, "No joke, you know, starting to wonder if maybe you haven't got what it takes any more. You now—buying me a drink and saying how about coming along to spend the night—you'll never know what a nice feeling that gave me."

She sat quiet a moment, self-absorbed with contentment, then poured me the rest of the coffee. "And speaking of jobs, I think it's only right to tell you I've always worked *most* of the time. Spells off—but never so I have to let just *anybody* pick me up."

I nodded, giving a hitch to my chair.

"And never mixed up in anything—not what you'd call a real *bad* jam. There was the time in the club we *all* got taken in—but that was just the job. And a couple of times when they roughed me up—but that was because I *wouldn't* play along. More or less, I've been careful."

"One of the best, Mad. Written all over you."

She sat tense a second or two, not sure whether to believe me, then gave a big, happy sigh. "Just so you understand. Moving in on you fast like I did the other night, it's only natural you could get wrong ideas."

"One of the best—I've already told you. And that's the way I'll always remember you."

I leaned a little on the last words and then watched to see if they had got through, the same as I would watch sometimes, the rifle still at my shoulders, to see if I had got my rabbit.

Good shot: a little flicker and contraction of the eyes, as if someone was throwing sand. Then quickly, voice sharp and right again, "That's what I mean—*exactly*. Don't want you to go round remembering me like I was some no-account old tramp. Same as me—something maybe on the radio'll set me thinking about that horn of yours and I'll say to myself well anyway the old girl sure knows how to pick them."

My hands itched to shake her. "But you don't, Mad! Your right ones are all wrong. Bill was wrong—I'm wrong—"

"Oh yes, Sonny, I can pick them." Face alight as if the sun were rising. "Same as if I went into a store to buy a ring and picked a diamond. Real whopper, way out of sight, a couple of thousand, say, and me with a couple of tens, but still it would be good picking .... I did that once—not even the two tens—just wanting to see."

The smile settled on me, serene, indulgent. "Far too good for me—out of sight by a mile. Just like the man in the store letting me try on the ring for a minute and holding it up to catch the shine."

And then, forehead wrinkled as if she were doing sums, "Although come to think of it it's not the same, because shine's just shine and then it's gone. And you, Sonny, you're *never* going to be gone. Something so good I'm hanging on to tight. Those big feet of yours—just wait and see. Fifty years from now they're going to be clumping along right beside me."

She disappeared a moment, underground, came up with another smile. Fragile, guardedly blissful: what had gone on down there I would never know. "Like today in Harry's— there you were, telling me to stop slopping the soup and get out of the way of the hands a little faster—and then all the way home and in the store helping me pick out the steaks, pointing to the good ones—every minute, Sonny, watching me, right there."

A three-layer smile: first the triumph, the invincibility; then a wistful little pull, regret that things could never work out the way she wanted them; and finally, just the corners showing, a furtive, irrepressible little hope that some day, despite all odds, they would.

"You're not just a fish, Mad—you're an *insane* fish. Nobody ever tell you?" I laughed and looked past her, remembering. "Fins won't do—you've got to have legs. Me, too—a long time ago—only I was smarter. Didn't take so long to learn it's rough going for a fish on shore ...."

I I

"YES, SONNY—WHO KNOWS? An insane fish—perhaps
that's what started *us* on our way. One that wouldn't stay in
the sea where it belonged and insisted on climbing up the
rocks and onto the shore. Insisted—and *succeeded*. Did the
impossible—*got there*. Made a new body for itself—lungs
that could breathe, feet that could walk. You see, don't you,
the magnificence of such a delusion? Imagine what all the
other fish said, how they tapped their foreheads with a fin ....
Just remember that you, too, can do the impossible. Just
have the courage to laugh at common sense ...."

Her name was Dorothy Whittle and she used to hold my
hand.

"Loose, my dear boy, *loose!* Just as if someone had taken a
hammer to it and broken every bone."

And her long, damp, big-knuckled fingers would palp and
squeeze and nuzzle it, like feelers testing in the dark for
edibility. "Tension exhausts. Learn to save your strength for
the big moments. Keep relaxed until it's time to *strike*."

Her voice would rise on the word, strident, incendiary, as
if she were coaching a young Jupiter on the art of hurling
thunderbolts; and in demonstration, releasing my hand, she
would hold her own a moment or two poised high above the
keyboard, index finger rigid, aimed, then plummet down like
a rocket of wrath and retribution on some upstart mortal.

Ping! Not even a singed spot on his pants.

"You see what I mean? Without relaxation there can be no poise, and without poise ...."

Here she would reach for my hand again, and I, in anticipation, would wave and wobble it a few times—well out of reach—to let her see its bonelessness; then scuttle up the scale *prestissimo* to show that further palping, thanks to the efficacy of her teaching, would only be a waste of time.

"No, my dear boy, *no*! Slowly, smoothly—slowly, *smoothly*—the good steed Impetuosity must submit to the reins of Discipline."

She had a town a day, arriving by the morning train and returning home late in the evening to her own town farther up the line. We were Saturday and my time, because I had to ride in seven miles on Isabel, was two in the afternoon.

Lessons were in the dining room of the Metropolitan Hotel. At one time Mrs. Riley, the veterinary's wife, had placed her living room at Dorothy's disposal—her contribution to the town's cultural flowering; and in return (lunch and dinner were also included) Dorothy had paid Mrs. Riley five dollars in cash and given free lessons to her two daughters. But with small-town inevitability, word got back to Dorothy that Mrs. Riley had remarked at choir practice it was little wonder Dorothy's husband had disappeared with another woman; the mystery was how any man with that much enterprise and gumption had taken up with such a dreary piece of teeth and leather in the first place. In response to which Dorothy, while informing parents and pupils that lessons would henceforth be given in the Metropolitan, let it be known that the Riley girls had repeatedly taken peppermints and silver from her purse, and hinted that only the bits and pieces collected by a veterinary in the course of his professional duties could account for the frequency and flavor of Mrs. Riley's stews.

And yet there was a spark, an urgency, an area of rapture. She couldn't play Beethoven but she knew how he should be played. And somehow, entreaty, temper, tears—plus hours, I would swear to it, on her knees—she somehow whipped me into shape to enter the provincial festival with one of the early sonatas and carry it off with a resounding ninety-nine.

"It's a gift, Sonny, God-given. You mustn't thank me."

She and my mother were both there. My mother beaming that her son had won, had had nice things said about him, but beneath the little flutter of surface pride with scarcely an inkling of what was going on. (Had she known that lessons were going to lead to fugues and sonatas instead of "Trees" and "Danny Boy" she might not have made such a fierce stand in the first place against my father's disapproval.)

Dorothy, in contrast, was taut with jubilance and the effort to control it. She wore a grey tweed coat with a bit of rabbity fur around the collar and a hat ablaze with yellow daisies. Dabbing at trickles of perspiration—it was May, and hot— she had made a doughy mess of her make-up and the hat, shaken by emotion and applause, had slipped down tipsily over one eye. As we edged our way out of the auditorium after the competition, she seized my arm and whispered, "*I will rise on the wings of eagles.*"

On the steps, the adjudicator overtook us to announce we were having lunch with him. A big, florid man with a bushy forelock and an overwhelming English voice, he took charge of us like a kindly collie, coming to the rescue of three addled sheep. And yet, for all the skill with which he put us at our ease, he was not at ease himself. Through my tongue-tied awkwardness I sensed the constraint—sensed, too, even while eating my lunch and trying to feel successful, what lay behind it. Guilt: the charm and assurance couldn't quite conceal it. He had gone too far and he knew it.

I daresay in all his career he had never come across anything quite like me. He wasn't prepared. He let his enthusiasm run away.

Fifteen and just a hair's breadth off six feet, wrists half way up to my elbows in a mail-order suit a year too small, stumbling across the platform to the piano like a drunk to a basin; then crouching over the keyboard in an agony of nerves for at least a minute after the bell had rung. During that minute he, too, likely crouched, wrinkling with embarrassment for me, setting himself for disaster. Perhaps he glanced at the list of contestants and for an instant, reading *"Peter McAlpine, Mallard,"* conjured up one of the lonely, false-fronted Main Streets that he had wondered at through a train window or seen from his plane like a litter of boxes tipped out by some other plane. Perhaps he turned questioningly to a member of the Festival Committee, only to receive a pained, disowning stare .... And then, instead of disaster, Beethoven. More than the notes: shape and control. Even, perhaps, a hint of insight, understanding. And surprised, carried away, he did what it was his responsibility as an adjudicator not to do: instead of listening to Beethoven, he listened to me. To a big, lumbering farm boy in a suit that didn't fit. Generously, marvelling, he judged me against background and opportunity.

Something of it came through when he mounted the platform to give his adjudication. "It is difficult to award marks to a performance such as we have just heard. Difficult, unfair, presumptuous .... If he were my pupil I might suggest a few changes, but only because there is a tradition telling us how this sonata should be played .... To him, and to his teacher ...."

During lunch, adroit, blandly attentive, he devoted himself to Dorothy and my mother. Dorothy, between soup and cutlet, remarked nervously on the universality of the masters, and my mother, warming to him, confided that Bach and Beethoven were away over her head and often made her feel like throwing the kettle at me. He nodded understandingly, touched his lips with his napkin, then turned to me.

"What about the rest of it? The other movements?" Abrupt and sharp, probing, almost hostile, as if he suspected me of trying to slip something over him. "Can you play them all, or just the first two that you prepared for the festival?"

Dorothy was ahead of me, breaking her words with nervous little tufts of laughter. "I know exactly what you mean—like reading just the first two acts of *Hamlet*. I talked to Peter about it and we did, more or less, work right through the other movements, but there was so little time—"

He made no sign of having heard her. "The other two— how much work have you done on them?"

"Not up to speed but I know what's in them—how they go."

"And what other Beethoven do you know?"

"The last two of the *Pathétique*, the first three of the *Moonlight*—" faltering, lying a little, dropping a spoon.—"A bit of the big F minor, not nearly up to speed of course—"

"You mean you don't play a single sonata—all of it—as it should be played?"

He studied me critically a moment, reconsidering the ninety-nine. "It was a fine performance. It puts you in a very small, very special class, and I meant every word I said. But you must understand that you're running terribly late. That is, if you're going to make a career of it. I know students your age who can toss off half a dozen of the sonatas—to say nothing of all the others—reams of the moderns."

At the time I felt it more for Dorothy than for myself. Without looking at them, I watched her fingers pinching and rolling bread crumbs with the erratic, desperate movements of ants rescuing eggs that have been scattered by a boot.

"Now I do believe you have the makings of a fine musician—an artist, and I don't use the word lightly. I appreciate, too, some of your problems. I am sure you have worked tremendously hard—"

He broke off, looked over my head a moment with a perplexed, slightly desperate expression, as if wondering how he had gotten into this, then came back glaring. "But not nearly hard enough. You must give everything you've got to it—make every sacrifice. For years .... Above all, get away."

I met and held the glare a moment, then said, "I think what you really mean, I'm running too late."

"My dear boy, that is *not* what I said."

Dorothy saw to it, of course, that I kept on. That summer, just as we had planned, I worked at the F minor; and that winter I settled down to more Bach and some of the early moderns. But the doubt was there and growing. Sacrifice for what? What kind of future?

Another year .... I had long outstripped Dorothy; all she could do was listen and nod inspirationally. Crops and prices seesawed; as fast as we paid off old debts we ran new ones.

"London," he had said. "Be sure and let me know." But at this rate I'd be lucky if I ever got as far as Winnipeg.

And there was a shrewd, practical streak. Sacrifices were fine, so long as they led somewhere. Like a good farmer, I had an eye for yield.

Not, give me my due, that in my unknowing, small-boy way I hadn't made them—even grown hard making them. For me, too, there had been an urgency—something that whipped and tugged, kept flashing signals from the other side, as if I were a stray. Now, looking back, I can only wonder. A farm youngster of sturdy, Scotch-Presbyterian stock—why couldn't he have just got hold of an accordion or thumped out "Turkey in the Straw"?

"You must have faith, Sonny. Faith in yourself and faith in this gift which truly comes from God. There's a future for you—you have responsibilities—"

Unlike her, I reflected, instead of a town a day I might eventually end up with a town of my own. If things went well, I might even establish myself in a little prairie city, Regina or Saskatoon, build up a class of pupils and perhaps, to supplement my income, find a church where I could train the choir and play the organ.

And in town, meanwhile—only an hour away on Isabel—there was Larry Turnbull and his clarinet. "Any time—come up and I'll run through some things for you. Have a go at it yourself—why not? One of these days we may be able to use you."

"Of course you're running late—and so to catch up you must just work a little harder. Of course only a fool would try—so go ahead and be a *big* fool!"

She was always reading a book and extracting a message from it; and the one with the bit about the insane fish was so appropriate to *me* she was sure she had been "guided" to it. "A gift like yours—it doesn't just happen—there's a purpose somewhere—a will far stronger than yours or mine—"

And Mad was saying, "Sure I'm a fish—Mad the Tuna—sure I'm crazy—but I'm getting something I'd never have got if I always watched and played it careful. And who knows?"

A little pause, eyes shining again as if she were holding up more diamonds, "Maybe we'll both stay in Montreal and every so often you'll say to yourself not much doing tonight— might as well give the Fish a ring. See how she's doing—maybe we can flip fins a while and have a nice cup of coffee."

12

IN THE MORNING, just as she was ready to leave, she brought out the two ten-dollar bills again and laid them on the table. "No back talk—you've got your tooter, but there's still lots of other things you need. Just look at those shoes, will you—no wonder you keep coughing."

Since I had no others, I sat half an hour in a little shop on Bleury Street while they were being re-soled. There were four shoeshine stools facing me, and always at least one customer. My feet on a newspaper and my toes tucked in to hide the holes in my socks, I tried to meet with nonchalance the eyes looking down at me, and remember I had a clarinet. Mad had done her best with the socks but the darns had torn away. I needed new ones. And rubbers—sitting here with the wind coming in in icy gusts every time the door opened, I was coughing again. Soles, socks, rubbers—six or seven dollars for my feet alone. A couple of shirts; gloves—just in case somebody wanted to hear me. Big feet and nerves were bad enough. I didn't want numb fingers too.

A day or two ago, twenty dollars would have been a fortune. Now, in my pocket, it rubbed in my poverty, doubled my frustrations. Before there had been a balance, a kind of resignation. Socks and shirt matched; bare hands were part of it. But now I swarmed with needs like vermin.

Buying socks and getting fitted for rubbers I felt hangdog, ugly. Instead of restoring me, the money made me a fraud. I watched the faces of the clerks, intercepted glances, and for indifference read contempt. In one of the stores I met a mirror and swerved. I wanted a cup of coffee and went home without it.

Swerved from the mirror, but not quite in time: a glimpse of furtiveness, shoulders that cringed. It was a minute or two later, in the street, that I felt the impact. Sonny McAlpine—big-time, in lights—remember him? And the recognition panicked me.

No—not that bad! All the way home I tried: *no—not that bad.* Just the light, imagination. After all, Mad was satisfied, and she'd been around. She knew her men. Not likely to pick up a down-and-out tramp and think she'd found a right one.

Mad, though—who was she? And what had happened to me that her approval carried weight? She knew her men all right. She knew dimensions.

Worse even than the mirror; for a while it even scared some energy into me. I practised for an hour, made coffee and went for a haircut, came back and put on one of the new shirts. Over a hundred clubs in Montreal: one of them must be looking for a clarinet. Even the ones I had visited already—somebody must have got sick or fired or gone away. The agent first: it would remind him. And at least I looked more presentable than the last time. He might make some calls.

Behind the sudden drive, the little spurt of will—was it still panic? Or a secret wish to get it over with? For I was tired; I hated Montreal; I wanted to go home. But I had committed myself—pride again—and it was a point of honour, to fight as long as there was fight left in me. I wanted to give up, but guiltlessly, absolved of responsibility. I wanted to look myself straight in the eye and say, "What more was there to do? They did hear you—they did listen. It's not your fault you couldn't give them what they wanted."

Sagging and souring, homeless, bruised—I wanted to go back to being a big frog in my little puddle again, to be known, needed, talked about. But I also wanted insurance against the days I might look up a yawning, bedraggled little Main Street and say, "If only you'd had the guts to stick it out a little longer."

My lucky day: the agent was in a good mood. A hook-nosed, owl-eyed little man with a gritty, up-to-my-eyes-in-business voice that he kept whirling round him like a lasso; harried, jumpy, playing it up a little. He found my card and studied it a minute, exactly as he had done half a dozen times before and said yes, a clarinet was sometimes a problem. Later on, in the spring—resorts opening—

"Nothing now then? Weekends—just standing in—"

"Well, it's still a problem—always seems they're looking for a saxophone .... There was a club in the east end just yesterday—somebody slipped and broke something. No harm in checking—in case they haven't found a saxophone. Sit down a minute—I'll call from inside."

I slumped onto a chair, not with any hope that the club might be interested, but simply because all at once I shrank from facing the street again. Not a chance: calling from inside so I wouldn't hear. Probably not calling at all; just his way of getting rid of me. Or they'd have found somebody already. Maybe later—a couple of months or so. And in the east end what could they do with me anyway? I didn't speak French. Slip somebody something—buy yourself a job. Maybe Charlie knew what he was talking about.

But he was back, rapping on the counter and fluttering a bit of paper. "Here's the address and ask for Raymond. No promises but he sounded *very* interested. Nice lively little place—understand they're turning them away. Fixed them up with a dance team from Haiti a while ago. *Very* satisfied."

Leaning on the pencil, he underlined what he had written. "Dancing and a four-or-five-piece band. He's never used a clarinet, but he'd like to hear you. Flexible .... Now it's a long way, but he won't be there till four so you've plenty of time to take the bus. Straight along St. Catherine as far as Delormier."

I walked. It was a raw, bitter day, and I had it coming to me. For the socks and rubbers and gloves I had let Mad pay for; for the cringing little snap of hope with which I had taken the address, like a clap-sided dog snapping at a bone.

St. Catherine, Delormier—half a dozen enquiries, half a dozen turns—and finally a flight of stairs even more splintery than Mrs. Painter's. A stale, hard reek of last night's smoke and liquor, then a big grey room lit by a dirty skylight. The ceiling was festooned with green and yellow streamers. Two palm trees stood at the side of the stage, with big gilt stars suspended over them. Some of the tables were piled on top of one another. An old man wearing an apron and a woollen cap was sweeping up sawdust. A woman with a pyramid of black, wiry-looking hair came towards me and said something in indignant French.

"Raymond," I replied, holding up the clarinet case. "For the band."

"Not yet—maybe half an hour." She came nearer, relaxing into English and smile. "Something to drink while you wait? ... Over here—he's finished sweeping."

"Thank you—a beer." I smiled too, with all the affability that cold and unease would permit. Waitress, singer, part of the set-up—best keep on the right side of her, at least for now; smile along for what she might be worth.

She brought the beer, the purple-shadowed eyes crinkling out of sight behind the smile. "Sixty cents, please—maybe cigarettes?"

"Thanks, I have some." I held out a dollar bill and then, as she began an elaborate fumble in the pocket of her skirt, waved her away.

Poor guess! Catching the grimace-like smile with which she acknowledged the tip, I realized how little chance there was that a word from her, for or against, would carry weight with Raymond. Poor guess—poor Mad! Her tips probably ran ten or fifteen.

A long wait and a small bottle—I drank slowly. All the time knowing. Not a chance. In a dance band the clarinet is the aristocrat. A place like this they would have a guitar, saxophone, and drums. Maybe an accordion—maybe two guitars. With a clarinet you're tops or nowhere.

She came back and emptied the ashtray—smiled at me, at the clarinet, at me again. I smiled back, looked away. Couldn't she read the signs either? Part of the place as a half-starved cat is part of its alley—could she have been taken in by a forty-cent tip?

Not likely. Would the cat waste time sniffing a beer cap, a bit of orange peel? Could it mean then—the hope burst in me sudden, violent—that she saw me as a prospect, somebody worth knowing? Had she overheard Raymond? Was there really a job?

I took the clarinet from its case, raised it to my lips and played silently a moment, then put it away again.

What a laugh for Dorothy if she knew? It had been such a solemn decision to make the compromise, step down from the heights to play the clarinet—to play it in a dance band. Bestowal, consent—like a plain, good girl resolving in great moral torment not to hoard her treasure, and then discovering that nobody wants it, not even offered free.

A double compromise: one foot in and the other out again. It was the practical streak that had finally got the better of Dorothy and her exhortations to do as the upwards-striving fish had done; but it was a furtive loyalty to the old belief—a relapse—that had nosed me towards the clarinet. Quality: from the very first I knew. There was Larry, of course, to teach and persuade me, to say why not? what have you got to lose? But any other instrument and I would probably have tired of it within a week. For the clarinet meant salvage: bits and pieces from the ruins big enough to glue. The negative of the dream: scratched and smudged a bit, but go ahead anyway. Develop it and see what's there. Popular and blues—Mozart and Brahms—there were roads in all directions.

Isabel, though, not Dorothy, was to blame for the condescension with which I yielded, for the upstart insolence. Dorothy was a fool—big enough for even me to see. Isabel, in contrast, was wily, hard—the disdain and intolerance of a thoroughbred. "Larry Turnbull Number Two? It's entirely up to you. But if you have other plans, get on with them. The bigger the better—nothing half way. The sooner the better, too, or you'll be running late again."

In a voice that carried. The little Main Street halls and basements where we played—the paper Christmas bells left hanging all year round for decoration, seats stacked along the wall, big sunburned boys in pointed shoes—the voice every time was louder than the band. "What you wanted? Satisfied? Ready to settle in?"

The same when I came East—she was always nipping at my sleeve. Filling in on weekends, Saturday night pick-up bands, a few days out of town, besides helping me eat they might have meant contacts, nods, a way of inching in. But the head went up and the hoof came down—"That's not what you're here for. If small-time's your size then go back where small-timers belong—where you'll eat well and the girls will tell you you're wonderful."

And now, waiting for Raymond, I could still hear her. "You've made your pint of beer last long enough. There's nothing here for you anyway. All the way from Saskatchewan for plastic stars and palm trees? Why not the old Christmas bells?"

But this time—sulky, belly-minded, plebian—I stood her off; and eventually Raymond came.

All in all, he was a rather nice little man. He stood smiling a moment with his eyes tightly closed as if hoping when he opened them again I would have disappeared, then called for two beers.

Neat, small, immaculate. Black, wet eyes, black, lacquered hair; small black moustache, exact as a stencil. And all wrong—your fingers itched to rough him up. In a dishevelled untidiness, the dainty insignificance of his face would to some extent have been lost. In its well-groomed setting it looked exposed, laid-out—a preserved specimen of something that hadn't quite matured.

"Clarinet?" He nodded pleasantly towards the case, then raised his glass. "I think I might have chosen it too. But not too popular .... Didn't you bring your saxophone?"

"Who said anything about a saxophone?" I seized my glass with an impulse to smash it, set it down carefully. "The call you got about me—didn't he say clarinet?"

"Yes, but I thought you always doubled. I mean if you play the clarinet don't you play the saxophone too?"

"I don't."

He spread his hands, soft and creamy, hatched with shiny black hairs, then brought out cigarettes. "Yesterday I called for a saxophone because mine's in hospital. When your man called back today, well, I just took for granted ..."

He spoke with a slight French accent that gave his voice a precision, small and careful, exactly like that of the moustache. He spread his hands again—an appeal for understanding—and I subsided, took a swallow of beer. "Until your saxophone comes back—at least till you find another—"

"I'm afraid this isn't the place .... Our clientele—not quite right for it."

The hands again and a little smile: very sorry—what can I do? "Most of the time it's fairly noisy—rough. A clarinet wouldn't have a chance .... But now that you're here why not tell me something about yourself, your experience."

"Why?"

He brought his head up quickly. The big black eyes narrowed. Then, in a puzzled, slightly reproachful tone—after all, he was saying "no" very gently, wasting time and beer on me—"There are other clubs—I might be able to put in a word for you."

"You haven't heard me? What kind of word can you put in?"

"But you were recommended ...."

"And these other clubs—they *do* have the right clientele?"

He took it well—so well, so forbearingly, that for a minute I wondered if he might be afraid of me. My size, my scowl—if he might just be humouring me, playing for time.

"You'll admit the clarinet doesn't fit in everywhere. Now if you were with a group, if it was a question of a band with you in it ...."

"You'd be so glad to have us you'd fire *your* band on the spot—is that what you mean?"

"I mean by yourself my band wouldn't know what to do with you. To use you to advantage it would have to make itself over."

"For a few nights—never mind using me to advantage—just to fill in."

He ignored this: a slight flutter of his eyelids like dots on a printed page when a dirty word has been omitted. "Where you probably belong is in a jazz group. It's not easy. A good group takes time—has to grow."

"And how do you know where I belong? I came for a job—not to hear about jazz groups and how they grow."

A smile and a shrug. "I like jazz. Once I even experimented—right here. It lasted three nights. That clientele again."

Not in the least afraid of me. Little head high, imperturbable, oddly dignified. "If things work out I'll be opening another place—maybe six months, the fall. My own. Here I'm just manager, doing what they say." He glanced around, his face twisted with distaste, so that the little moustache seemed more than ever like a stencil, not on quite straight.

"Just a basement probably to start off with—I've got my eye on one. Young people—students—that kind of clientele. For the first year I'll be satisfied if I break even."

He leaned forward, hands expansive now, sharing. Already he had a boy on the drums who was coming along. And drums and clarinet—well, wasn't that a good beginning? The essentials? When the agent said clarinet he took for granted he meant both clarinet and saxophone. And the way he had described me, not slick but sincere—*very* sincere—with experience, a band of my own out West somewhere. Well, he had thought while I was playing saxophone here the drums and I would get to know each other, and if I turned out to be what he wanted he knew another boy for the piano.

"You thought all that in the thirty seconds or so you were on the telephone?"

Weariness, frustration—all at once I was ready to put my head down and blubber, and a snarl helped stave it off. "Before I've played a note—before you've even seen me—straight into your goddammed basement to start growing with a jazz group."

"The basement's been there a long time. All ready—you and your clarinet just had to step in."

"And what am I supposed to do? Admire it? Say it's a nice basement? I want a job. I'm broke. It's a good four miles and I walked—"

"I'm sorry—I've explained about the saxophone—the misunderstanding." Standing up, he flicked open his wallet and held out two dollars. "I've wasted your afternoon but at least you can take a cab home."

For a second or two the old Sonny towered over him. "You and your goddammed two dollars—you know what you can do with them!" And then, all in the same instant, the bills were in my hand and I was out the door and down the stairs with them. Why not? Wasn't his money as good as Mad's?

But I walked again. Four miles and the wind even colder— more than ever I had it coming to me. Because he had been on my side. He liked jazz—he liked clarinets. Through the stars and palm trees and gigolo-sleek hair, that much had rung true. And I might have played along. For a few minutes— tossed back the ball. Instead of snarling that his basement was empty, I might have stepped in and listened, had another beer. And then some other day, when the tables and chairs were in and the lights on, gone back to meet the band and find out what it's like to grow.

13

IN CONTRAST, Mad was good. She arrived on my heels, pink cheeks and shining eyes, bursting with importance at having a man to come home to; and at the sight of my haircut and new shirt she let out a squeal and threw her arms around me. "Just like you'd stepped out of a movie! Now if I could only take you out and show you *off* to people!"

And at the same time the fear again, the little flicker of unease that was becoming familiar. How much longer? Job hunting? Found one?

But my response—lips on forehead, hand on breast—was right, enough, and as I stepped back the fear vanished in another blaze of smile. Reassured: cup running over. A big, warm lump of a woman who would never grow up and never grow bad, not if she lived a hundred years, not if she slept with a hundred right ones. After the harpy in the club, greed to her fingernails, she looked fresh, guileless; and urgently, abruptly, I wanted her again. To forget the street and day. To wipe out the humiliation of the snatched two dollars. In satisfying her, to feel righted and restored.

"Oh Sonny—you mean right *now? Before* supper?"

She stared a moment: six years old and just told to go out and buy ten cones. "Talk about things coming true! Doesn't it just show you, though—you can be so crazy and so right!"

And then drawing back a little, wetting her lips and taking a deep breath, "Sounds sort of funny maybe, but I'm going to say it anyway. Because there's no sense missing out on things just for the sake of being shy and backward."

I waited. She wet her lips again and looked at my chin. "You being what you might call an any-time-at-all sort of fellow—well, I just think it's sensible to let you know that that's me too—an any-time-at-all sort of girl."

She looked me hard in the eye a moment, then expanded, "You know how people get so set on having a special time for it—*bedtime*. Well, nothing wrong with having it all day to look forward to, but *sticking* to bedtime seems to me's just missing out on an awful lot of fun."

Another deep breath while her eyes returned demurely to my chin. "What I mean, you never need hold back thinking it won't seem a good idea to me—like I've been holding back on you sometimes. You know—scared you'll start saying to yourself that's all that woman *ever* thinks about."

She paused a moment, head tilted thoughtfully. "Same as bacon and eggs. Nice and tasty—fill you up—how come people never think of them except for breakfast?"

"It's settled then—any-time-at-all Sonny and any-time-at-all Mad—bacon and eggs whenever we feel like them."

"That's right—Sonny and Mad!" Her voice leaped. She reached for my hand and squeezed it hard. "Just today at work I was saying to myself again how nice they go together. *Sonny and Mad—Sonny and Mad—*"

Shying quickly, I thumbed her to the bed.

"All right—all *right!* Just a minute till I turn out the light. Lucky I didn't get started making supper. First time in all my life, I think, I've ever had it right *before* supper."

That was the trouble: it left a long evening.

Fifteen minutes and there we were—she flat on her back and still hopeful; I flat on reality like a fish washed up on the shore.

With the merest dregs of gallantry I lay still and let her nestle against me and stroke my arm, once even responding, cupping a breast as if it still held interest. But in a few minutes, seeming to sense the indifference, she sat up suddenly and said, "Now for a real *good* supper. Tomorrow's coming, remember, and you've got to keep in shape."

She had just finished dressing when Charlie knocked. Tired of his own company again; he would like to take us out for dinner.

She was curtly inventive: it would be nice, only she was just ready to get our own supper, everything in the pan, and as soon as we finished Sonny had to settle down to work. At least a couple of hours. Maybe a job coming up tomorrow—looks like it might be good. But cutting in ill-humouredly, I overruled her. "Why not? A good meal's just what we need—both of us. Cooped up in here .... it's starting to seem like years."

For all at once the room was small and smothering, and the prospect of the evening alone with her made me want to smash something, break out and run. The manoeuvring, physical and mental, to keep out of her way; her eyes on me, admiring, as I practised; every half-hour or so the motherly, "How about a nice cup of coffee?" Without meeting her eyes, I said, "You too—you look tired. You've been on your feet all day."

She flinched, whitened, then said easily, "No—just you and Charlie go. Tired feet is right, and it'll mean going home to change."

But Charlie was insistent. A steak and a drink would set her up, and her dress didn't matter. He knew just the place—no arguments.

Insistent, not just perfunctorily polite. Seeing her coat on a chair he picked it up and helped her into it and then, with a suggestion of a bow, respectful, formal, handed her her purse. She hesitated, glancing at me for instructions, and I said, "Of course—it's still early. Plenty of time to practise later on."

I threw in the bit about practising to help her save face. The look of appeal I smiled down coldly—a smile that felt like an arrangement of string and pins. She nodded, bunched up the collar of her coat, and started down the stairs ahead of us, step heavy, shoulders sullen, as if she had just received a sentence and were being escorted to her cell.

In the restaurant she was still a prisoner, still accusingly morose. She twitched me away when I tired to help her off with her coat and then, bundling into it defensively, lit a cigarette. Her own—Charlie's proffered pack ignored. Nothing to drink, thanks. Just coffee later on.

Charlie smiled expansively, a good host, seeing everything and nothing. "Better, isn't it, than sitting home listening to the radio?"

"Sitting at home at least I wouldn't have to look at phony logs." With her cigarette she waved disdainfully towards the wall. "Look like they're made of tin and a bit of paint slapped on. Couldn't they find real ones?"

"Trying to make it look like an old French farmhouse—I think that's the idea."

"French tables, too, I suppose. Knotholes you could stick your finger in. They even been cutting names and initials."

"All part of it, Mad—what they call atmosphere." Our scotches came, and raising his glass, dismissing her, he smiled. "To the job, Sonny. Glad to hear about it. Looks promising?"

I shrugged in embarrassment, keeping my eyes on the drink. "I don't know—he wants a saxophone but maybe he can fit me in. Crummy little joint in the east end—not very important anyway."

He nodded sympathetically. "So many of you to be fitted in—it's always tough. And the buyers—what are they interested in? The package, Sonny, not the goods."

A twist to his mouth. Very tough, very cynical. "Not one in a hundred knows the difference anyway. Clarinets or tooth paste."

"So all I need is a sharp suit and a pair of alligator shoes?"

"They'd help although, by the sound of it, you'd do better to have someone pick them out for you. I told you about the corners."

I finished my drink quickly and sat quiet a moment, concentrating gratefully on the progress of the glow and telling myself not to mind him. Candy-pink shirt and black tie, sunken eyes and a lick of hair across his forehead: the youthful look was spurious, but the little boy peering out from behind it was the real thing.

"You look beat, Sonny, and so you feel beat. It's as simple as that. A crummy little joint in the east end—naturally that's where you head for."

"Leave Sonny alone." It was like a club on a skull. "I told you before—he's going to get along fine—no help from anybody. When he needs you to worry for him he'll let you know."

"Right—he doesn't need either of us to worry for him." He smiled and made a little smacking sound. "Knows where he's going and one of these days he's going to get there. But there's no harm showing him a few short cuts. Unless you'd rather slow him down so you'll have more time to enjoy his company."

She snapped her purse open and shut and sat silent, no match for him and knowing it. The steaks came. I caught the twist to his mouth and understood why he had wanted her to join us. But I didn't rally to her. I wasn't loyal. She was behaving badly, and I made no move to help.

"I hope you're both hungry." Good host again; smile impartial. "We'll have to do this often. I know a lot of places."

"And I'll lay money on it a lot of them Sonny wouldn't be found *dead* in." The club again. We stopped eating a moment.

"Maybe you're right—there are quite a few for that matter I wouldn't want to be found dead in myself." He shrugged, smiled indulgently, then with his head slightly lowered looked hard at me. "Maybe it's the reason I do certain things and don't do others. At certain times and in certain places .... Let's say why I never take chances—never play with loaded guns."

The eyes sharp and small. The voice like a scratchy pen, underlining a clause in a contract.

A moment's silence and a strange room: holding the door open, watching while I entered and sat down. And this time I didn't say, "Not so fast, Charlie. There's no contract and the job's all yours."

Not even to myself. The implication of an understanding reached, a common interest—it didn't register as presumptuous. Neither response nor rejection. On one level I was intact; on another, reconciled. A wheel had turned. A cog had found a groove. What he had suggested was no longer unthinkable.

"And one of the places I don't intend to be found in, just in case you're interested, is the room on Ste Famille Street."

For me again. An arrow pointing to the big-time. Short cut straight ahead.

But it still didn't make sense. If he needed someone to watch the door and whistle for trouble, wouldn't he do better down on the Main? Where they grew and trained, had the same sour, crafty minds?

"Not that I'm complaining about Ste Famille Street. Nova Scotia and Saskatchewan—what better neighbours could you ask for?"

Because I was so big and raw? Because so much Saskatchewan was sticking out nobody would ever think of connecting me with a "job"? Planning to work behind me, use me as a screen?

Too simple. Besides, he already knew it was what I suspected, had seen me shy.

"Except, of course, for the clarinet. This morning—" He leaned a little towards Mad, lowering his voice confidentially, "Two and a half hours—non-stop. Then *he* went out—made me wonder if he could hear what I was thinking."

The clarinet? A future, perhaps? Cut me in on something now, and I might be grateful—useful—later on? Flattering—I licked around it a few times—but it wouldn't hold. A clarinet's future wasn't that good. Besides, he had heard me for the first time only yesterday.

"In any case, Sonny's particular. Young man with a clarinet and a destination—only the best places. Clean-cut, clean-living—only the best places and only the best roads to take him there."

Envy? A little curl to his lip as he talked made it possible. The chance that I just might make it on my own terms. Envy because—comparatively, at any rate—I was healthy, uncomplicated; because, despite the corner I had worked myself into, I had a big country faith in both myself and what lay ahead. Because I believed—as simple as that—that I played a good clarinet and that the world was fair and discerning enough to eventually give me my due. A big, stubborn lunk with no idea of the odds against him, up to his eyes in small-town smugness—somebody had to bring him down to size.

A kind of innocent—at least by his standards—and as such, even a spotted second at the bottom of the bin, I had perhaps made his fingers itch to smear me, pull me down to join him in the mud. For there were times when Charlie left you wondering—a note struck too hard, too quickly, a falter in the eyes as they retreated—if he mightn't have started out on the side of innocence himself. And who more than a fallen angel would resent the rustle of even imaginary wings?

"No Mad, he doesn't need either of us. Good lip, good nerves. Steady—it'll take a lot to rock him."

He was looking straight at me and between the twitches of his smile derisive, thrown like a net over what he was saying to make sure nothing flabby or soft slipped through, there was unmistakable approval. The smile a failure—the meshes too wide.

Steady, taking my time: perhaps that was the answer. For even scared—even jumpy, mean—I always gave the impression of control. Mask, false front: I never let on. And no one ever seemed to see farther, to suspect what lay behind. Perhaps because I was big: the jittery little impulses that started somewhere deep inside me, brain or belly, were exhausted before they got far enough to twitch a lip or eyelid. Even as a youngster, eleven or twelve, I was always the one sent to town with my father when there were signs he needed watching. "Stay close and keep him out of the poolroom. Speak right up and say it's time to do the chores. You've got a way with him. He'll listen."

Trying to persuade him not to go in—there was a blind pig in the back—sometimes helping him out, with an interested little crowd of Main Street loungers looking on; head up, eyes front, ears burning—was that how I acquired it, the stolid coverall that now, in Charlie's eyes, qualified me for a job as his assistant?

"You'll have competition, you know. That big, slow, easy look—God knows why, but a lot of them fall hard. Just wait—tooth and claw and the feathers flying."

It was the same coverall, a few years later, that had given me the band. The day they took Larry Turnbull to the hospital I stepped in to play the clarinet, and within a month, shy, green, full of butterflies, I had taken over. My band: they said so. Not in so many words at first; rather a kind of deference, a nudging into place. And not because of the way I played the clarinet. Not bad for eighteen, they conceded; at the same time, not by any means did they think of themselves as second-raters. But I was dependable, sure of myself, didn't rock. I took nerves and gripes and upset schedules in my stride.

Didn't rock—not likely to rattle in a jam. That was it, perhaps, plus a little of all the other things as well—including even a dash of unpolluted friendliness and good-will.

Guile or good-will, though, it didn't make much difference, for as we sat watching each other I saw the fear again. The attack—always getting his licks in first—what other word was there for it? The bright, sunken eyes like lookouts at the entrance to a cave, the curl to his lips, the on-and-off smile: a system of defences, wall after wall, behind which the same little boy was hiding.

And since he was afraid, there was nothing for me to be afraid of. Whatever he might do, whatever the situation, I would be a match for him. As simple as that. And as stupid. As if you saw a snake and reasoned that since it was no longer than your arm and wriggling to escape, you could pick it up and run no risk of being bitten. Sober, too: steak and coffee and just one double scotch.

I met the smile, companionably, tractably; and satisfied, with a knowing pull to his mouth, he turned to Mad. "But the places I was talking about were restaurants and you've likely got some favourites too. Next time we'll let you choose."

"I sure know some a lot better than this one." Inflexibly hostile, without the words to thrust or parry, she could only keep on whacking. "Why even down home in Nova Scotia, even in the little places, everything's all slicked up and smart. Tables with nice shiny tops, pink and green and yellow."

He considered this a moment, nodding gravely. "You'll admit, though, there's something to be said for the wooden tops. Look—initials—just like you were saying. Here's a set of them inside a heart—young lovers. Sonny—why don't you cut yours and Mad's? A good chance—nobody's watching."

"Because he's grown up, that's why. And got better manners."

He was still bringing out the worst in her, deliberately and gleefully, and I was still aloofly disloyal. Without raising my eyes I said you don't eat tables. If the steak's good the restaurant's good.

"But there's no reason, Sonny, why you can't have both. Good steaks and nice tables."

She took my loyalty for granted. No question as to which side I was on. If I didn't speak up for pink and yellow tables it was because I didn't know their virtues. She would have to convince me.

"Doesn't matter what you're eating—a nice shiny table makes it twice as good." She tried to turn and face me, and finding it awkward, began waving a fork for emphasis. How to run a restaurant and put money in the bank, plus the art of making people feel at home. The man coming in alone, for instance—like as not it's because he hasn't got a home. "So what's he looking for? Just plain good tasty food and someone friendly. Somebody to take a little interest—time to say you're looking fine."

A practical side to the lady: it was starting to show. She could manage a restaurant all right and a little over. Just give her time. Crack the whip, keep people on the run. A restaurant and a lot of other things once she got her hands on them.

"Same as everything else, you get on to all the little tricks. Like fixing plates—a bit of this and that, a pickle or a radish or a slice of beet, and you can cut away down on the meat. And what's more, leave people thinking what a *good* meal it's been."

"And those poor lonely men without a home—fine way to be friendly, cutting down on the meat they're paying for."

I said it sourly, without smiling, and made a sign to Charlie. She wasn't starting and goddammed restaurant with me to help fix bits of beet and radish on the plates, and once and for all I was bloody well going to let her know it.

"Sorry—I'd forgotten," Charlie said quickly, signalling in turn for the check. "A job coming up—you've got to practise."

And then to Mad, "Why don't you and I go somewhere else? You haven't had a drink yet .... Let Sonny settle down to work—"

She looked round at me, wide open with appeal, then with a shrug brought out her compact. "If Sonny wants to be alone a while that's fine with me." Absorbed for a minute in her mirror, cool, self-possessed, puckering her lips. "There's a couple of little jobs it's time I was doing over at my own place anyway."

Worse than the appeal: I said quickly, "I don't suppose I'll practise more than half an hour anyway. So if you can stand it that long—"

"*Stand* it?" The voice like a flood of light, as if I had turned a switch. "Easiest standing, Sonny, that's ever come my way."

Charlie held the door open for us. "You make a wonderful pair. Somebody ought to write a story for the papers—'The Domestic Life of a Clarinet.' With pictures."

For Mad it was triumph again—undiluted, not a flaw. "All right, Charlie, run along now and have your little drink." Waving him away blithely, she took a fresh grip of my arm. "Sonny'll be in the papers all right, and it won't be you he'll need to write the story."

But for me it was exactly what he had intended. Arm in arm along the street and up the stairs—doors opening, eyes peering out; accidentally, or did all the house know now?

Then inside the room and posing for the camera he had turned on us, re-writing the captions for the pictures. There we were, domesticity itself. The bed with the pillows and blankets still in a state of any-time-at-all upheaval, the old cracked dishes, the milk bottle on the window. *They Make Their Dreams Come True—Prairie Farm to Ste Famille Street—*

I picked up the clarinet and stood motionless a moment, posing again while the camera clicked; and then, still clutching it, as a child would clutch a toy, flung myself onto the bed and ground my face into the pillow.

"That's right—have a nice little sleep and don't worry about anything." She came over to the bed to pat down the pillow and take away the clarinet. "It's early still—lots of time to practise. And after a while we'll have a nice cup of coffee."

Without looking up I squirmed my back and shoulders in acknowledgement. There was the creak of the floor as she tiptoed away, the faint, dry click of the clarinet being laid on the table, another creak as she sat down to her mending.

Silence for a minute or two; then she began again, testing, in a whisper, "Oh Sonny, I nearly forgot—down at work today I was thinking what'd be a good lunch for you—" but I lay carefully still, pretending to be asleep. For this now was a private misery that I had to lick and scratch alone. All the fine beginnings, all the big dreams—time now to make the final gesture, lay them out like corpses in a morgue.

But I had forgotten Isabel .... Two or three times around— touching the waxy faces, making sure they were all in place, spitting on myself for what I had done to them—and suddenly there she was, hell-bent for leather, tossing years and corpses as she had many times tossed me. For she, too, had been in on the beginnings and, whatever or whomever else I was laying out, I wasn't laying out her. A witch of a horse: from the rock her hoof had struck there would always flow a clear bright stream, never the bitter waters of remorse and failure. They had been good, brave beginnings, and that was what they would always be. The wind through her mane would always have a sting of sky and wonder.

14

"I SAY SO and your father says so—*that's* who says so. For the last time, you're not riding her in any race. Not if there was a chance of winning a *thousand* dollars."

"But what's the difference? Every time I ride her it's a race anyway. At the fair there'll just be other horses."

"That's silly talk. It's not a race *unless* there are other horses."

"Oh yes—Isabel always races. And I'm not going to fall off just because people are watching."

"That's it—they don't just *watch.* They yell and whistle and throw hats—and to start the race they fire a gun. She'll go crazy—you'll never hold her. And there'll be other horses bumping into you and other men maybe even trying to hit you—"

"How? We'll be way ahead—how are they going to bump *into* us? Or *hit* us?"

"That's enough. A lot of good your hundred dollars will do you if you break your neck."

"The hundred dollars is the *prize.* How could I win it if I broke my neck?"

"And none of your smart aleck back talk either. You're getting to be as big a show-off as she is."

"I suppose if she threw me right at the finish I could do both—win *and* break it."

"Anyway, it's something you won't have to worry about. She'll be in her stall and you'll be in the potato patch. *Hoeing.* Run along now—that's final."

Of course it was no such thing. After a good show of resistance, stretched out nearly a week, they finally said I could *go* to the fair; and since it was a bad year and they themselves were staying at home, they even said I could go on Isabel. "But mind what your father's telling you. You tie her up when you get to town and you *keep* her tied up."

"Anyway it's seven miles," my father said, "so she'll be in no shape to race when she gets there .... I don't know why you're so set on going. I've told you already—a dollar's all you're going to get to spend."

Consent? I wasn't sure. They had done it before, threatened hair-raising punishment if I ever dared ride Isabel and then, when I finally disobeyed, looked relieved, as if all along they had been secretly ashamed of me.

Not that it mattered. Consent or not, I was riding her. I needed the hundred dollars. With the crop shrivelling up it was the only way. My father might confiscate it—to show his authority, bring me down to whipper-snapper size—but only temporarily. My mother would have the final say.

Luck was with me: it clouded up the morning of the race and there was a brief, drenching shower. (At the breakfast table, as the first drops spattered on the windows, we had a clash of prayers: they wanted rain to save the crop and I wanted sun to save the race. Mine got through.) The rain left the air fresh and cool and she covered the seven miles at an easy canter, without so much as working up a sweat.

I wasn't in favour of the canter but there was no holding her. With a fling of her head she gave it to me straight what she thought of fussy little boys who always listened to their mammas. The road, I persisted, was muddy and she'd be tired before we got there; she snorted back the rain had barely been enough to lay the dust. In any case, it was too far to walk. She wanted to get there and see what was going on.

"I know you'll win all right. It's just I'd like it to be an *easy* win. I don't want you finishing in a lather and having people say you had to work for it."

This time she let a bit of froth fly back to catch me in the eye—don't worry, I won't disgrace you—but mollified, none the less, settled to a gentle, rocking-horse lope. At the same time there was a warning: better not try to hold her in. If she had to fight she'd be in a lather *before* the race.

She also hoped I wouldn't disgrace *her.* Carry yourself with assurance; try to sit up straight. Whatever you do, don't gawk or let your mouth hang open. After all, she had a reputation to think about: an outlaw, very dangerous. She didn't want people saying it needed only a little boy—a skinny, scrawny-looking one at that—to handle her. Another splash! Better not try putting on airs, either, unless you want to be sent flying. Right in front of everybody—and this time so it hurts .... There was a good chance, of course, she'd send me flying anyway—just for the hell of it.

We arrived. The man at the gate said, "A dollar," and straightening indignantly I said, "What for?"

"To get in—what did you think for? Horse and rider one dollar."

I hesitated a moment, awed by his threatening look and at the same time outraged by the injustice—after all, weren't we part of their fair, performers?—and then, starting to dig in my pocket, could find only ninety cents.

The man got sarcastic; Isabel got furious. No doubt about it, she was accustomed to escorts who paid their way with style and flourish. She stamped and gnashed the bit a moment—a dozen pairs of curious eyes on her while her rider fished for a dime—and then, the simplest way out of an unfortunate situation, swung her head round and sniffed my shoe in bland surprise. Who was it? How had he got there? Not that it mattered—there were so many today who didn't know their place. Best, perhaps, just to ignore him.

But inside the fair grounds, after I had finally found the missing dime, she made it up to me. All the easy things that looked dangerous: flinging her head up and baring her teeth;

giving a scandalized snort and skittering sideways at the sight of a red-headed woman in a purple dress; glaring with coal-hot eyes through a forelock in outlaw disarray; rearing to slash at invisible challengers and then to trumpet a victory neigh that for seconds made the fair stand still. All for me, to make them stare and say, "Did you ever now—just like she was a bicycle! What kind of mother do you suppose he has? He can't be more than thirteen!"

Even the band struck up, as if they had been watching too and appreciated that music was our due. A march, and a good one. Clang and bumph and sparkle—they had been practising. It brought out the sun and waved the flags and put four-four allegro in everybody's shoes.

Another snort, a twitch of the ears: we're doing fine but now you're sitting *too* straight. Try and relax a little—loosen up your shoulders. That's it—and whatever you do don't smile.

What on earth, I wondered, made her think I might!

A little farther on—she took me there; she knew her way around fairs—a man was sitting at a wooden table in the shade of a soft-drink stand. The office—where you entered for the race. She reared again as I made a show of reining her to a halt and came down stuttering her heels dangerously. Another snort, frothy and mild this time, ears pricked forward as if the soft-drink stand might also be selling oats, and then—a professional performance, polished, timed to the second— thrust her nose out towards the man sitting at the table with an expression of amiable curiosity.

"We'd like to enter for the race," I said, politely and firmly. "The one that pays a hundred dollars."

The man stood up and came towards us. Even keeping my eyes fixed on him, I could feel the whole fair starting to crowd around.

"Who's we?"

Voice and eyes hard, knowing; the face a solid frown. A front, I told myself swiftly—just doesn't want to show that he's impressed.

"The mare and I. We came alone."

He walked slowly around us while I did my best to look indifferent and at ease. "Not bad," he said at last, coming back to where he had started and reaching out familiarly to scratch her between the ears. "How old are you?"

"Thirteen—thirteen past. But I ride her everywhere—to school—every Saturday to town .... Have you never seen me?"

Fear that my age might disqualify me put a sputter in my voice, and with a sharp tap of her foot Isabel signalled silence.

"I don't know. I was watching you ride in from the gate and if that's the way she's going to carry on out on the track—"

"Oh no—she's raced before—lots of times. There's nothing to worry about."

Not looking at the crowd made it bigger. It listened attentively, in complete silence, and everything I said seemed to be picked up as it came off my lips and then played back like somebody else's voice, magnified a hundred times.

"Does she act mean like that often?"

"You don't understand—she wasn't acting mean. The band and everything—it just made her feel good."

"Well, it looked to me a lot more like acting mean than just feeling good. Does she ever throw you?"

"Only when she wants to."

The crowd pondered this a moment. Isabel declared afterwards they even stopped eating hot dogs and cones. Then, cautiously, the man said, "And you don't think she might want to now?"

"When she's racing? Oh no, she'll want to win."

He reached out absently and scratched her between the ears, then took his hand back and scratched his own chin. "I still think you're pretty young. Does you father know?"

I hesitated a moment, then spluttered again. "Of course— he even helped me saddle her. My mother too—"

Isabel gave an approving cock of her head and simultaneously tapped her foot again. In the circumstances the lie itself was all right, but I was making a terrible mess of it. "He gave me a dollar to spend and if I'd slipped away without telling him he couldn't have done that—now could he?"

The crowd pondered this too. The man's eyes narrowed, still suspicious, and in anticipation of a demand for proof I said, "They took it away from me at the gate just now. The whole dollar—just to get in."

"You mean you paid your dollar and now you're broke?"

"That's right. The man said horse and rider one dollar."

"Well, that takes care of *that*!" Relaxing, a sudden relieved look on his face, he took a deep breath and wiped his neck and forehead with his handkerchief. "Sorry to disappoint you but you can't ride if you're broke. The entry fee is five dollars."

"I didn't know, but it doesn't matter." Easy—the solution so obvious I scarcely felt the flash of panic. "You can take it out of the hundred—afterwards."

"Come again?"

"When we win—just give us ninety-five."

Silence for a second or two; then hoots and howls of laughter. Outraged, Isabel spun round with a threat of heels to clear a respectful distance, then for good measure snapped at a lank, loose-jawed youth whose hoot had been particularly offensive. He put his hand to his face, lost the cone he was eating, and staggered back ignominiously into the crowd. Silence restored and status re-established, she faced the man in charge again, muzzle cajoling, neck still arched and proud.

The man scratched again, her ears, his chin, and she edged forward a little to nudge his elbow. He knew horses, and she knew men. There was an uncertain moment, his tongue running over his lips; then he said firmly, "Sorry, we can't do it that way. There are seven other entries, and everybody thinks his horse has a good chance too."

"But just look at her—she'd have to *try* to lose. It would be harder than winning."

"I know just how you feel and I wish I could help." His eyes ran over her admiringly and I saw their corners take on a conspiratorial pucker. But catching himself in time, turning back to the table and giving his pants a hitch, "Anyway, you're on the young side. There'll be another race next year—and next year I'm sure you'll win."

"Hold it!"

A short, red-faced man with an enormous belly pushed forward, a five-dollar bill in his hand. "If he believes that much in his horse he deserves to be staked .... There you are, young fellow—you're in. And I'm sure you'll win this year."

Of course we did—by three lengths, not even trying—and afterward, when I paid the stranger his five dollars and explained we had raced because I needed the money for music lessons, he told me he was a musician too. "There's a big dance tonight—everybody in for the fair. If you're not in too much of a hurry to get home, why don't you drop around and hear *us*? Just tell them at the door you're a friend of Larry Turnbull—you won't have to pay. And who knows? Some day I might have a job for you?"

"I'll have to phone," I told him, "and talk it over with my mother. She gave me strict orders, you see, *not* to race. But since it's over and we've got the money ...."

So far as my mother was concerned, I simply *informed* her I was staying in for the dance—with ninety-five dollars in your pocket you don't say please and may I—but I did talk it over with Isabel.

She agreed that the man himself was all right. Obviously a drinker—the smell and the belly and the red face—but he rang true. A good heart. As for the music—that was something for me alone to decide. And as for the job he hinted at—even supposing I *wanted* to play in a dance band—better not take it too seriously. People talk a lot and make a lot of fine promises. Sometimes you believe them, play along .... and then it's too late .... "All kinds of angles, all kinds of tricks. When you make a deal with somebody like that you never know what you're letting yourself in for. Just take it from me, Sonny, if he's got a job for you it's a dirty one. You'll find yourself in trouble fast .... And there you are, lying there not listening to a single word ...."

15

"YES, MAD, I HEARD YOU. And there's nothing to worry about: Charlie and I haven't any plans."

"Oh yes, he's got plenty. But never mind now—I've got a cup of coffee ready for you and a nice little sandwich. Up on your feet and wipe that look off your face."

"But we just had dinner—"

"Three hours ago—it's half-past eleven."

She went out to the gas-ring for the coffee and was back while I was still rubbing my eyes.

"That coffee tonight was terrible; this'll help you get rid of the taste .... You know you can always tell a restaurant by their coffee. Good safe rule—gives them away every time."

I took a sip of hers and tried again to be honest. "I just wish, Mad, you'd find a good safe rule for judging your men. You're only bringing out the heel in me."

"Some heel you! Little baby one—haven't got your teeth yet."

She laughed, clapping her hands, then sobered abruptly. "If you just knew what some of the real ones are like. Not just the teeth—the minds. This fellow Charlie, now, with his jobs and fancy invitations—"

"Charlie doesn't need a clarinet so he doesn't need me. There's no job."

"All right—not another word. But waving money in front of you when you're broke—I can't help feeling scared."

"He hasn't waved it yet."

"He will, though—I can smell it coming. And if you'd just sit tight and take things easy for a while—no time at all they'll be running after you with jobs, and in the meantime what's wrong keeping on the way we are?"

I drank my coffee without answering. So many reasons they jammed.

"Good for both of us. Sort of two birds with one stone—giving me a good time and coming through a bad spell yourself. *Three* birds, come to think of it—so you won't need that fellow Charlie either."

"You're starting again—"

"No, just eating with him tonight set me thinking about your meals. Supper's all right, but I'm worried how you're making out at noon."

She paused, leaned forward with a wink. The restaurant where she was working—a couple of times a week anyway—why not come down? Crowded around noon, Harry busy with the cash. Nothing to it—a nice big steak or a plate of roast beef and just a cup of coffee on the check. Supposing he does notice—everybody makes mistakes. Rushing every way what do you expect? Who is he? Never set eyes on him before—just some jo—

"Not that kind of jo."

I pushed back my chair and stalked off to the bathroom and for a long time stood clutching the edge of the basin and staring into the mirror. What kind of jo, then? A steak for the price of a cup of coffee—or stud service for the steak—what was the difference?

She was even cleaning the bathroom for me—my domain—and I wasn't indignant about that. Dirty walls, a cracked window thick with fuzzy dust, linoleum worn through to the boards, but bath and basin shining. I looked around, then back to the glass. Vanity without guts—that kind of jo.

I went back to the room and to please her drank another cup of coffee and when we went to bed had another piece of tail. Leisurely and conversationally this time: comparisons with the girls out West and the boys in Montreal—compliments flying—but the knife, nonetheless, had turned.

And with it a key. The next door was open.

For it was clear now—what I was, what I had become. Therefore nothing mattered. Therefore I was justified.

Long after Mad was asleep I lay alert and tense. Numbed by the face in the mirror and at the same time stung. Shake it all off, make a fresh start—it was more than time. Anything, anybody—at least listen to Charlie, hear him through .... The country boy again, the innocence. I had seen and lived so little I thought it was rock bottom in the glass.

16

BUT THE NEXT AFTERNOON, defiantly, I took my clarinet and went back to see the agent. A chill in the air: he had had a call from Raymond.

"Some unpleasantness, by the sound of it. I didn't quite understand."

"Some."

"*Very* upset—never had it happen before." To avoid looking at me, he took off his glasses and polished them briskly on his sleeve. "He hopes I'll be more careful who I send another time."

"I'm sorry. I had to wait—and it was a long way for nothing."

"It's all right of course if you can afford it. I just wish I could." He put back his glasses primly and looked past me with an expression of sour, martyr-like endurance. "Not affording it, in fact, is the way I keep going here—not telling people what I think of them. And considering what I've done for you, the trouble I've gone to—it seems you might co-operate to the extent of being civil."

As if on cue, a haughty queen swished in, opulently fat and flaxen-haired; and as if to demonstrate what he meant by "not affording it," my benefactor hurried round to welcome him. Hand extended, the sour look transformed to one of pleasure and surprise. *Very* happy to see him looking so well, *very* happy the trip had been such a success; and then to me, with a quick glance as he shoulder-patted him into his office, "Why don't you come back in a week or two? We'll make some calls for you."

On the street, I sauntered a little distance, as if it were spring and mild; and then at the first corner halted to let the wind, furious at the thrust and insolence of buildings, do its worst with me. Better that way, shivering, wincing, so I would think only of the cold. So when at last, unable to stand it longer, I ducked and ran uphill to Sherbrooke Street, it would still be the reason, still the cold; so I needn't know—dog with tin can tied to tail—I was running from defeat.

At the house, just as I started up the stairs, I met Charlie coming down. He looked at me in silence a moment, then seized my arm and swung me around. "It must have been rough. You look as if you need a drink."

I went meekly. "Just cold. Not used to the big city yet—I still stop and look in windows."

"Forget the windows—take a minute for the view." We had reached Sherbrooke Street again, and hunching his shoulders against the wind, he drew up and pointed. "Gives you a better idea what it's going to take."

It fell from Sherbrooke Street in a clutter of construction and dilapidated houses, then reared up cut-out black and arrogant against a dirty-yellow sky. The lights were on and coming on, as if an alarm had rung and insect guards, sting-eyed-alert, were springing to their stations; and between us there were mile-deep barricades of cold.

"It's what you want, isn't it? What you came for?" And then with a glance at the clarinet case and moving on again, "Just remember it'll take a lot more than that."

But his voice today lacked its usual bark, the dog-shaking-a-rat irritation, and over our drink he looked dispirited and tired.

"Big night?" I ventured. "Out on the town with somebody?"

"Thanks to you." He watched me morosely a moment with blood-shot eyes, then sipped his scotch as if testing for poison. "You and Nova Scotia—when you left me last night I decided it was time I went out and found one too."

He took another sip, still dubious, and then with his lips curled, as if the taste had puckered them, half-hissed, half-whispered, "Jesus, Sonny—how can you?"

Not putting it on this time; the disgust as genuine as the bewilderment. "A couple of hours all right—get it out of your system. But the *morning*—waking up and *looking* at her—"

"She's always up before me—looking fine."

"You mean you're satisfied? She's what you want?"

"Let's say she's useful. I'm getting through the winter."

"And if you hadn't found her?"

"I'd probably be on my way home by now. I told you the other night—I can always wire for my fare. But I don't want to go. Now that I'm here I'd like to stick it out at least another year."

"A lot longer than a year, Sonny. As a matter of fact you've got no choice."

With a slightly coy smile, fingers gabled, he paused a moment and leaned back as if expecting me to be impressed. "Oh yes—you can buy your bus ticket and take the body back; visit your friends for chicken dinner and put the blocks to some of the local beauties; even start up your little band again—but you'll never fit in. You'll never be one of them. Because all this time, whether you know it or not, you've been growing. Same as me, Sonny—you're the growing kind."

He beckoned the waiter to order me another scotch, then nodded confessionally and spread his hands. "Speaking from experience—I tried."

"*After* the gas station?"

"About two years after. A couple of fumbles—nothing serious—but I started to lose my nerve. Bad dreams—bullets and the police and my poor bloody corpse on a slab in the morgue."

The laugh collapsed: the sound of a shoe on eggshells. "Scared, Sonny—scared sick. You're the only one I ever told.

Scared and starting to get low in cash—hungry .... So one day I rang the bell and said just passing through, thought I'd drop round to see how everybody's doing—"

He gulped the rest of his drink as if trying to wash down the memory, then smiled wizenedly. "Big day! If you could have seen the calf they killed! *Oh my boy, my poor boy, the good Lord has heard my prayers!* And then the old man, all choked up again just like the day in court he sent me to the Farm—*It's good to have you back, Charlie, really good. Everything's going to be different now, you'll see.* And naturally brother Big Prick had to join the celebration—*Hi-ya fella—how ya doin'? Long time no see.* Intellectual of the family—lawyer, egg-head—talking down to the black sheep to make him feel at home. And all three of them with their little knives out, sharpening them up to whittle me down to size."

He pushed back his chair and stood up as if to start pacing, as if gall were driving him, then glancing round with a startled look, seeming to realize where he was, slumped down again. "I'd come back, broke, so they had me. We'd see who was giving the orders! Never mind the Farm—it was two years since I'd run out and Brother Prick could smooth things over—but there was a price. I wasn't going to disgrace or embarrass *them* again. They'd always kept their little heads and noses high, and that was the way they were going to keep them. All those years of work and sacrifice—no young punk like *me* was tracking mud up their stairs."

First a job that his brother arranged for him with another law firm. *Charlie, be a good fellow and get us some coffee. One black, one no sugar, two the works .... Oh Charlie, I forgot my pills this morning—you wouldn't mind, would you? It's nearly lunchtime, and I get such terrible heartburn. Here's the address, and tell Miss Tiddelty-tits I said to give you your bus fare.*

Six weeks and another job—arranged—with a real estate office. Three weeks and another—arranged—with a trust company .... Careful to tell everything and nothing. Not a name or detail that might ever serve to trace or trap him, but making the point, even as he spat on them, that his family were of means and some importance. Leaning on it a little, snobbishly proud, that at thirty-three his brother had been a full-fledged partner in his own law firm and *could* arrange jobs; and that his father, whatever his work or position, "was so used to all these stupid little jo's running for him he thought it just took one of his big-shot looks to make me run too."

He ran the last words into a laugh, thin, derisive, almost a giggle—*ever hear anything so ridiculous, somebody trying to make Charlie run!*—and then, an abrupt change of key, yawned and glanced at his watch. "Time, Sonny—I've got to see somebody .... See him and look him over. I can't wait all winter for you."

Something in his voice this time, a weary, it's-up-to-you finality, made me say quickly, "Give me a couple of days. I want to sleep on it."

"A couple of days—and then just be sure you wake up." Himself again, the bark back in his voice, his eyes snapping cold and bright. "It's a big town—take another look some-time. Plenty of places to go if you've got the guts."

Disowning—he liked people who did have guts—and striding ahead, eyes front, heels clicking, he seemed trying to give the impression to anyone who might be watching that he didn't know me. On the street he turned a moment, raised his hands as if to seize my arms and shake some sense into me, and then with a shrug, pulling his chin and ears into his collar against the wind, strode off ahead again.

We walked perhaps half a block in silence, keeping our distance. Then there was a bus stop with two girls waiting and he slowed, smirked at them, came to a halt. Run-of-the-mill blondes, passably, insipidly attractive—the kind that if you happened to meet you might make out with but that on the street would never draw a second glance. I looked from them to him, puzzled, wondering for a moment if they might be friends.

He was smiling. Leer, grin, grimace—something like a snap-shot of a smile taken at the wrong moment, in the wrong light—or as if while smiling normally he had been impaled, suddenly frozen, and this, the bared teeth and deep creases, was all that remained. Head still drawn into his collar and arms pressed tight against his sides, rocking slightly, he seemed poised to spring. A lick of sandy hair had blown loose and fluttered from his forehead like an antenna, searching for an opening to attack.

"Hi, there! You don't look like you've been getting much lately. How'd you like to come along and make a night of it?"

They swung towards him a second—eyes rounded, faces flat, an expression less of fear or outrage than of incredulity—and then, pivoting again, stared fixedly at each other, as if that way they might shut him out.

"Satisfaction guaranteed—thrills to remember!" His voice rose like a barker's. He took a step towards them, leaning back a little, his hands to his groin. "Don't just stand there drooling—it's all for free. Plenty for both—hump you to the eyes."

I moved in fast and grabbed him—hard, expecting a struggle—but he came away in my hand easily, like a weed without roots, almost as if he wanted to come, as if he were the one being set upon and baited and I had come to his rescue.

"They're only bags, Sonny—don't take it so serious." I strode off, furious, shaking, and he broke into a trot to keep up to me. "All the same—just because they got it. Think they can make you sit up and beg like a dog—" He was out of breath and the words were coming in wheezy spurts. "Not a brain—just that! Trying to put you down—like it gave them the right—think you'll come sniffing anyway. Didn't you see them? The way they looked at us?"

He stopped suddenly, wheeled round, and afraid he might go back and start in again, I stopped and wheeled with him. But it was only to spit at them, shaking his voice like a little fist, "Dirty bitches—who'd want you anyway?"

A block or two farther on, at Sherbrooke and Ste Famille, we separated, and watching him strut off towards St. Lawrence, head up as if he no longer felt the wind, dapper and assured again, I tried to be tolerant, understanding. What was it like on the run? What kind of woman *could* you have? Twenty years of them—how much loathing finally built up inside you? And Mad in contrast—Mad and her barndoor-wide devotion—did the sight and sound of her rub a raw spot? Was he envious?

But for all that something had rubbed off—something warped, ugly, sour—and I walked on feeling soiled, contaminated, as if I had been in on it too. All evening—like getting something sticky on your fingers, honey, glue, then picking up the clarinet—the smear of his grinning face persisted, clung.

Even asleep: for hours I ran frantically, trying to find the bus station, always the wrong street, always a dead-end; and when finally I arrived the two blonde girls looked at my ticket and said it went the other way.

If it's only enough for a real ticket! Awake, turning away from Mad, I whispered the words into the darkness like a sick prayer. *Back home—Toronto—anywhere ... just enough to start over, start clean—*

17

BUT AGAIN I DELAYED.

In the morning, as soon as Mad left, I went down to shovel off the steps and sidewalk; and when I came back he met me on the landing and suggested we go out for breakfast. It was a good chance—early and clear-headed, time to listen again and test for tricks or flaws—but confronted by the smile I lost my nerve. Sorry, not today. A cup of coffee and then I had to see Mrs. Painter. The furnace again—I promised her to see if I could find out what was wrong.

I said it awkwardly, the lie showing, and his smirk sent me clumping down to the basement as soon as I had finished my coffee in an effort to save face.

Mrs. Painter stared when I asked her if there was anything she wanted done, hostile and uncombed, her thick squat body with its neckless head like something made of clay with clumsy thumbs; then with a croaky laugh she stepped aside and nodded me in.

"Hungry—so that's it. Sit down and I'll see. I think the coffee's still hot."

She cut short my protests. "Bacon and eggs or sausage and eggs—you don't look like you've had much breakfast. Let's say sausage and eggs—time they were used up."

And then she suggested that while I was waiting I bring my clarinet. I had promised her apparently, and a good old-fashioned hymn for a change wouldn't hurt me. My mother would be pleased. "Shall We Gather at the River" or "Bringing in the Sheaves."

I needed the room; I needed her good-will in case she found out about Mad. Nothing for it but to pull a willing smile and tiptoe back upstairs.

It wasn't very good clarinet, listless and thin, holding out against the pop and sputter of the sausages about as well as the small, anaemic light bulb was holding out against the January morning.

"Real nice—now go ahead and try another. I'll hold back the sausages. Do you know 'In the Sweet Bye and Bye'?"

Progress for you—Main Street to Ste Famille. A broom and shovel for my bed and "In the Sweet Bye and Bye" for my breakfast. The light was dim, but I could see myself again.

"Brings back the old times. I'm not getting to church these days and anyway it's not the same." She put the plate of sausages and eggs on the table and poured a cup of coffee. "You sit there playing like a good Christian boy, but I'm afraid you're not."

She poured herself a cup of coffee and sat down facing me. "Oh yes, I know. A couple of them have seen her again, all curled and tizzied up and the place reeking with her scent. A boy like you from a good home—don't you realize what she's doing to you?"

"If she was the kind you mean—after money—she'd hardly be coming to see me."

"Sluts—all of them! A pack of scum!"

The words struck like the back of a bony hand, while she sat apart, in stolid calm.

"I've seen plenty in my time and I've thrown plenty out. They don't get away with their tricks in my house."

As if finishing off another eviction, she leaned back and slapped her hands together. "And don't worry—they'll get what's coming to them. They won't end up just old and ugly like the rest of us, but full of corruption and disease. Showing off their fine clothes—turning up their nose at good hard work and decent people! Just wait—there'll be a day!"

"You've got her wrong. She works hard—six days a week."

"And the nights she stays—you mean to sit there and tell me you never sin?"

We raised our cups and watched each other over them. "The Sweet Bye and Bye" had got me nowhere.

"Not that I blame you. You're a man like the rest, and the way you tell it it's what she wants." She sipped her coffee with a whistling, sucking sound, holding the saucer under the cup in case of drip. "It's no use anyway. I've been running out her likes for thirty years and you might as well kill cockroaches. Squash them till you're up to your knees—they still keep coming."

She sat quiet and glum a moment, cup and saucer still at her chin. "So if you're so set on ruining yourself just go ahead. Me, I'm through. I'm not even worrying any more about the heat. Anybody gets cold can move. Up and down, trying to keep people satisfied—all these years a lot of good it's done me."

She put down the cup and saucer and with a grimace moved into a rocking chair. I said cautiously it was probably just time for a rest and someone to help her.

"It's been time for five years but they've been trying to beat me down and I've been holding out. Scared—your bit of money doesn't last long when you've nothing coming in. And suppose I live to be ninety?"

I thought of saying I hoped and was sure she would—hesitated, afraid I couldn't bring it off.

"I've been holding out for thirty-five thousand and now I'm giving in and taking thirty-two. I'd have got the thirty-five if I'd just hung on a while, only it would have meant putting in another furnace. Nobody to trust—what's an old woman to do?"

"You mean you've sold?"

"They've had the house on each side now for a couple of years, waiting for me, so they can go ahead with a big fancy apartment house. Swimming pool—I'm glad I won't be here to see it. I could have held out till October and got the summer rent but they turn their lawyers on you, talking fast, all their big words, and you get so rattled and tired."

"Even thirty-two thousand, though—it sounds like an awful lot of money."

"That's right—sounds like a lot. Start spending though, and you soon find out how long it lasts."

(Was this, I wondered, what Mad was afraid of? Why she preferred the hazards of the street, the forlorn hope of a right one who would last? Skinflint Cora and her diamond rings—had she read the signs?)

"The price of everything—and now I'll be paying rent besides. I'm sixty-six so there's not much more work left in me and suppose like I say I last another twenty years. The doctor says my legs are starting to come along. That means the chances are I will."

She sat erect, at bay, gripping the arms of the chair as if the doctor were about to attack. Already he had helped her legs.

"All that money, though—won't there be a lot of interest?"

"Some. Good rates and it's not so safe. And low rates are low."

Reaching for the clarinet, I said politely she would feel better in the spring. No more furnace troubles, no more people like me—

"The first of April—out you go. They're starting right away to tear down. Sometimes I think I'd have done better just with somebody to take over, so I could have kept a room."

"You say that as if you're afraid you're going to miss it?"

"After thirty years?" She paused a moment, the creak to the rocker carrying on. "I've always said soon as I had the time I'd take a trip—far, to remember—but prices today you don't know what to do. The older you get the more things go wrong with you, always needing doctors and hospitals, and it helps if you can pay for extras. Pretty soon I'll be needing somebody to fetch and carry."

"I'd take the trip—one to remember."

"Your age, it's easy. I used to do things too. Thirty-three when I married a no-good drunk and gambler—eyes wide open, everybody telling me—and a couple of years later when he fell under a truck I was so glad I cried. Not sorry, glad. But maybe if I'd known what the next thirty had in store I'd have fallen under something too. Furnace and stairs and taxes—people not paying their rent and getting drunk and giving you a bad name—"

"I'd risk it anyway."

"Last summer I was in hospital and the bed next to me there was an old woman paralyzed all one side. Couldn't eat by herself, needed help. They'd bring her tray and leave it, and then by the time somebody came to spoon for her everything would be cold. One day it was mushroom soup. They tried to make her take it, and she fought and spit it out. Cold mushroom soup—by the time they finished it was in her hair. That's what I mean—makes a difference if you've got your own nurse."

"Your problem then's to break even? So your thirty thousand lasts just as long as you do—none left over?"

"Why shouldn't I break even? I've got a son—good money, runs a garage—and all he and his wife ever do is send a ten-cent card at Christmas. Never come near. Things going wrong and nobody to put in a word for you—"

She looked at me with the same glum eyes, and thanking her for the breakfast I slipped away. Charlie was in the hall, leaning over the banisters as I came up the stairs and smiling. Not a word—just smiling.

18

THERE MUST HAVE BEEN A MOMENT when the key clicked and turned—a moment of decision, involving *me*—but when I go back I find only the door, first closed, then open, never the act of opening it.

There must have been a path or trail of some sort, firm beneath me all the way; but trying to retrace my steps, to part the bushes and jump the rocks, is like trailing an unknown quarry whose tracks suddenly disappear and then, away on, resume; as if it had wings or were capable of enormous leaps—some kind of monster kangaroo.

Less leap, though, than suspension. Common sense, ambition, the way I had been brought up—everything said *no*. I knew better. I had a clarinet and a future—a stake in going straight. But there was a break, a blackout, a dead path—almost as if I had been slipped a drug.

A temporary derangement, then, brought on by worry and depression. Paralysis and flap. Things were too much for me. I cracked and jammed.

Tempting, but it won't stand up. I wasn't in a corner. I had a place to sleep. At the worst I could have written home. There was even an improvement now that Mad had stepped in: I was cleaner, better fed. I was squeamish about accepting her help but, as she kept reminding me, I could consider it as a loan. Besides, it was between ourselves; no one need ever know. And if there really was an inner rectitude involved, a private sense of what was right and fitting, then what about Charlie? How did I come to terms with him?

Circles. I don't know. Perhaps in every lapse there is a step, blind and unwilling, that springs the trap. Perhaps no man, the tangle of his fears and hungers bared, is guilty. But the old Presbyterian streak survives, and I don't get away with that one either. Non-responsibility stands up to it like a cotton shirt to a prairie blizzard. Morally, I take my medicine.

In any case, a few days later, here I am. Sonny McAlpine from Saskatchewan, level-headed and practical, a farmer's son, with big plans and big dreams for the future; here I am in a Montreal tavern, corner of Sherbrooke and Bleury, listening to Charlie as he tells me how he plans to make a thousand fast and easy.

And I am a good listener.

"Right now I've got five little jobs lined up. The way I work—slow and careful—time to figure out the angles. This one now's been shaping up the last couple of months. *Developing.* Not big—just right to start on. Somebody like you on the green and jumpy side."

The voice patronizing but kind. The eyes still critical, slightly dubious, like hands at a sale feeling the hide and muscles of bull. Then back to himself, complacently, "Can't go wrong—so easy in fact I sort of feel ashamed. *Too* easy—a good job is one that keeps you thinking sharp and fast, so when it's over you've got a feeling that you've pulled a real one. Something worth while."

"Something that brings out the best in you."

It pleased him. The hard, wary face collapsed a moment, and the lookout eyes went in. "Let's say I don't like taking candy from a kid."

He sat quiet a moment, enjoying the picture of himself that this little exchange had conjured up—a rather fatuous look in contrast to the usual front of glass-eyed foxiness— and then, whipping in the smile as a neighbour-conscious housewife would whip in a dirty towel left hanging out the window by the children, he tensed a little and said, "This one, though, is no kid. A smooth old Jew with a smile as big as a double deal. And he thinks he's one up on *me*. That's the laugh—he thinks he knows *my* game."

The smile was better this time, sharp and sly, a look of professional competence, a reassuring hint of reserves. And I caught myself hoping that this was the real Charlie, that I was teaming up with someone who in a tight spot wouldn't have scruples, wouldn't waver.

"Jeweller—at least that's the front—sells and repairs watches. A little place up north on Park Avenue, back a little from the sidewalk. An outside stair—squeezed in behind so you almost miss it. Sits working away right in the window—been at it I'd say a couple of hundred years .... Well, this day I happen to be passing and he looks up and I catch his eye. Click! Just like that I've got a feeling that there's something funny going on. The eyes—the way he had his neck stuck out. Something worth while—I got the smell of it even before I went in."

He repeated the click with his tongue, then smiled to himself a moment, nodding. "A few cases of cheap stuff spread around—brooches, cuff links. Worse even than it looked from outside, dirty walls, junk lying on the counter. Sure, you come across a place like that sometimes but it's not run by somebody like him. That nice sleek smile and the eyes all the time doing a frisk job—going through your mind like an old whore going through your pockets."

He put his lips to his beer without drinking, something the way a horse idles its nose in the trough after it has drunk its fill. "And I said to myself it's a front—a set-up—a fence if ever I saw one."

He broke off and studied me a moment—another frisk job, another bull. Then, a curl to his lip, "Know what a fence is?"

I nodded, clutching my glass, wanting to yell at him just to tell me what I had to do. At the same time it registered that the sneer meant he was sure of me, knew I had signed on.

"Just passing, I say, but maybe it's the place I'm looking for. Bargain hunting—a watch for my sister in Toronto—birthday coming up. But right now I'm short—laid off and you get behind."

Spinning it out, enjoying himself. He didn't have a listener every day. "Naturally, he smells me too—just the way I want it. Knows there's something, figures it might be worth his while. So yes, he's got just what I'm looking for—somebody brought it in for cleaning and never came back. Twenty dollars—all right, a present for a little girl, let's say fifteen. Fair enough. She's going to be crazy about it, I say, and beaming like Father Abraham himself he says so you're from Toronto. Always thought Toronto was such a fine place nobody ever left it. Snicker snicker—big joke. And now you think you'll stay in Montreal a while?

"A while, I say. In and out—I've got friends."

Again I clutched my glass. He was revelling in it, would go on interminably. It was a workout, a toning up of all the muscles of his conceit and I was his victim, a kind of punch-bag. And he kept watching me as he talked, half-smile, half-sneer, as if he knew my hate and were revelling in that too.

"Out of town—for somebody like him that's important. Maybe a connection—help him keep the stuff moving."

He dipped his lips into the beer again, then began blowing the little floes of froth to the side of the glass, pursuing and manoeuvring the ones that eddied back until, except for the white ring around the edge, the surface was completely clear. For as he talked he was expanding, asserting himself, coming into his own: he had a right to indulge his moods and temperament.

"On the boats, I tell him—most of the time Montreal and Toronto. Friends in both places. Now and then to Detroit."

"But *my* part, Charlie! I'll take your word for the master-minding."

A moment's silence; a slight flicker of his lids to let me know he had heard.

"All ears like I say—maybe a connection. And I keep talking, trying to sound like a big wheel and all the time making sure I don't. *Get it?* Not nearly so tough or sharp as I'm letting on. Easy to handle. For somebody like him a pushover."

"But he knows you now—he's seen your face—"

He sucked at his teeth a moment with a puckered, squelching sound. "You think I intend sitting on his doorstep till the police get there? So he can identify me? Getting him softened up—that's what's important—not afterwards. He's got a safe—we want him to open it and bring everything out himself. It'll be that much easier."

"But your description—it'll be a lead—"

He stretched and yawned, went back to blowing his beer. "The police, Sonny, won't be interested. Old Abraham's not worth it. Read the papers—a couple of dozen little jobs like this every week. You think they're going to start a big manhunt when somebody like *him* comes whining about his rings and watches? Chances are he's got a record anyway."

He gave a soft, private laugh, then came back tolerantly. "Not a chance in a million they'll ever bring us face to face, and even if they do—well, he's blind or crazy, because that night I wasn't even in Montreal. Alibi—foolproof. I was in Toronto."

The eyes bright and expectant a moment, then exasperated. *"Toronto*—ever heard of it? The night it happens—how can they pin it on me when I'm out of town?"

I sat staring blankly. (*The face changes on you—all at once it's somebody you don't know!*) He gave a sharp, stuttering rap with his knuckles. "Not one chance in a million but that's the chance Charlie never takes. You don't realize how lucky you are. I pack a bag and tell Mrs. Painter I'm going to be out of town a couple of days. I've got a friend in Toronto—we do each other little favours. I address a postcard to her, send it to him and he mails it back. I'll be longer than I thought—be sure and hold my room. That one chance in a million—postmarked Toronto."

I lit a cigarette and tried to look at ease. "All right, you've got it all planned. Now some details—what we do—"

"He's expecting us—everything open. Customers. We just walk in."

"But I'd like to know—"

"You'll get the details at the right time. Now back to where we were: I tell him a couple of the boys I know are getting married and out he trots his diamond rings. Half a dozen of them—not bad. Just a small business—can't afford to keep much in stock but let him know a few days in advance—

"Well Sonny, I've been back three times—looking at what he's got, asking prices, beating him down, saying maybe—more or less showing my hand. That is, showing what he *thinks* is my hand."

He paused impressively. To hurry him I nodded. "Two of a kind—he accepts me. I've been letting him see through me, spelling it out. Now he's satisfied—so busy figuring out what cards I've got he doesn't realize it's not cards I'm playing. Out to pull a fast one, slip something over him—sure, he knows and he's not worried. Both of us with tricks up our sleeves—he knows who's going to win."

I finished my beer without looking at him. "All right—and what are yours?"

"Surprise. The place closed, nobody around and everything spread out in front of us—and then a gun in his ribs."

A twitch to his lips, a still, glassy stare. As if he had just pulled off the job, inflicted defeat.

"And where do I fit in? And if we're customers why don't we go like customers? In the afternoon, before he's locked up?"

"Because you'll have just got into town and you'll maybe have to leave again the next day. One of the boys who's getting married—I'll phone him. Maybe we're working together—maybe I'm taking a cut. You want a ring yourself but you'd like to see what he's got because you'll be back in a week or so and some of the other boys may be interested. Another connection. He'll be interested too."

"All this just so he'll let us in?"

"And open the safe—and lay everything out on the counter. Brains, Sonny, instead of dynamite. Not so messy—not so much noise."

I looked at him dully and said "When?"

"Tomorrow—about eight. Relax and leave everything to me."

"I won't see you around the house then? You'll be going to Toronto?"

"Caught a plane this afternoon. Mrs. Painter knows. Back the day after tomorrow."

"Where do we meet?"

"This'll do—seven-fifteen. If the paper's right there'll be snow. Probably a storm. The forecast's windy."

"And that's all? Here at a quarter past seven?"

"Better without the details—so you won't spend the time going through them in your mind. Just take it easy tonight with Nova Scotia—I don't want you dragging. Wait till tomorrow night after it's over. The next day you can both sleep late—won't have to send her out working for a year."

His face told me I had winced. "Then a quarter past seven," I said, and went out alone.

19

AND I HAD ROUGHLY THIRTY HOURS. All that time what was I thinking?

Sometimes I try to blame Charlie. He was smooth; he knew how to talk his way around me; how to humiliate and sting. Something about the eyes—the queer cold way they had of coming forward in their sockets, the flat stare. Hypnotic, I try; he had them fixed on me as a snake fixes on its prey.

But such poor prey. Another that won't do. The offer was an offer. The answer was up to me.

And Charlie himself; not a mystery man. Life size, just twisted. Perhaps a smart crook, lying low; perhaps a clumsy one, at the end of his rope and desperate. I don't know. There was a kind of authority at times, a poise, that could argue for a record of successes; also—for one instant I saw it—a whip of speed and fearlessness. Even the vanity—childish, up like a balloon—it didn't necessarily mean he was an amateur or fumbler. Beneath it there probably seethed a little hell of envy and insignificance, but the itch could have been the fuel.

I don't know. I'm from the farm and a prairie Main Street where people are exposed, comparatively simple. Easily taken in; not fit to judge. In any case, speculation about Charlie is not what matters. The blame comes back to me; not only how I consented but also, more important, how I justified the consent, made it seem rational, necessary.

Roughly a day and a quarter. Not hungry, not sick, not concerned about anyone belonging to me. Quietly doing my chores, shovelling and sweeping, playing the clarinet, watching a movie that evening with Mad and afterwards, contrary to instructions, helping myself to a second piece of tail. All that time, what was I thinking?

Somebody else and we're at a loss, uneasy. Chilled, even, as we try to imagine ourselves making the decision, taking such chances. Why? Put to it, might we? And then, even as we shrug it off, we make a furtive bow. The all-or-nothing throw—some part of us responds, admires. The fellow's been places, done things that we, perhaps, if we dared admit it, would like to do. Why? What was it like out there? And still again, why?

But I, who have made the trip and crossed the border, come back with blank pages.

Clues? The way I worked around the house that day, the diligence with which I handled shovel and broom—perhaps it was to remind the big-time Sonny where he was, to rub his subconscious nose in the rancid smell of failure, to make the point that only a drastic remedy would do .... Leave it for the record, anyway.

And practising the clarinet—at least for the first half-hour, when it was disciplined, conscientious practising, everything taken slowly, painstakingly—perhaps that was evidence too: that he was serious and worthy, deserved something better than the broom. An attempt to clear himself, make certain that a charge of shiftlessness or delinquency would never stand, to put the blame on circumstances. He had betrayed nothing. It was the other way round.

And that night with Mad—especially the second time, when I didn't really want it: in part it was to take the sting out of some of the things I had said on the way home from the movie and to stave off the long night ahead; but there was disgust, too, self-contempt, as if I were deliberately piling it on. "Here we go again—Sonny and his half-wit broad. One for the dinner, two for the show."

We had quarrelled after the movie. Hardly a quarrel; the movie had put her in a domestic mood, and I had slapped her down.

Something about a nice little house with the whole front wall a window—wouldn't I like one like that too?—and I had said Jesus, no, if I had the price of the window never mind the house I'd be on the first bus out of Montreal.

"Oh, I didn't mean a house in *Montreal*," she had begun, and then, understanding, went abruptly silent. Her head dipped. As we walked along her fingers bit my arm.

But a few minutes later, at a cafeteria table, over cherry pie and coffee, she was expansive and assured again, complacently critical of the pie. "Shoeleather and goo—the stuff they get away with in these places! First chance I get *I'm* going to make you a cherry pie. Sunday, maybe—I'll bake it in Cora's oven and run over with it while it's still hot."

"Your siren sounding?"

She sat still and white a moment, then let out a whoop of laughter, "That's right—*whoo-oo, whoo-oo!* Mad the fire engine, coming with her cherry pie. Ripping and roaring and the juice flying—*whoo-oo, whoo-oo—*"

"Never think it's time to you had an oven of your own?"

"Some day maybe. Things'll work out."

"Not the way you want them. And never fooling around with the likes of
me. You just haven't got that much time."

She raised her cup to her lips and held it in both hands a minute, as if it were something alive that needed warming.

"I keep trying to tell you, Sonny—I never had it so good and I don't suppose I ever will again. It's not going to last—I know—so I'm making the most of it while it does. When it's over—well, then maybe it'll be time."

She looked up and past me, gave a toss to her hair. "Maybe I'll start thinking about the oven, maybe not. Don't suppose I'd ever bake a pie to eat alone."

"But all the time you keep hoping—a happy-ever-after ending with me coming to my senses and realizing I'll never be able to get along without you."

She nodded, sipped her coffee. "Same as people are always hoping, Sonny. For something good—like taking a trip or finding a purse full of hundred-dollar bills. Hoping it'll happen and at the same time knowing it never will."

She reached out, smiling, and touched my finger tips with hers, eyes gentle and patient, almost as if she were trying to console me. And yet even in the smile they were there, tendons of will and wanting like the veins of a leaf when you hold it up against the light; and for a moment it seemed the wanting was a mouth fastened on me, sucking, leechlike, and my impulse was to tear it off, jerk free.

"Once and for all, Mad, let get things straight." I leaned forward, my face ugly, my fork dinging on the table. "I don't want your cherry pie and I don't want your nice clean friendly little restaurant. Right now we're shacking up but we're not teaming up. Got it? There's even less chance than there is of taking a trip or finding hundred-dollar bills so for Christ's sake *stop* hoping."

"Well, if you don't want my cherry pie I'd better go and get you some more shoeleather. Sure need something to fill up that hole inside you. Sounds of things it's getting bigger."

She was smiling again when she came back with more pie and coffee, solicitous, unshaken. I ate a mouthful or two in silence, then pushed the plate away. "Listen, Mad I know you'd make a good cherry pie, a hundred times better than what we're eating now—but pie's not what I want. I can't settle for it—try to understand. I'm after something different— that I've been after for years—"

"You'll get it, too. Soon—I can feel it coming. Just keep strong and well and stay away from people like Charlie."

"Never mind Charlie—we've got to talk about us."

"That's what I say, too—never mind Charlie. Never mind me, either. I'll get along all right. Just get that pie and coffee inside you and tomorrow'll be another day."

I woke through the night and found her sitting over me. Defensively, like an animal watching over its young. For a moment or two, not quite awake, puzzled, I lay motionless and watched her with my eyes half-closed, pretending to be asleep. She was resting on an elbow, her other hand on my shoulder. The light from the window caught her hair and gave it a faint, brassy glow; her face in contrast was hard, chalk-pale, gouged with shadow. Something like a head in a child's scribbler: the features drawn in clear outline, the hair a daub of yellow paint. She looked haggard and worn. The mouth was twisted, bitter, the chin thrust out defiantly. She moved her head slightly and her eyes snapped brightly and glassy, Moved it again, and I saw that she was crying.

What do you do? There was an impulse to draw her down to me again and feel the misery within her ease and melt, but there was also the awareness that it would be a kind of treachery, a pledge I could never fulfill. For her chances with me were like mine with Beethoven and a career. Not her fault, not mine; just the way things were. I liked her body; sometimes I even liked her. I recognized the good things: the spirit and bounce, the big-hearted laughter; her faith in the "right ones" that somehow skirted silliness and always came out shining. Count after count she had the edge on me—above all, she was big enough to crash—but no matter what her virtues, and no matter how fairly I acknowledged them, she would never be anything more to me than someone for fun in bed.

And hadn't I been fair? Right from the start hadn't I told her what she could expect? If she picked the wrong "right one" and suffered for it was it anybody's fault but her own? After all, you've got to take your own measure, come to terms with what you are. It's easy to want, to dream; the pinch is adjusting to what you have a right to. Jazz and the blues in exchange for the other—what I really wanted—that hadn't been easy either. Hadn't been—*wasn't*. For you don't get away with a couple of bad days, a single wrench of renuncia-tion. The ghost of a might-have-been goes with you all the way, clinging to your back like an Old Man of the Sea, sneering at the deal you made. Even though it was the only possible deal this side of lunacy—still there's the whisper, "What was the hurry? How could you have been so sure? Supposing you had given yourself another ten years—supposing you'd been right all along—"

So let her cry, let her learn. Let her do it the hard way, like the rest of us, come to terms with second best. In the meantime, though, what do you do?

I scratched my hand and coughed, as if stirring in my sleep, then lay still again; and at once, like something wild and shy slipping away at the snap of a twig, she turned her back and sank stealthily onto the pillow. And then we both lay still, straining to keep from touching each other, listening to the branches and the whimper of the wind.

For me, too, it was a bad time, with the moments of doubt piling up and gaining like wet flakes of an early snowstorm that melt as they fall and yet gradually thicken and spread until the earth is white; and now I wanted not only to comfort her, feel the defeat and silence spring alive, but also to be comforted, to yield to the devotion and draw strength from it in turn. But I lay tense, resisting. "I'll make it up to her. Some way—maybe tomorrow. If things turn out all right— a couple of those goddammed hundred-dollar bills."

20

Tomorrow was snow.

Charlie had said a storm was forecast and in the morning, as soon as Mad had left, I began going to the window, sometimes just to glance out, sometimes to stand waiting a few minutes, staring out through the branches at the soft, ashy sky.

Compulsively, without knowing why. What difference would it make? How could snow help? I didn't ask myself, just concentrated on it—*snow*—as probably a soldier concentrates on the condition of his rifle without thinking how or why or to what end he may be going to use it. Giving it importance, as if the success of our venture depended on it, staring into it but not through it, so that the venture, like a barn in a blizzard, was just there, just a blur, just visible.

All day: for there was a wind blowing little spits and skiffs of old snow off the roof and out of the crotches of the branches before the new snow began, and from my first trip to the window I was intent on discovering which it was, old or new; anxious when the wind lulled and street and tree were unobscured, elated when a flurry whitened out the view and hissed against the window.

Between trips I practised. Carefully and conscientiously at first, keeping time with a hidden metronome; then lapsing into flourishes and flutters, exploratory, as if I were trying out the clarinet for the first time, discovering what it could do; and from there to idling along with bits and tunes of my own invention, sometimes a little show-off cadenza, sometimes just a note or two, hung on, wavered—what it pleased me to call "improvising"; the same sort of thing that in the old days would bring my mother banging in from the kitchen with an indignant, "Enough of that! Either do it properly or go out and help your father."

For it went a long way back, before I knew such a thing as a clarinet existed; before my first lessons with Dorothy, when I was stumbling along with the occasional and dubious help of a neighbour; days when the major-minor diatonic forthrightness of "Old Black Joe" and "Rock of Ages" was a strait jacket into which I couldn't fit, neither I nor the prairie world around me; and at such times, like a cat trying the furniture for the right texture to scratch on, to ease the itch in its claws, I would leave off practising and for a few minutes go exploring on my own.

The mystery was that my mother always knew. Up to her eyes in work and worry, she never seemed aware of the piano except as a tiresome din or tinkle, Bach, Brahms or Schubert all the same, all going nowhere; but the instant the "fooling around" began she pounced. "Your father and brothers up since five—do you never think? It's not just that it's costing money. When you're in here playing you're not doing your share."

At that, I yielded to the impulse seldom. Even when I was alone in the house, I would catch myself almost as soon as I began. My own overseer, as quick to pounce as she was. For with her milk I had absorbed her values and no less firmly than she believed in hard work, thrift and discreet self-betterment. Frills were not for farmers; I knew; and a dollar was a hundred cents. Besides, there was the practical incentive. Hard work might some day take me away from the farm. Mooning never would. "You must climb the mountain," Dorothy kept reminding me, "if you want the view. And the very highest mountain, where *you* belong, it's a long, steep climb."

Now, though—today of all days—I felt release, exhilaration. I was good. Half a dozen notes came out and hung together—made something. I worked them over a time or two, shaped them—took pencil and paper and wrote them down. Back at the window I hummed them silently, watching the little spurts of snow. Then, taking up the clarinet, I played them again, tossed them to the piano, listened approvingly to what it did, repeated them on the clarinet with a variation, shared another variation with the drums.

Good. Just let myself go, be what I was, do what I could. The farm and the sonatas and Dorothy's metronome were all a thousand miles away. Improvise—let go, yield to what you feel, project it—wasn't that the way to make good jazz? To be away out and at the same time in control—an elastic round your neck letting you lean out eighty-nine degrees but always pulling you back to vertical? I had the discipline— a *feeling* for it, right to the marrow of my inner-directed Presbyterian bones—and wasn't there a vagrant streak as well? All my prairie common sense and caution notwith-standing, hadn't I picked up and taken to the road? And here at Ste Famille Street, grubby inside and out—for all my protests was I minding very much? Permission granted, wouldn't I be right at home? There was a voice nattering about decency and self-respect, about amounting to something, but farther in—my own room and the door closed—was I listening? Right now—wasn't it a way, perhaps, to thumb my nose at the rules I had always lived by? No need to go home. I belonged to the world around me after all. Dissonance and drift—they weren't alien. I had come a long way and I was going a long way farther. You did what you could, put your feet where there was firm footing. The ground varied, smooth and rocky, bog and sand. The feet were always yours.

And I had good feet. On the way up you couldn't afford to be finicky about where you put them. Good feet and a fair share of guts. Tonight—with Charlie—that was going to take guts, wasn't it?

I gulped a second, as if a snowball had caught me with my mouth open, then began to play again.

Another tune out of nowhere, smooth and brisk this time with the reckless lilt of the disinherited. Just a snippet of a tune, just a shrug, a couple of phrases, but something could be done with it. A tune worth listening to. Out of nowhere. Out of me.

Isabel would approve—just as she had approved when I took the law into my own hands, heedless of warnings, and saddled and rode her. For that matter, once I had done it, hadn't *they* approved too? After you've done what you want to do and got away with it, don't they always approve?

I turned to the window and watched the snow again, went back to the clarinet. The "fooling around" was good now, valid. It was as if my recklessness in joining Charlie had cleared a course, washed out restraints and obstacles. As I played, as skips and runs turned into tunes, as tunes did tricks, idled and bounced, ran backwards, on their heads, I felt dilated, sure. Like a bronco that has jumped the bars of its corral—good, firm earth beneath him, the road open to the sky. Tonight—what lay ahead—that was only an incident in the landscape, a bush, a rock, a badger-hole, to be taken with a snort, a flash of heels.

Meanwhile the snow was establishing itself as new snow. A flurry, dense for a second or two, then subsiding, as if someone had taken a swipe at the roof with a broom; an interval and then a spit, a spray; and then another interval. New snow—it must be new—the roof and tree couldn't have held so much. And the sight of it reassured me, confirmed the confidence, the sense of just beginning. For somehow, by a sleight of mind, I had identified with it, linked it with my fortune—as if it were something precious, life-giving, to be prayed for. Rain, I could have understood. At home on the farm we sometimes did pray for it, watching the sky for a cloud as a believer would watch for the Second Coming. But snow—even feathery clean and sparkling in the sun—was winter, bleakness, cold ... a looking-glass world. I had taken a step too many, stumbled through ....

A knock interrupted. "I heard you playing so I knew you must be in, and I thought you could maybe see about the tap."

I had met her a few times on the stairs but we had never spoken. A thin, rope-necked woman with a straggle of greying hair and big purple shadows under her eyes that seemed to run down and droop her mouth. The voice matched, soft and apologetic, yet with an accusing whine. "When you want to wash something and leave it in the basin to soak the water gets cold. On account of the drip. It's the cold tap leaking."

As she spoke her eyes rolled sideways to see past me into the room and I knew that the tap was a pretext. A pinched, avid look, as if she expected to see Mad flat on her back with her legs up, waiting for me to resume. "No, there's no one here." I stepped aside to let her see into the room. "I'll speak to Mrs. Painter about a washer for the tap."

"Oh, it doesn't matter." Eyes flickering, flattening—something between fright and fury as she realized I had caught her. "It's just that the water gets cold so fast—like I say, the leak—and knowing you were in on account of the music—"

She backed away swiftly, hands spread in a gesture of self-effacement, and vanished down the stairs.

Not that it mattered. They were all strangers, meant nothing to me. In a couple of months the house itself was coming down. But it was time I was on my way. High time. I wouldn't even come back. Just to leave Mad something and pay Mrs. Painter—just for my clarinet. Shake the dust off, blow the stench out of my nostrils. The stench of squalor—on my hands, in my hair and clothes. Tomorrow I would strip to the skin.

21

SPARKING AS HE WALKED IN: a motor running on its own, out of control. Cutting down, holding himself in—this was a public place, a tavern—and still not able to bring his feet quite level with the floor.

The same with the smile—fixed and drawn as if the skull had started to grow and the skin were straining to hold it in. The cheekbones were pressure points, white as if frost-bitten. The eyes stood out round and glassy: a tip of the head and they might roll.

"Ahead of me and drinking already. Good—that's one beer I won't have to pay for."

"And I don't want another, so the one you paid for yesterday will be the last."

"Touchy tonight—that's good, too."

The chain appeared, wrapped and unwrapped itself around his finger, then struck the table with a sharp, disintegrating smack, as if in striking it had killed itself.

"Just the way I want you—because you're still a little on the soft side and that could mean messing up the job. Ugly and mean—so you'll run to catch and kill."

As the chain struck again lips and eyes tensed, drew together in a silent crunch. "Anyway you've brightened up at last and here we are."

A shot of something, I wondered—I'd read sometimes they did—and I put my hand protectively across my glass. The chain whirled again, like an extension of his finger, tongue or sting.

"Brightened up and all set to go. After a while even the big dumb ones from the farm catch on."

A thrust of teeth through the smile; then the chain like a red-hot lash across my hand. I winced, bunched myself, gripped the edge of the table. More threateningly, perhaps, than I knew, for with a smooth deflection—like saying see, it's only fun between friends—he whirled the chain again and brought it down across his own hand.

"What's wrong, Saskatchewan? We're *partners*." He ran the word into a whinnying laugh, his head back as if he were gargling. "We're stepping out tonight—on the town. Get with it and have fun."

Another smack on the table; another bite of jaws and eyes as if he were killing something that had reared to strike. And at that, still holding himself in. Like his walk: as easily as he could have taken ten-foot strides, over tables and chairs, he could have beaten me to a pulp.

"Now to work." The smile vanished as if dried off in a sudden heat. "No instructions—nothing to go over and remember. Just do what I tell you—*when* I tell you—and do it fast."

He took a small, neat drink of beer, as if he were swallowing a pill. "Nice easy little job—just your size. Like rolling a drunk in an alley."

A pull to his mouth, disdainful; another sip of beer. "Maybe if you handle yourself all right tonight I'll cut you in again—something bigger .... We know, we know—" The whinnying laugh again, his hand up warding off my protests—"You're coming out just this once because you need a few fast bucks and as soon as it's over you're going to be clean and noble again. One of the good guys—but who knows? Maybe when you get the feel of money in your pocket and start to spend—maybe you'll smarten up a little more."

The mixture—that was what silenced and held me—the contempt and the concern. The two voices—sour and sneering, counselling and big-brotherly—that both rang true. "We'll make a good team. We've both got the goods. You don't know how to use yours yet, but I'll bring you along .... Only first, you've got to trust me—stop snivelling—looking so goddammed scared! You hear—*trust* me!"

The voice ripped like saw-teeth. It was as if he had caught the bewilderment in my face and read it as resistance—an affront to his efficiency, his infallibility. He slammed his own glass down so hard the beer splashed frothily over his hand; then bending forward, his sleeve soaking up the slop, he seized and slammed down mine.

"But nobody's twisting your arm. Go on—run home and let your broad look after you—give you your thrills and fill your belly too. Most of us have got to pay for our fun but you it's the other way round—butter on one side, jam on the other. So run along—if butter and jam's what you like. For recreation sweep the stairs. Because I don't like scared people. They make me jumpy. And I've told you already I don't take chances. I've got a lot more to lose than you."

More to lose than Sonny McAlpine! I stared and took it. Our eyes met and the little spurt of anger buried itself in the truth like a bullet in sand.

"All right—if you're coming we'll get ready."

Only contempt now. Undiluted, one hundred per cent proof, almost as if in doing what he wanted me to do I was failing him. His voice had a snap, competent, assured. Adhesive tape and a penknife appeared.

"Just half an inch on the cheek—and some blood smeared around to make it look real."

A quick tiny jab of the knife before I could ward it off and the pain of a mosquito bite, then a long, crackling laugh.

"If you could have seen your face just now—I must have got at least two drops. What's wrong? Scared of blood?"

Another laugh, snapped off in the middle like a stick across the knee. "Hold still—nobody's paying attention—

we're just a couple of drunks. There—couldn't be better. Just enough blood to show around the edge."

"For Christ's sake stop the clowning!" I put my hand up to the bit of adhesive tape he had slapped on my cheek. In the same instant, the chain whirled and caught me across the knuckles.

"Leave it, you goddammed half-wit—it's for your own good. We're not going to kill old Abie and when it's over he'll be talking to the police." He leaned forward again, rapping on the table, his voice hard and quick, rasping. "All the details—what you were wearing, how big, how old—and the one thing he'll be sure of is that bit of bloody tape."

"Talk about half-wits—you mean it's supposed to be a *disguise*?" My hand moved involuntarily towards the patch, dropped as the chain whirled again.

"Right—a disguise. Better than a handkerchief or turning up your collar. Take it from me—that's all he'll be able to tell the police—your face was cut, taped up—like you'd been fighting. Look at this—"

He brought out a pair of black-rimmed glasses, slipped them on and leered at me through a cracked lens.

"Get it? I put them on when I visit him and they're all he ever sees. A pair of glasses with a crack—never me. It bothers him. He keeps looking—a couple of times I've seen him wet his lips, all set to ask me why I don't get a new pair. But I slip in ahead and he's left with the question—getting bigger, pushing *me* out of the picture. Nothing left but somebody with broken glasses."

Chair tilted back grandly; his face set in wrinkles of self-approval, as if he were looking in a glass.

"Up here, Sonny!" He tapped his forehead and then, raising his glass, blew at the froth as if it were a fly. "Ideas—getting in first. Once I heard the cops questioning a woman about a man who'd been selling phony insurance and do you know all she could remember? He had a hat and a blue tie with little white dots and a funny smile."

"So there's no danger? I'll be safe because I've got a bit of tape on my face."

All at once I felt lost. Not even fear—just a slow, grey heave of nausea, a conviction of disaster. Not a chance—his eyes a pair of crystal balls in which I could read only doom. And at the same time acquiescence, almost an impatience to get it over with.

"Can't we go then? Isn't it time?"

"We don't *need* the tape and glasses. They're just to prove something. Watch the papers tomorrow—you'll see. One man wearing broken glasses and one with a bloody face."

"And this idea—you thought it up all yourself?"

Face and voice must both have been completely deadpan, completely bled: it seemed to please him. "And plenty more coming along—good ones. Another two or three years—you'll see. Don't be surprised some day if I take this town over."

Meant it, believed it. A sick, ten-year-old trying out his little schemes like kites or glue-and-paper boats. And the chances were he had worked well: kites that would fly, boats that would stay afloat.

"And there'll be a place for you, too. God knows why—just because I'm so goddammed soft and you're so goddammed helpless. Or maybe instinct."

"You mean you've smelled me out?"

"Could be—like the queers say it takes one to know one. Underneath, Saskatchewan, if we dig for it, there's maybe what I'm looking for. I think so and tonight I'll know. I'll be watching. Every second—every turn—and you know why? You know why tonight's important?"

"You just told me—because I'm so goddammed helpless."

"Because you're going to waste—using your guts for shov- elling snow and frying hamburger. Lots of headaches, I said to myself, but you're hooked. Time you took over. He's your boy and he needs a hand."

He meant this too. The voice had warmed, gone crumbly. And momentarily, a respite. I yielded to it. Perhaps because, only a moment before, the spitting hate had unnerved me with its threat of worse to come—like something bristling in your path that as yet has only snarled but any second may spring.

And I thought swiftly, desperately—at least it's not a trap. He not just using me for the dirty work. On my side, a partner. Maybe we'll bring it off after all.

"We've been here half an hour—isn't it time yet?"

"Twenty minutes." He glanced at his watch and smiled, placid and unblinking.

"First time it's always the same—always in a rush. Later you like to take your time. The job itself—get the feel of it. Seeing how things work out—coming your way. Same as a game—you're in to win but it's fun while you're playing too. All right, let's go. Relax a little and you'll enjoy it this time. You can afford to. You're with Charlie."

As I pushed back my chair the chain came down again: another spark of pain, a drop of blood.

I straightened slowly, staring at the blood as it swelled compact and glistening like a berry, then broke and trickled across my hand.

"Coming?" The voice had a crunch of bones again. The lips made a small, peremptory grimace. Wiping my hand on my trousers, I stumbled out after him.

22

THE SNOW WAS THICKER NOW and the wind had fallen. The street lights with the big ragged flakes whirling round them were like rows of dandelions gone to seed. We waited a minute at the corner of Sherbrooke and Bleury, the light against us, watching a truck and half a dozen cars struggle up the hill with spinning wheels, and I said, "Do we take a bus or a taxi?"

"A *bus*, Sonny? A *taxi?*" He turned and stared, his shoulders hunched and a hand against his cheek as if the night were cold. "Let's take a big breath now and start all over. First of all, we're on our way to pull a little job—remember? Second, when we're through, we don't stand on a corner waiting for the bus. Third, if we took a taxi and asked him to wait he might start thinking too hard and head for the nearest phone booth. The dawn yet? One of those little outings where we arrange our own transportation."

Head drawn in low against the snow, he started across the street. I followed sullenly, a few paces behind, like a slapped little boy trying to show his independence. It ran through my mind I could still walk out, still say if you're going to be so snotty about it you can do your own job. But I didn't think of it as something I should do, the right thing, important for me. Still the sulky little boy, I only imagined the effect it would have on him, what the eyes would do, the way the chain would whirl. There was no real question of walking out. We were embarked on our little trip together and he was in command.

"Smile, Sonny. Charlie's here. You can lean on him."

We had turned a few steps up another street and were stopped beside a Chevrolet. The ugliness had drained from his face. The voice was friendly again. "Everything planned—nothing left to the last minute—that's Charlie." When we were inside he even gave me an affectionate dig in the knee. "A well-oiled little operation—going to be so smooth and easy you won't be able to remember tomorrow how we did it. Like it happened when you weren't looking—behind your back. I don't believe in spending money till it's in your pocket, but all told, cash and rings and watches, I'd say a thousand easy. Each."

I sat hunched forward, my hands between my knees, trying to believe it.

"And you don't have to worry—conscience or anything like that—don't have to feel guilty. Ten to one it's all stolen stuff anyway."

I didn't answer. He waited a minute and then began crisply, "I phoned and he's expecting us—no trouble getting in. And I've told you already—you're one of the boys who's getting married. Like me, you've been working on the boats. You shake hands and say pleased to meet you. Big and friendly, sort of stupid. Put him at his ease."

The snow slapping wet and sloppy on the windshield; the wiper at a brisk *allegro.* "Nobody *likes* a metronome, Sonny. It's just to keep you steady. Because sometimes, you know, you're inclined to take the bit in your teeth and run away. It's a good horse that runs away but it's not good *for* anything until it's trained, learns to obey."

"You've got the right face—friendly but not too friendly—holding out just a little. He'll look you over and you'll look fairly satisfactory. Not the type somebody like *me* would take for a partner—get it? Chances are I'm planning to pull a fast one on you too. It'll put you more or less on his side—

make him feel safe. He'll figure there's no harm in letting you see the stuff."

I was slow. We were topping the ridge on Park Avenue, between the park and the mountain, before it struck me that the car was probably stolen.

"So we'll hope he brings it out. He will anyway when he sees the gun, but it'll be that much easier if it's all spread out in front of us. Now this part's important so listen carefully. There's a little opening in the counter—sort of a gate, you've got to duck—but I want you instead to go *over*. Jump—the same second I pull the gun. No rough stuff, just a little show to help get the idea across we're ready to be tough—just to get things rolling. Do it fast and the size of you sailing through the air he'll think all hell's broke loose. He won't think. His eyes'll just pop. He'll be paralyzed."

The flakes swooped to meet us, seeming to gather speed and recklessness, like suicide swarms of white hornets.

"We can't waste time so I've got a little sack for you. I'll slip it to you later. First, you do *him*—everything straight into the sack. Try to hold on to the stuff or put it in your own pockets and you'll start fumbling."

Glib. An uneasy feeling he had read it in a book. I was to be thorough. Every pocket—side, hip, jacket, vest—and everything into the sack. Letters, pencil, comb, matches—*everything*. Plenty of time to sort it out later.

"Except keys." We stopped for a red light and leaning back and turning his face towards me he jabbed me in the knee again. "Any keys you pull out you just drop so he can find them afterwards. No good to us, and I don't play mean."

"Like a good hunter—kills only what he can eat."

"And I never hurt anybody—unless it's necessary. If somebody gets smart ideas about holding out you've got to smarten him up—naturally—but never keys. Smashing things—all right. Sometimes. Gets their nerve, helps show who's giving the orders. But never just for the sake of smashing things."

"And you remember all this while you're doing the job? You never lose *your* nerve?" In an effort to prove to myself I hadn't lost mine, I let the sarcasm show. "You never get rattled? Do something you didn't intend to do?"

"Sometimes I pretend to lose it, so my man'll pick up his feet and get moving. If there's a gun pointing at you you want a steady finger on the trigger."

"And the gun's empty anyway?"

"The way I work—always empty."

And now another fear: that I had put myself in the hands of an amateur. Had he ever been on a job before? Or was it the big hour of the mixed-up little ten-year-old, trying out one of his master plans? The ring of smug, handbook authority made me wonder sickly.

"Watch now—on your right—we're nearly there. We're going to drive past, then double back on the next street and park. See the vacant lot on the corner coming up—it's two doors farther .... There's the sign, *Watchmaker, Jeweller* ....

"Now when we come out—after—we cut across the vacant lot to the back alley. Parallel to the street—got it? And then right—to the end of the alley where we're going to park. Remember now—*right*—to the end of the alley, naturally not losing any time—"

I relaxed, confident and almost grateful. The glibness had given way to precision. The voice had lost its jumpy edge, gone alert, cold. He'd been there all right, done his practising. Professional—nothing to worry about. Butterflies, perhaps, but not nerves.

"Look at that snow, Sonny—just what we ordered." As we stepped out of the car he turned his face to catch the flakes and held out his hand—for a moment curiously young, absorbed, like a boy watching the first snowstorm, jubilant at the prospect of snowballs.

And then turning to me, his face still alight with small-boy eagerness, "Something about you, Sonny—makes me feel good having you along. Like I was starting all over—things starting to go right. You too—when you find out what I've got planned."

And then back to the snow. "Couldn't be better—couldn't have picked a better night. Enough to keep people off the street but not enough to tie up traffic. We'll make it easy make it easy .... Be sure now you've got it: across the lot, then *right*— up the alley and here we are."

He slapped me on the back, gave a strange, almost happy laugh, and then craftily screwing up his face again felt for a package of gum. "Here you are—I'll hold out my cigarettes and you'll say no, you've been smoking too much today. Instead you'll take a stick of gum. Big and dumb and simple— he'll relax even more. Chew it as if it was a treat."

I shivered and sickened again: another hint from his "Handbook for Holdups." But already his hand was on my elbow, assuring and at the same time determined, as if he had read my mind .... A few seconds later we were there.

23

IT WENT LIKE THE PERFORMANCE of a well-rehearsed play in which I was a last-minute substitute. I had been told the action, given my lines, and now I walked on blindly, dazed, to find every movement expected and responded to. It wasn't quite real; I didn't quite believe it. Therefore I felt no particular concern about the outcome. It was only a role; therefore there was no danger. The trouble was the role itself; it wasn't right for me, and I was certain to handle it badly. Something like wearing clothes that don't belong to you, don't fit. I was more embarrassed than afraid.

The door was locked. In response to Charlie's knock the old man opened it.

A wave of stale, sour air that in contrast to the clean winter night seemed almost visible; then a half-dark, cluttered little store, divided lengthwise by a rough, bruised-looking counter. There was an opening cut into the lower part of the counter, leaving the top intact, and the old man, just as he was supposed to do, ducked under to get back to his side—except that instead of ducking he went with arthritic slowness then came up jerkily, as if worked by rusty springs.

A shaded gooseneck lamp was turned to throw the light on the table where he had probably been working and now, swinging it around, he thrust his head out half across the counter and peered at me.

But instead of me—exactly as Charlie had said—he saw only the bit of tape. His eyes, like quick, nervous flies, hovered and settled on it, hovered and settled, and watching first their wheel, then their sudden, stingless dart, I felt anaesthetized, invisible.

"So you want a ring for your girl friend? You want diamonds maybe? Or plain gold?"

A sly, shifty old man. Slightly fawning, slightly contemptuous; face and eyes a wrinkled mesh of wariness, the nose a thrust of forthright greed. And still again Charlie was right: it was guile against guile, a devious old fox trotting out to sniff and snap at one of his own kind.

"I think our friend here's got a lot of girls on his mind." Charlie—wearing the black-rimmed glasses—accompanied his shrug with a conspiring glance of tolerance. Young fools—what do you expect? Good, though, for a few easy dollars. "I think I told you—in the summer, same as me, he's on the boats."

"That's right—the boats." With a tittery little laugh he floated them out, wobbly as pea shells. No boats, of course, but he would play along. "So you know other boys? And they got girls?"

Before I could answer, Charlie brought out his cigarettes. The old man shook his head without looking at them. I said no, I'd been smoking too much, and after searching through my pockets for the gum, methodically stripped the paper off a stick and began to chew.

"It's getting late—and all this snow." Exasperation starting to show; fingers drumming on the counter. "Maybe you could show him something—give him an idea about prices."

And to me, "When do you go back? Tomorrow?"

"If I find what I'm looking for. A ring and a watch—" And then to the old man, "But if you've a minute I'd like to see what you've got—I'll likely be back a couple of weeks from now."

Charlie looked pleased. A bright pupil, learning fast. "If you two can get down to business then. I've got some things to do myself tonight—"

A ring and a watch from under the counter—another ring, two or three watches—others from the drawer at his hand, others from a safe that had a shell of old, knotty boards around it to give the appearance of a cupboard.

I tried to look dubious, knowledgeable, pushed one away he was holding out, and he said shrilly, "Use your eyes and read—*Omega*. Thirty dollars I ask—any store you pay hundred—"

"I know—but what shape's it in. Does it work?"

"Does it *work*, he says! From Switzerland!" Snatching the watch away, he held it up to my ear. "You deaf ? Listen, does it work!"

Things blurred then a little, shadowing around a sudden clarity within myself. Performance—*doing it*—point of no return—zero at the end of the countdown—irrevocable as a take off to another planet; a clarity in which I saw not only what I was doing but the absurdity, the hopelessness—

"Jesus, you ought to be able to make up your mind from what's here. Some of it doesn't look too bad. A couple of those rings—I know somebody who'd be ready to come across with some pleasant little favours—"

Voice bland, slightly bored; foot knocking against my ankle. Perhaps to signal that it was almost the moment, perhaps just to remind me to keep sharp.

"Why not? Let him see what I got." With an indulgent grumble the old man spread his hands and shuffled over to the safe to bring another box. "Tell your friends on the boats—next time you'll maybe buy me out." Another titter, weary, contemptuous. "Here—take this one today—twenty-five dollars. A gift. Show it to your friends and tell them I've got more."

Another tap on my ankle, Charlie's hand at my side, groping to find mine—something thrust into it and his voice flat and leathery. "The sack—got it?"

A second or two of silence—long enough to miss a breath and hear the purr and snuffle of a car going up the snowy street—and then his voice again, harsh, ripping, "All right—put them up and stay there. *You*—over!"

I didn't see the gun come out, only the snake-whip of his hand. In the same instant, as I leaped, there was a glimpse of round, marble eyes and a fish-mouth scar of lip cutting half-way to his ear. The counter had been faintly bothering me—could I clear it with a single spring or would I have to clamber up with hands and knees?—but his voice batted me over like a ball.

For a second or two exhilaration—so easy! light!—and at the same time, fleetingly, contempt.

Retaliation. Peering out from his smelly lair the old man had sized me up and labelled me with such professional dispatch—a dolt, a stooge; a bug, perhaps, for his craw—and now it was my turn. As I landed beside him and for an instant met his eyes, stranded in the terror of his face like dead fish-eyes, I was abruptly, brutally, on Charlie's side. *With it*. In for the kill.

Cool and deft as I went to work, possessed by my own greed. Everything half mine—*everything half mine!*

A wallet, a roll of bills fastened with a rubber band; some twenties in another pocket, thin and flat. Coins and cigarettes, letters, matches, bits of paper, a handkerchief, a pencil stub—it was like picking berries in a hurry, a storm coming up, with a bag instead of a pail and no time to separate fruit from leaves. A gold watch in his vest pocket, attached to a chain and fastened somewhere inside his clothing: a moment's fumbling, then Charlie's gritty, "Jerk it for Christ's sake, *jerk!*" And in the same instant, hand responding a if a button had been pressed, the watch was plucked and in the bag.

"Leave him now. What's here on the counter—over there on the table. See what's left in the safe."

The words were hard-nosed, staccato, as if the gun were firing them. The eyes fixed on the old man had such a white-hot, icy glare that as I cleared off the counter I involuntarily kept out of its way, hands extended, body curved, as if it were a high tension wire.

Hands running on their own—swiftly, well. The counter, the work table, two or three more cases from the safe. As a measure of my efficiency, not a word from Charlie to instruct or hurry me. Until "That's it—over again. Here—I'll take the sack—"

One hand outstretched while with the other he kept the old man covered.

"Give it a yank!" As I touched the floor he motioned with his head to the telephone at the end of the counter. "We don't want any calls."

Just one yank: a little ripping sound, a whiff of plaster. And then Charlie again, to the old man, "If you don't want to get hurt stay right where you are. Stick your nose out and you may get hit. There's somebody covering us across the street—"

He spun around, leaped for the door. I followed, in my rush flattening and jamming him, and as we backed away and disentangled ourselves he cursed and jabbed me with his elbow.

A slap of cold night air. In the same instant the crack of a gun and a hot little nick of pain. Foot—heel—slam and stumble. Across the lot then right to the car .... Tape and blood and a stick of chewing gum .... *Relax, relax, just leave it all to Charlie.* All the angles, everything planned—everything but a little shelf or drawer somewhere and another gun that wasn't empty—

 **24**

"G OT YOU?" Perhaps I had lurched against him; perhaps, without knowing it, I had let out a yelp. "Not far—you'll make it .... Somebody's at the bus stop—*run!*"

Running .... Not so much pain as a drag on my foot—and at that, perhaps, not so much foot as mind: response to the awareness that I had been hit.

The gun again—a blunt, little popping sound this time, smothered in the snow, as if he had fired straight up; and then a shrill, old man's yell, frightened and furious, hunted and hunting, like a lost hound.

"Run, for Christ's sake! *Run!*"

Charlie had gained a little; at the jab of the words I drew even. A few yards neck and neck across the vacant lot, thinking of the car at the end of the alley—time yet to get away—and then a shout behind us, voices, a pack, and another jab from Charlie. "*That* way—separate! Wait at the first street—I'll drive round for you."

No time to question, argue—already somebody would be phoning the police—and at the bottom of the lot, obeying as a horse obeys the click of a tongue, I turned left up the alley, away from the car.

Long legs—lucky. Big jumps ... hit, but just the heel. By the feel of it not serious. And dark in the alley and all the snow .... Getaway .... Another shout—hundreds of shouts—howling, baying ....

And then at the end of the alley a street light and a spinning daze of snow. Sudden—like stepping out of dark wings onto a stage; and the snow, somehow, instead of concealing, seemed to whirl the light around me, as if to make my entrance visible.

With a sharp breathful of it, light and snow, I recoiled into the shadow of a wall.

A wall and a little recess—completely hidden. But somewhere behind me there were still the voices, shouts, and this was the way they would come. Not loud—not approaching—not yet—

A little crowd gathering outside the store; probably just standing around, listening to the old man, extracting drama; uneasy about taking off up a dark alley in pursuit. But any minute now there would be a patrol car—and they had seen me turn up the alley—

The street in front of me was too bright. Even with the snow. Deserted, silent as a country road—but if someone happened along I would stand out all the more. If a car passed—six feet two and limping—

I reconnoitered, peered. On the other side of the street the alley continued. So better perhaps if I crossed the street and kept straight on. When they got this far, not seeing the alley through the snow, they would think I had changed course, turned up the street—

Charlie, though—he was to drive round and pick me up—and this was where I was supposed to wait .... And then up on Park Avenue there was the sudden sputter of a car having trouble with the snow and with a single leap, airborne, hoisted by fear as by a giant boot, I was across.

Crouched in the shadow of another wall, trying to control the fear, to think clearly. Crazy to wait. They might turn up the street; just as likely they might keep straight on along the alley. Any minute now .... The patrol car would drive along the street and not seeing me would know I had crossed. Crazy to wait—never mind Charlie. Running and scared when he said he would meet me with the car, no time to think. By now he would realize the risk: better for us each to try to make it on his own. Follow the alley then a few more streets—then maybe a bus, a taxi—

As I hesitated my foot began to waken, fine cracks of pain running through the numbness, up from the tread, like cracks in a sheet of ice. I lifted and turned it, experimentally, and there was a little squelching sound. When I looked down I saw a dark patch on the snow and then a trickle of dots, each precise and black as if my foot when it moved were throwing rivets.

I ran—just ran. For a long time mindlessly, as probably a wounded animal runs, concentrated on flight, escape, to the exclusion even of fear or hope of safety. And yet, at the same time, on another level, aware. The alley was not dark—I had been wrong before—but white and dim, with only blocks and bars of heavy shadow, like an intricate, haphazard scaffolding; and as I ran I leaped and veered to keep on shadow, as warily alert as if my life depended on it—one false step and I would go plunging.

Aware, too, of my foot—that the pain had receded again. Wondering detachedly if some survival instinct were dulling it so that I could run faster; also wondering about the blood, if I were losing more or less by running, if the effort contracted or opened the wound—multiplying the little splatter of drops I had just seen by minutes and trying to work out how long I would be able to keep on running.

Somewhere in it a pause and a jog. Two women—both swaddled and hurrying and fat, laughing as they stumbled along, kicking up the snow with big, furry boots. Just as I emerged from the alley onto another street and was about to cross. I pulled up short, frozen, unable even to retreat to the shadows of the alley. They shuffled along a little distance and then, with more laughter and a great stamping of feet to knock the snow off their boots, turned into a doorway and disappeared.

I waited a few seconds, then turned up the street at a careful walk. Thinking vaguely it was good tactics—that turning up the street and then taking another alley would put the odds in my favour. They might make the same jog and turn up the same alley, but it would be luck. So if I kept on, changing streets and alleys—

Walk, though. *Walk!*

No one in sight, but there were windows. A man running along a quiet, snowy street, a man with a limp; somebody might pick up the telephone. It hadn't cost me an effort to run; there had been only slight pain; but still I knew that it was a crooked, floundering run.

And then a car. Coming along behind me—a soft, growling roar as the wheels spun in the snow, the very slowness of its approach making it sound undeviating and relentless—aimed at me. *Walk, though, walk!* As if you hadn't heard it, didn't care. Straight and easy, careful not to limp .... Just going home from work .... just stepped out to buy cigarettes—

When it passed there was a black, spinning moment, and then the sweat started trickling from my armpits and the strength went out of my legs like the air from a slashed tire.

Relief, a soft, unknotting bellyful of it and another wave of blackness. I staggered, clutched a lamp standard; then for a long time stood watching the blood creep out from my shoe and eat its way into the snow.

Presently, tiring of that, I lifted my foot, slowly extending and swinging it so that the drops fell on clean snow, as lost and absorbed as if I were off alone somewhere, miles deep in prairie .... There was a rabbit once that I shot with my .22 and fascinated by the vividness of blood and snow I held it by the feet and made patterns with the scarlet drip; square, circle, cross; until at last, my arm tiring and the blood beginning to clot, I dipped the nose to give the last tip to a star ....

Another car, coming towards me this time, strings and an old-fashioned waltz on the radio. Nothing to be afraid of— not a police car—but I straightened and walked on carefully erect, away from the rabbit and the blood.

The sweat cold now. My leg a hip-boot filled with dirty water and a sharp pebble in the heel. Not afraid, just cold. *Walk, though—keep on walking.* Nothing for it but to keep on walking. Lucky—such a lot of snow .... Hidden in it—lost, alone .... Couldn't have picked a better night ....

Starting to thicken, gain, clogging the eyes and nostrils as if I were venturing too far, into forbidden territory. A flick at my ear and then away, another, sharper, on my cheek; then a thick hard slap to cut my breath and fill my mouth—

More cars that didn't matter, and once a boy gasping and laughing behind a dog tugging at a leash; and then, in the same instant, the mouth of an alley and a distant siren.

Panic again—a spasm that sent me flapping up the alley like a wounded crow. Perhaps a hundred yards until I tripped and came floundering to my knees in the snow and darkness. It was deep snow here—knee-deep, drifted—and as I struggled it kept fluffing up around my face and working up my sleeves .... Struggling and not wanting to struggle—spitting, groping—reminding myself that the siren could have been an ambulance or a fire, that if it was a patrol car they wouldn't have announced themselves .... Safe here, safe and still—the siren fainter now, gone. Just snow and dark and shelter—starting to turn warm ....

25

... SPITTING SNOW, picking myself up and shaking it out of my sleeves while twenty feet away she stands there, demurely watching me ....

Skilful—head first into a snowdrift where it wouldn't hurt me, less than a quarter of a mile from home. And not even to toss her head and gallop off so that Millie, watching from the stable door, would think she had done it in a fit of fright or meanness. No, just to *stand* there, ears perked in puzzled innocence, blandly transferring all the blame to me. What was wrong? Why had I deserted her? Just when we were getting along so well—

Moralist. A bit of the Presbyterian despite her record. A firm stand against pride that wasn't justified. For only a minute before, a little drunk with the realization that barely turned twelve I was actually riding her and holding on, I had let slip the thought that at last I was both her master and my own. Presumption! Nerve! One thing to be able to ride an outlaw; another to be accorded the privilege of riding one. And high time, for my own good, that I learned to appreciate the distinction.

... spitting snow ... sore spots but nothing serious. Considering the record, a lot luckier than I deserved. For a year now, dutifully, they had been warning me: all the lurid details of the mangled and untimely end in store for me should I even take it into my fool young head to ride her. So I was getting off easy. At least no splints, no undertaker—

What a liar, though! After all the promises! The way she had worked to convince me that the record was a slander! Nuzzling, coaxing, pleading: "Just once—just try! Ask yourself what I would gain by throwing you. And remember you're twelve. It isn't as if you were a *small* boy."

And then how many times, temptress, had she borne me to the mountain top of my vanity and guilefully, with all the world spread out before me, talked of fortune and acclaim.

Over there, three miles away, the schoolhouse. What a sensation to come galloping up on *her*, the notorious outlaw, instead of jogging along on hairy-legged old Pete!

And town the other way, the cupolas of its grain elevators just visible on the horizon; where fairs were sometimes held and races run ... The prize, they said, sometimes a hundred dollars, and with a horse like her I naturally would win. Well, then—

What a liar, though! Head first into a snowdrift, spitting snow .... And *not* just to escape her stall and stretch her legs as she pretended. A sly streak; pure perversity. Just for the satisfaction of bringing me down a peg or two, showing me who was who.

For the will was like the shapely, high-flung head. Her pride was at stake; I had to be reduced. With the first coaxing nuzzle of her lips she had committed herself, and that as a male I was still at such a rudimentary stage made it doubly imperative she emerge the victor. Bad enough to be defeated by a man—but a boy, a skinny twelve-year-old—

... spitting snow ... down my neck and up my sleeves and nostrils. And my foot sore, a far-off numbness round an apple-pip of pain as I struggle out of the drift and start after her.

Motionless, sniffing in my direction until I have almost reached her; then, head and tail up, trotting pertly home. Waiting for me at the stable door, curious but cordial, Millie beside her, goggle-eyed. Neither of them the least impressed that I am limping.

... curiously, though, not moving—not an inch. Walking and walking and still right where I landed in the snowdrift. Up to my ears, a powdery smother of it .... And here now, tired of waiting, they've come back. Both of them. "Up on your feet. It's nearly dark and you're going to catch your death of cold."

Walking again, limping. Putting on the limp a little, because with Millie there it looks better, makes my spill less a laughing matter—and Isabel, as if believing me, puts her nose out, all condolence, and feels me tenderly where I'm pretending to be sore. So far as she is concerned, however, she can make no promises. There's been one fall, she explains to Millie, and there may easily be another. She can't be responsible for my horsemanship.

"Your ears are frozen and your mother knows. You're really going to catch it when your father comes. You've been warned a hundred times."

"No—because all along it's what they've been wanting me to do. They'll approve. Once you've done something and got away with it they always approve."

"But you haven't got away with it. You're still stuck up to your neck in a snowdrift and just look at your frozen ears!"

"Not my ears—my foot. It's running blood and I can't walk straight."

"Your foot's all right—stand up and walk. Lie here in the snow you're going to freeze to death. Stand up and walk, stand up and walk—"

And Isabel too joined in. "That's right, before you freeze to death ... stand up and walk, stand up and walk—"

26

MY FOOT FELT A LONG WAY OFF but I could move it. Tied on, paining by itself, not properly part of me, but obedient.

Not a very bad pain, I reassured myself. Dull, hot, manageable. It was there, steady and grinding, but I could think my way around it. There were more important things. It withdrew with the effort of standing up, came back stabbing. But permissively. I could walk.

Walk and think. Even think clearly. A cold, two-dimensional clarity: what had happened, what to do. There was fear, alert, proportionate, but no panic. They would call it an armed holdup—empty or not, there had been a gun—and if they caught me I would be sent up for four or five years. So hide, lie low—try not to limp. A long way to go yet back to Ste Famille Street. Nothing for it but to keep on walking.

Still snowing. Only an occasional car, with the driver intent on the street, peering through a plastered windshield. But one might be a police car and the second man, no matter what their errand or destination, would tie me in with the description broadcast on the radio. So alleys whenever it was possible. On the street, when a car was coming, steps and doorways.

Twice I actually did—turned off the street and went up the steps, making a show of stamping my feet just as the two women had done, as if I, too, were home and knocking off the snow before going inside.

Another time, when a car seemed to slow as it passed, I turned and looked up at a window and waved.

And then the weasel wariness began to slacken and I trudged on stolidly. I resigned myself to the pain that struck each time I brought my foot down and even let it give me pace and rhythm. *Walk don't limp—walk don't limp—keep walking straight or you'll get five years.* A stab of pain with every step like a pencil beating time. *A long way to go yet— Sonny and Mad—a long way to go yet—Sonny and Mad—*

I tried to stop but my feet picked up the words and lilted them to fit the pain. *No damn the bitch—not Sonny and Mad—no damn the bitch—not Sonny and Mad—*

Ste Famille Street—the stairs, the door, the bed where I could throw myself and collapse—I fastened on the moment of arrival and moved towards it like a tired spider along a single strand of web. Concentrated on not admitting that the pain was worse, on bracing myself to meet the throb without limping.

And then like a blow in the face there was Park Avenue again. The very place. Without noticing, I had come back— had just crossed the vacant lot. A scrabble of fear at the trick my feet had played on me, an impulse to turn tail and run. But a bus was coming, chuffing its way slowly through the snow, and carefully controlling the limp, I turned *up* Park Avenue, in the wrong direction, and passed the jewellery store.

Safer—would look better. Of all places, they wouldn't expect to find me here; and in the same instant, sickening at my forgetfulness, I felt my cheek and ripped off the bit of tape.

Quiet, blank; door closed, light out; snow piled four or five inches deep on the step. How long ago? How many hours had I lain in the alley? Where was he now? With the police, talking, describing? Or home again, in there at the back somewhere, frightened, trying to sleep?

I walked on to the next intersection, then crossed and came back along Park Avenue on the opposite side. Slowly, staring, the pain withdrawing again.

The window, small and narrow like a house window; the little sign, *Watchmaker, Jeweller*, pallid and extinct-looking in the snowy light; the grey wooden front sliced by shadows from the outside staircase; then the door opening and a wave of warmth and musty air; the gooseneck lamp, the long wooden counter—

Different this time. I was there.

The first time it had been a dumb show, a pattern of movements: two steps this way, three steps that; over the counter—everything into the sack; but now I was alone, on my own. The mindless, numb resolution had dissolved. I entered again, quick and raw.

Arrival, entrance: the old man creaking slowly under the counter, holding the watch to my ear and saying "Listen, does it work!" Then the fear flickering on his face like a light when the bulb is loose in its socket; then the feel of his bony, jack-rabbit hips and thighs as I went through his pockets, hands swift and unerring as a pair of beaks making time on a bit of carrion.

Sonny McAlpine's hands: I had been there.

Not remorse or guilt, just awareness. I had been there. The feel of the things in his pockets—the coins, faintly sticky and warm, the handkerchief damp as if he had just cleared his throat. Sonny McAlpine's hands: they would remember.

And the fear: at the time it had been gathered in my throat and contained as in a capsule, local and confined, not in the way of will or purpose, but now, the capsule broken and the poison free, my legs went limp with it and my belly crawled with nausea.

Slowly, staring: finally I had passed. The street brighter now, lights and neon signs and snow all spinning round me, spiralling up to the centre of the sky.

And flowers: suddenly at my side a windowful of them, blood-dark carnations and white and yellow roses, inches away, flawless and cool like flowers in paradise. I halted and rubbed my hands against the glass, then pressed my forehead on it, soaking up the cold. There was an impulse to smash the window and enter, protest exclusion; but it was muffled and dull, like a bell under water; and weariness collapsed it. Instead I bent and scooped up a handful of snow, held it to my face until it melted and began trickling down my neck, then went on walking.

27

"OH, SONNY—I've been so scared—hours and hours waiting .... And your hair, will you—the snow just *packed* in! Shake it out and here's a towel and I'll hurry up a cup of coffee."

"If you'll look at the stairs first—" Without meeting her eyes I made a movement with my head. "In case somebody sees it—there may be blood. Never mind the steps—it's still snowing."

She took it in instantly. She had brought a towel and was holding it out to me: now, snatching it back, she vanished without so much as a click of the door behind her.

I waited without moving except to tilt my head forward, so that as it melted the snow dripped onto the floor.

"Just a few drops—it's all right." She leaned against the door a moment, panting and flushed as if she had done the stairs—down and up and a wipe on every step—in a single breath. "You're sure nobody's following you?"

Still without looking at her I nodded. "It's a good four hours. I've been keeping out of sight."

"Then we're all right—we'll just lie low." She drew a deep, racking breath and squeezed hard on the towel, as if to keep from wringing her hands. And then efficiently, regaining control, "All that time it's no wonder you look so terrible. Sit down quick and let's see."

She backed me onto a chair and dropping to her knees began taking off my shoe. "There—not so bad—" Another deep breath; she had been preparing herself for something worse. "Just about stopped bleeding—maybe a little when you walk. Sit there and I'll go wet the towel so we can clean it up and see."

The blood washed off, it looked reassuring. Somewhere between a graze and a gouge; on the fleshy, underside of the heel, about an inch long and a quarter of an inch deep. (The bullet had struck my shoe just a little above the heel and ripped a long, slanting hole through the sole.) Bits of sock and leather packed in; a few rags of skin and flesh that when pressed back into place left a meaty, purplish welt. Once, riding Isabel too close to the pasture fence, I ripped my calf on the barbed wire—something like that.

"Oh Sonny—I never saw anybody shot before—a real bullet—"

Her face was white, her voice nearly a sob, and I barked irritably, "Well you've got eyes—it's just a scratch. Nothing to howl about—just let me get to bed."

For it seemed trifling now—scratch was right—and all at once I was embarrassed at the way I had staggered in and asked her to wipe the blood off the stairs—*fugitive enters, wounded, desperate.* "I just don't want anybody knocking at the door to find out who's been hurt. If I start answering questions I may come up with the wrong answers."

She watched me a moment, motionless, unblinking, then said sharply, with a slap of anger, "No—you're not to talk like that. You don't mean it. You're not to pretend."

"Pretend what? It'll be in the papers tomorrow—if somebody saw blood on the stairs he might start wondering—"

"Tough and hard like that—that's what I mean. Like you didn't care. It's not you any more."

I shrugged, and feeling the flesh around the wound repeated, "Just a scratch. At the time I hardly felt it. Afterwards a little—trying to walk so it wouldn't show."

She looked at me a minute longer, holding my foot as if it was something she was about to lay on an altar, then put her head down and began to sob. "I'm so scared, Sonny, and so glad there's nothing to be scared about. All mixed up—split right down the middle. I just knew something had happened—getting so late and him not in his room either—"

"Well I'm not dead and the cops haven't got me so for Christ's sake shut up and go to bed." My nerves jumped. I wanted quiet and rest and darkness, not hysterics. "We can talk about it in the morning."

She took it white and silent, as if her hands were tied, and I had struck her. "A couple of days," I said, softening, trying to sound offhand, "and it'll all be forgotten. Nothing to get upset about—just one of those things."

"No, Sonny—no!" Her voice blazed. The clutch of her fingers made me squirm. "Something so bad you're never to forget. *Never!* Half an inch more and it could have hit the bone and lamed you. A better shot and you'd be stretched out cold."

I slumped a minute, then reached for her hand. "I know, Mad—I'm scared too—and tomorrow I'm going to be a lot scareder. So just give me a little time."

"You mean somebody *does* know it's you?" Her face leaped to bay. The kneel sharpened to a crouch. "Tell me, Sonny—I got a few dollars. We can squeeze in at Cora's tonight and tomorrow we'll get another room."

I reached out again and rubbed my knuckles on her cheek. "Nothing like that—I just mean I've been busy—on the run. No time yet for the scare to sink in. But don't worry—it's there all right and it'll catch up with me. I won't forget."

"Sure, Sonny—everything's going to work out fine." She pressed her forehead on my knee a moment, then rose abruptly. "Big-mouthed me, preaching away and you just about passed out and nearly frozen. Off with your clothes now and into bed—I'll get the coffee going—"

Strong, quick, competent. A little explosion of function and importance—the assumption of a role. While the coffee was boiling she dried my hair and helped me undress; while I was drinking the coffee she bandaged my foot with a hand-kerchief and settled it on a pillow. Then, slipping into her coat, she said she was going over to Cora's for iodine and aspirins. "Where else? It's away past one—everything closed. What's getting out of bed when somebody's nearly had his foot shot off? I just don't know how you did it, Sonny—honest I don't. A night like this and losing all that blood—"

Not a question till she was back and dabbing on the iodine. Then, curtly, "And your friend, where's he?"

"I don't know—we had to separate."

"After you'd been shot—you mean he *left* you?"

"Not exactly—there wasn't time—"

"Time for him to figure out what was the smart thing for Charlie."

I told her how it happened, how instead of waiting for him to drive around and pick me up I had panicked and started running.

"So why's he not been here then looking for you? Seeing how you made out? I've been listening and waiting and leaning over the banister all night and there's been nobody."

"He'll have to lie low too. Maybe tomorrow."

She finished bandaging and straightened. "You mean you *believe* that? That he'll be back?"

"Unless they catch him. He'll have his things to pick up—and I think he'll want to pick me up too."

She drew back a step, screwing her eyes up as if to get me into focus. "And that's what you want?"

"It's what he'll want. Good partner, good stooge—he'll want to keep me."

"Not now—not him. Not when it didn't come off like you planned it."

"It almost did—except for this .... He'll be back all right—just to show me what a smart fellow he is, and how smart I'll be to play along."

She stared down at me, nostrils twitching in disbelief. "Sure he's smart—smart enough to know he'd never get around you twice."

"He didn't exactly get around me. He asked me and I went."

"You say that funny—like you're sticking up for him ....
Like you'd changed—on his side—"

She edged away a few inches, then came back and touched
my forehead with her finger tips—a careful, hesitant touch,
as if feeling for something in the dark. "Right this minute
you ought to be hating his guts for playing such a dirty trick
on you—grinding your teeth and swearing you'll get him—"

"No use, Mad, hating *his* guts. He made the offer, I went
along."

"It wasn't a fair offer. He caught you at a bad time."

"Maybe. In his own way, though, I think he meant it to be
fair .... At least he wanted to prove something—show me.
What's the use of being a mastermind if nobody knows? And
who else has he?"

I shut her out for a moment, groping for my own answers.
"He'll be back—because there's still something outstanding—
because I haven't acknowledged him. He's not going to be
satisfied until I make a little bow."

"I don't know what you're talking about but if he does
come don't touch the money. It's dirty—just like him." She
knelt by the bed and shook me, one hand on my arm, one on
my thigh. "Even if you've been counting on it to do things—
don't let him through the door. Sly and wriggly—you can't
stand up to him. Just one look and you can tell—the mouth
and the funny way he works his eyes—"

I laughed, tried to veer. "You ought to know better than to
judge people by their looks. See how I fooled you—big honest
country boy—remember? One of the right ones—"

"You think I don't know why you did it?"

She bit her lip to steady it. "Right from the first I've been
trying to tell you that it doesn't matter—that you can do
something to make up later on if it's bothering you—telling
you over and over I've been having such a good time—"

She stood up to find a handkerchief, blew hard into it and
then, head up and chin out defiantly, turned and faced herself
in the mirror. "Sure, just like Charlie said that night in the
restaurant, I've been hoping you wouldn't get a job for a

while—so it would last a little longer. But just because you're what you are it wouldn't work. Sit back and take it easy for a while? Not you—not Mr. Sonny! Instead you got to go out and do something terrible and crazy—get shot at—"

She knelt beside me again, stroked my hand a few times and then laid her cheek against it. "I knew you minded but I didn't know how much. I kept sort of hoping it was more than just having a time with me. I thought you felt safe, liked telling me things. But all the time it must have been hurting you bad—real bad—"

She was silent a moment, her breathing broken by choked-off little sobs. Then, quietly, "Sometimes I think the craziest things—how you'll be playing away in a fine big band and every once and a while, say Christmas, you'll come round to see how I'm doing or maybe send your picture if you're out of town—or play a piece on the radio and say this one's for an old Maritimer friend—and I'll feel so good just because you remember—because once I had such a good right one—"

Laugh at her, reach out and touch her cheek again—what else is there to do? The years ahead, the grubby rooms and the grubby friends and the grubby bars, clothes starting to scuff, face starting to sag—from the brave, silly babble you could chart her course as easily as an expert in such things could chart the trajectory of a missile.

And as she talked, I wanted her again. A kind of pity, an impulse to reach out and reassure her, bring back the glow; and at the same time a need to bury my face and find shelter, shut out my own streets, my own darkness.

"Did you *ever* now—full of bullets and everything .... Oh, Sonny—talk about being one of the right ones—"

And yet there was a difference. Trying to slow me: a pant in the voice, laughing, protesting, half in earnest; a hand pushing hard against my chin, half insistent—as if afraid that afterwards, lying awake in the dark, she too might start charting courses.

 **28**

THE NEXT DAY I hung suspended in a long, drowsy blur, rocking on easy waves of limpness and relief. The snow kept on, big-flaked, windless, and the padded stillness of the street gave a sense of safety and escape. It was like the day after a fever breaks, the tired, mindless lull before recovery sets in. I had never known such tiredness. Boneless and crumbly, as if I had been drugged; as if I were buried up to the neck in warm, damp sand.

Movements were journeys: hand to pocket, eye to window, finger to itchy ear—and journeys were to be planned, delayed, broken. And once there, was the return trip worth it? For a quarter of an hour the luxury of deciding. I lay and sat stone-heavy. Sometimes there was a throb of pain, a scratching grind, but distant, not very important, like trouble in another country.

And yet all the time within the torpor—systole and diastole—it was going on: first a blister-beat of panic, shame; then the cool, sweet slackness of relief. I had done it, been there—jumped the counter, filled the sack—but it was all behind me now, lost somewhere in the snowstorm, and everything was going to be all right.

Strictly Sonny's relief. A gopher whisking down its burrow with a snap of teeth just inches from its tail. No more than that. No understanding yet of what I had done to *him*, no inkling of the implications. If anything, he was less victim than I. I sickened at the memory of my hands going over him—it even seemed that the smell of his clothes, sweaty, slightly acrid, still clung to them—but there, at my own frontier, the shame was halted. Not what I had done to him; what I had done to Sonny McAlpine. The smirch; the finger. For Sonny's name now, even up in lights, would always be a dirty name.

Charlie, I sensed vaguely, had come off better. For him, the old man was a real victim. There had been a relationship. He had committed himself, as a fighter commits himself to his opponent, as a hunter to his quarry. He had planned the job, staked and risked himself, accepted the challenge. But I had only handled a body, emptied pockets and drawers.

In a slow, hazy way I kept thinking about Charlie, but for most of the day without involvement, trying to assess and catalogue him as you would think about someone you had lost track of years ago; and it was not until well on in the afternoon that the questions started drifting in. How had he made out? Where was he holing up now? When would he be back for me?

I was sure he would be back. So sure that I began to wonder if I ought to avoid him, slip away tonight—ask Mad to lend me enough to rent a room for a few weeks in another part of town. For she was right: it was dirty money, and if I took so much as a dollar I would be in, bound to him; the partnership would be sealed. But the last few days, dirty or not, I had been busy spending it—buying a ticket that would take me well out of reach of both of them—and I didn't trust my hands.

Charlie, too: he had made a bid for possession, fixed on my mind and will as flies, heavy with eggs, fix on the hides of cattle, so there would be no casual leave-taking, no tapering off to an indifferent you-go-your-way-and-I'll-go-mine. It would be a swipe, a slaughter, and as always I was squeamish. I wasn't afraid of his anger or vindictiveness, but

I shrank from the sight of it. He wasn't someone I could ever like or trust or feel at ease with, but in a backhand way he had become important to me. And besides, I had a certain faith in him, was satisfied that in his own sour, twisted way he was for me. *His* boy—giving me a foot up, helping me cut corners.

Mad, though, when she came at six, made nonsense of it all. She looked at my foot, checked to see if I had eaten, and then said, "Well, I suppose he's been and gone?"

She stood in front of me, arms akimbo, lips drawn together grimly. "A fistful of ten-dollar bills just to show you what a pal he is?" Our eyes met and the scorn gave way to a little cluck of laughter. "Oh Sonny—I thought it was us Maritimers that were the dumb ones .... But you now, not seeing through a slippery little rat like that—not even *wanting* to see through him—"

My face probably warned her. "Not that they didn't take me too on some of their rides when I first landed. When you don't grow up among them how can you know? This Charlie, now—"

Her glance wavered, went towards the door. For a moment or two it was almost shifty, as if she were afraid she might be overheard, caught talking out of turn. "Smooth, working you into a corner—I used to know one just the same. *Living* off people like us—the town's full of them."

"Maybe it's not quite so simple. I can't explain. I just feel he'll be back—if he can."

"You fool, Sonny! You big no-good goddam sloppy-gutted fool!"

She seethed suddenly, crouching and bristling, ready to rip the face off me. "He sets a trap for you and you put both your big stupid feet right *into* it! You get shot at and walked out on and there you sit still sticking up for him! Wait—maybe his door's open—"

She wheeled away and into the hall. "Come on—see for yourself." He hadn't locked the door and by the time I reached her she was pulling open bureau drawers. "For somebody that's coming back he's sure done a good job packing. All those fancy clothes! Here's a button and here's a couple of beer caps—you suppose he's coming back for *them*?"

And then she laughed, a clear, light-hearted, tumbling sound, as if she hadn't been quite so sure he had run out on me as she pretended, and had needed the sight of the empty drawers for confirmation. "If you could just see your face, Sonny—*still* sticking up for him, still making out a case. But never mind—" She took my arm and steered me out of the room—"There's lamb chops and peas for supper and a whole chocolate pie .... And I bought a paper so you can read all about last night and how you did."

The snow had made things busy: half a dozen of us all lumped together in one column. A filling station holdup, a fur robbery, a taxi driver given an address on a quiet street and then hit on the head; two armed men who succeeded in gaining entrance to a jewellery store on Park Avenue and escaped with an estimated three thousand dollars in cash and jewellery ... Fired several shots—one believed seriously wounded .... Blood on the sidewalk—seen staggering across a parking lot .... A woman robbed of her purse by two youths on her way to visit her sister. One of her assailants wore a beard ....

I read it several times, from start to finish, giving exactly the same attention to the taxi driver and the youth with a beard as to the man staggering across the parking lot. Identification came slowly, sickly. I had got away; not a chance in a hundred now they would ever know; but the paper gave it a setting, made it official, put me on record. No escape—I would always be the man running. Already I knew. And being would mean fearing: the freak chance, the one-in-a-hundred encounter. Charlie perhaps, caught or drunk, resentful I had got away. An oyster eye, a finger and a chain—he would always be there, on this bus, in the next doorway. A different kind of fear: not of simple things, like hunger or failure or the humiliation of going back to the farm, but of someone who knew, wanting something, waiting at the corner.

"What you've got to do now is forget, Sonny—forget all about it and start over."

We had begun our meal. Her hand slipped across the table to touch my sleeve, drew back and ostentatiously busied itself with a bit of bread, pretending it had never been away. "I've done far worse things and got mixed up with people just as slimy so don't mind me looking on. Talking about rides—it's when you're dumb and blonde and stacked so you don't need a sweater you get taken on some real ones."

Her mouth hardened. "Yellow and cheap—it's got to be easy or they run. Let them see your mind's made up and they leave you—even me they did. You it'll be no trouble at all because you're going real places—already as good as there."

She piled peas on my plate, then pointed the spoon at me. "And just suppose he ever does come back, or sometime you run into him again, straight off let him know. Tough and quick—no saying to yourself at least let's have a beer and hear what he's got to say."

Her voice had been ablaze with warning, now it tightened, crunched, just as I had sometimes heard his crunch. "He'll have plenty to say—all kinds of excuses, all kinds of offers for something big again. But it won't be big—just dirty and cheap. And that'll be you too, dirty and cheap, just as long as you keep knowing him."

Right—*dirty and cheap*—and I hated her suddenly for reminding me.

"What do you mean, no chocolate pie? The time I had snitching it out of the kitchen and then all those feely-fingered Frenchmen on the bus .... Oh, Sonny—you've got to get *over* things!"

29

THE NEXT DAY I SLEPT. Something like sleep—a long, grey, stubborn stupor which somehow seemed to be my choice: I could and maybe should get up—shave, eat, turn on the radio, and play the clarinet—but this was better. All day—as if awareness as well as exhaustion was catching up with me, and while the body rested the mind turned away, a hand across its eyes, getting its nerve back, steadying itself before it looked again.

I remember Mad shaking me at six and then giving a big laugh as I twitched awake: she had thrown back the covers and knocked some snow off her sleeve onto my bare belly. I remember her making a great to-do because I had eaten no lunch and hadn't even drunk my coffee—so I must have been up at noon and made the coffee. I remember her saying there was steak again for supper but I don't remember eating it .... Not ready yet: not time to look again.

The following day cleared slowly. My foot was stiff and sore, but in the afternoon I limped downstairs and shovelled off the steps and sidewalk, then came back and ate what was left of the chocolate pie and played my clarinet till someone underneath started pounding on the ceiling. Charlie didn't come. I went into his room and looked at myself in the mirror and sat on his bed awhile, then went out and bought a paper. More furs; a woman gagged and bound; the ubiquitous two youths escaping in a stolen car. Nothing about us .... Yesterday, perhaps: I thought about going back to ask the man in the newsstand if he still had the paper, wondered if he might be curious to know why I wanted it, and while wondering forgot.

My foot had begun to throb; I rubbed on more iodine. When Mad came home she doused it and then, enjoying herself hugely, gave me a thumping lecture about staying *off* my feet. I lay tractably in bed most of the evening, but with my face turned away, pretending to sleep. At bedtime she gave me soup instead of coffee and said sternly this was one night there was to be no goings-on. There weren't. She sounded as if she could be persuaded, but my back was aching from the snow and my eyes felt heavy and hot .... And besides, because the bed was starting to rock a little, I thought it better just to lie still and try to hold it steady .... Later that night, I dreamed again about the flicker.

All the way—from the dazzle of its wings to the bedraggled ignominy of its suffering that I hadn't even the stomach to put an end to—the furious beak and bitter eye.

It was May, and for a week or more I had been catching glimpses of it flashing like a whir of gold, a flight of feathered light; and gradually wonder had become a need to see and verify.

Not cruelty—just need. Desire that was at once innocent and unspeakable. To run the miracle to earth, lay hands on it, for all time make it mine.

So far so good—what better quarry than a whir of gold? But oh, Sonny McAlpine—of all things to use a gopher trap!

"You little bastard," my brother Allen said when he came and killed it. "You mean little bastard!"

When a gopher trap is set—the curving sides pressed apart and locked down, the tongue in place—it has a bland, wide-eyed look, just a little like a flower; then, foot or muzzle on the stamen-spring, the sides snap up and grip like jaws .... There is a light chain attached for staking, to make sure the gopher doesn't drag it down the hole.

By my time gophers were almost extinct—so rare that the sight of one would set my parents off on stories of the days when the fields were pitted with their burrows, and municipalities paid a bounty of two cents a tail—and the traps, four of them, hung rusty and cobwebbed at the back of the toolshed.

So let this much be said: I had never used one. I had set them experimentally, sprung them with a stick, plotted revenge on the old gander who used to come for me with a hiss and an unnerving flap of wings—but I had never seem them clamped on flesh and bone.

So it was to catch, not to kill—to possess and delight in, not to maim. The words are always there, always on the alert. At the drop of a feather they spring to their defence positions, like soldiers at the sound of a bugle. To catch, not to kill. I didn't know what it would be like. I didn't think—I just wanted.

It was a clear, sunny morning, unwrinkled, still. A first-morning-of-the-world stillness, sky and earth in conspiracy, up to something good. Blackbirds and meadowlarks, the smell of crocuses and willow—every step you paused to breathe it in and listen, to feel if it would bear your weight.

And then the flicker again, the sudden arrow-dazzle of its wings, splintering the morning like a glass, leaving behind it ruin and desire.

Ladder, hammer, trap—twice back to the toolshed for the right nails, the right saw. The nest was in a telephone pole, the entrance eight or nine feet off the ground. The hole had to be flattened at the base so the trap would balance on it, and the chain that was attached to the trap had to be fastened to the telephone pole with nails.

A kind of make-believe—perhaps that would explain it. The trap was all I had, all I could think of. I no more expected to catch the flicker than a dog, bursting from a farmyard in furious pursuit, expects to catch the passing car.

But half an hour later there it was. Head down, suspended by the chain, its leg mangled, its wings flapping feebly, ruffled and bruised. And the eye, just about level with mine, an unsparing, snake-hard little drill of hate.

I dreamed and woke, dreamed and woke: it was always there. Bright and beady, exactly fair. Mad was stirring in her sleep and scratching her thigh and a branch was rubbing on the window. "Dirty and cheap—dirty and cheap—there'll be no more roses for you."

Awake and not quite awake: the eye kept shining through the darkness and at the same time burning hot within me like a coal. "Catch and kill—cheap cheap cheap. Big-time Sonny and his name in lights—no more roses, no more gold—"

I began to struggle, to fight it off and pluck it out, to squirm away and at the same time reply; and then it was not the flicker I was struggling with but Mad; and she was shaking me and saying "Wake up—it's just me. Wake up and listen— you've been having bad dreams."

The eye was gone; the coal was still burning in my foot. I lay still a minute, trying to understand; then by way of expla- nation, casually, I told her about the pain and tried to persuade her to go back to sleep. But instead, springing out of bed, she switched on the light and threw back the covers.

There was a rim around the wound, hard, swollen, purplish. Inflammation—starting to spread—

"At home they used to say when a cut starts to hurt it's getting better."

"Maybe—it's got a hot look. We'll have to watch and see."

She wet and soaped a handkerchief, sponged the wound carefully and put on a clean bandage. "I'll get some peroxide in the morning before I go to work and you'll just have to keep dabbing it on. You boil out the germs that way. Maybe we'll be in time to stop it."

She brought a glass of water and some aspirins. "Drink lots of water and don't walk unless you have to. Try to get some sleep now. In the morning you'll feel like new."

She straightened, bent and looked again. "I've seen lots worse. My old lady once—broke a glass in her hand when she was washing it and had red streaks up to her elbow."

"I've seen them too—my brother Tom. Caught his thumb on the barbed wire and nearly lost his hand."

"Nowadays it's nothing to worry about anyway—even supposing it gets bad. They just take a needle and squirt something into you. A couple of days and you're fine."

A needle and a squirt of fear. "Penicillin—but you can't buy it." I lay taut, stick-straight, staring up at her. "You've got to see a doctor—he gives it to you—"

"That's it, penicillin." She looked at me sharply, then gripped my shoulder. "But time enough to start worrying when you need to. Running ahead of yourself—no sign of the streaks yet—"

"But you can't *buy* it—" I jerked my shoulder free from her grasp and sat up. "Even if you could you couldn't use it. It's a doctor gives you the needle—only a doctor—"

The fear caught. She crouched white and still a moment, then pressed me back onto the pillow. "First things first, Sonny—if it's going to take a doctor then it's going to take a doctor. Lots of them around. Just leave everything to me."

"No—" I sat up again and seized her wrist. "It's a bullet wound and he'll know. He'll turn me in—we were in the papers—"

"You think a doctor up to his eyes in operations and people dying's got nothing to do but read the papers? About the likes of you?"

"He'll have orders—it's not like an accident. Soon as he sees it he'll report me—"

"We'll find one that won't. There's a lot of funny people around town doing a lot of funny things. It's not going to hurt us just this once to join them. I'll talk to Cora—she knows a couple, and I think a young one too. Doesn't take much of a doctor, you know, to stick in a needle."

"No—they'll turn me in." Panic again, shameless, running wild. "Never mind Cora—don't tell anybody—anything—"

"Easy—you don't even *need* a doctor yet and chances are you won't. But you've got to think straight, just the same. If the time comes, you've got to trust me."

She bent and put her lips dry and strong a moment on my forehead, then pressed me back again onto the pillow. "Right now you're just played out—things starting to catch up on you. A job like that and then getting shot at and nearly frozen—not one in a million that wouldn't have cracked up right then and there. Me now, if I saw a gun coming—"

At the sight of her round-eyed, solemn face, I relaxed and laughed up at her. "I know—a real hero. Got any medals for me?"

"No, but I got something better. Not tonight, though. Go to sleep like I say and tomorrow maybe you can have two."

30

IN THE MORNING there was still just the purplish, rubbery ring around the wound and the wound itself looked clean and dry. Mad was up early, waiting outside the nearest drug store before half-past eight. She bought peroxide and gauze and more aspirins and after carefully washing the wound again dribbled on a few drops of the peroxide.

"Look at it, will you, boiling out the poison and dirt," she said gravely as the wound began to froth. "So just stay quiet and keep boiling away. Every half hour or so—and if it's not better tonight when I get home—"

She broke off a moment to slip into her coat and give a final pat to her hair before the mirror. "Nothing to worry about but you might as well start getting used to the idea .... And it's the truth: Cora knows all kinds of doctors and she's got all kinds of things on some of them. If penicillin's what you need we'll see to it they give you plenty."

I must have been already a little light in the head, for the moment she was gone I started playing the clarinet, first anxiously, with a sense of urgency, as if time were running out and one more idle morning might cost me a career, and then with elation and surprise, a sudden conviction that I was playing extraordinarily well, improvising as no one had ever improvised before.

Clarinet and peroxide. Faithfully, every half-hour, I dabbed a few drops on the wound and as it frothed and bubbled repeated after her, "Look at it boil now—boiling out the poison and dirt. So keep boiling away and tomorrow you'll be fine again, fine again—" Deriving assurance from the words, wanting to believe them; and at the same time ashamed of such childish trust, pretending to be only mimicking her.

Until nearly noon, and then I saw them. One about six inches long and two about four, extending up the leg like a fork with broken tines. And as if one of the tines had pricked it, the bubble of elation burst. Blood poisoning: I needed a doctor and the doctor would know it was a bullet wound and as a matter of routine report it to the police. I was sure of that. I had never read or been told that a doctor must report a bullet wound but now, desperately and crazily, I was sure. A holdup, a gun; the chase was on, and they were all my enemies. Dog and rabbit—that kind of fear. A cornered rabbit, no place to run.

There was the impulse. Even a little more. For I remember *returning*, coming *up* the stairs, the clarinet inside my windbreaker. I must have panicked and bolted and then, steadied on the steps perhaps by the cold, retreated.

And back in the room—much later, I think—I remember playing the clarinet again. "Jesus, Lover of My Soul"—sweetly, with feeling; pretending to jeer at myself: *shacked up with a broad, wanted by the police and playing hymns—JESUS is right!*—and at the same time thinking furtively it might help, could at least do no harm, just as earlier, dripping on the peroxide, I had mocked Mad and repeated like a litany the string of her motherly assurances. Not a secret faith, though, beginning to assert itself. Just rabbit desperation. Cornered, no place to run, it tries to climb a tree.

And like a rabbit I could only run. Nothing to fight with; no defences. Cornered. Nothing but to wait till they closed in for the kill.

On the street I had made a getaway, hidden, walked straight, made my way unseen to safety. They didn't know—probably didn't care—and still they had me. Trapped. Hole up and die or turn myself in. Hole up or send for a doctor—hole up or send for the police. Around and around it went—teeth snapped on tail. Doctor or blood poisoning, blood poisoning or the police.

Better hole up and get it over with. Because it would be over anyway. I had messed things up enough already. With a jail sentence thrown in—

Only she, of course, wouldn't let me. In a sudden, crazy rage I seized a glass and hurled it at her. Goddamned interfering bitch—she'd do it her way. Put me in jail for a few years like a chicken on ice—suit her fine. Every visiting day bring me cigarettes to show her devotion and be waiting when I got out with her legs spread and a nice clean friendly little restaurant ... Crooked doctors doing jobs for Cora and her whoring friends—suit them fine too to turn me in. One good turn deserves another—so when they're caught with their own hands dirty—

And the pain now, purring like a motor, driving me. Nowhere to run, and driving me. Pacing—the pain squelching up every time I brought my foot down as if I had stepped into a puddle of it, and yet pacing. Foot and teeth—a grinding itch in the teeth to bite it out, like a weasel in a trap trying to gnaw off its leg—

And then talking to Mrs. Painter and coming back up the stairs a second time. Why was I limping? I had slipped on the step and sprained my ankle. Where was I going now with my clarinet? To see about a job—not to hock it ....

But my foot hurt too much—I wouldn't go now till tomorrow .... Thanks but I'd already been rubbing on liniment and it was time to practise. She'd been listening to "Jesus, Lover of My Soul" and she wished my mother could have heard me. Montreal was a wicked city, but the good seed had been sown. Just get rid of that woman and keep clean—

"Because I can't *trust* my legs, understand? Some day there'll be the smell of her and not knowing how I'll be up there. And I don't want to catch you. I'm going to have a lot of time now for remembering and I want to be able to say well anyway there was the one that played the clarinet."

Clear and formidable a moment—a finger drawn across a steamy window pane—and then the room, the pacing and the pain again. Cursing Mad for interfering and not letting me make an end of it and cursing her for staying away so long just when I needed her.

She was very strong when she came and very frightened. That was clear too: how her face changed at the sight of my foot, as if she had gulped a drug.

"All right—into bed so you can rest properly. Didn't I tell you you weren't to go walking around?"

And I obeyed, frightened in turn by the sudden, sucked-out vacancy of her face and at the same time assured by the scolding authority. I lay meek and vaguely guilty while she bathed my foot again and yet all the time—as if outside myself, just looking on, uninvolved—kept thinking how the fear in her face made it old and drawn, how the anxious lines ironically spelled defeat, destroyed the bloom and bounce that were her only assets. And suddenly and idiotically I laughed out loud. Up against a right one like me with nothing but devotion? As much chance of making it as of finding a pocketful of her hundred-dollar bills.

"Stay there nice and quiet now till I get back. Your foot's got worse and we can't take chances. But we're not going to take any other kind of chances either .... It's a promise. First here's more aspirins and then try to get some sleep."

The pain that had kept me pacing now slowly turned the room. Mad came and went, fluid and lopsided like a reflection in a rippled glass. She held my hand a moment after I had swallowed the aspirin, and as the room carried her away my arm stretched out to follow her with elastic, painless ease; then, as if the air were being let out of it, slipped back compact and firm to normal size. I brought my other hand over to make sure it wasn't out of joint or kinked and she said, "Promise now you'll stay there. I mean if you start getting funny ideas—just say to yourself you're sick and not supposed to mind."

The room kept turning after she had gone, but I lay steady as its centre like an eye floating in a pool of pain and clarity. If it were all over when she came back—that would be the best thing, the kindest. Because it wasn't going to last much longer anyway; and if instead of running out I simply died on her, she would at least have a good memory. Which would be important to her. She was the kind. Important because now, good or bad, the memory would be there. She had said it to herself; she was never going to be rid of me. Good or bad, I would go up and down the streets with her, footsteps beating out in unison, "Sonny and Mad—they got a nice swing—Sonny and Mad—just like it was intended—"

The words went on interminably, in time with the throbbing in my foot. The pain kept putting out the light—after a while began shaking the house and hammering in the basement.

And then I understood: they were starting to tear it down. Of course—Mrs. Painter knew what was going on; now it was time to get even. Start at the bottom instead of the top, she had told them. That way they'll be trapped. No stairs—no way out. No heat—nothing to eat. She'd laugh and croak, "That'll teach them. They'll get a bellyful of each other now."

Mad, though, wasn't here yet—maybe there was time. If I could get to the stairs before she came and warn her—

31

I HAD JUST STARTED DOWN THE STAIRS when she appeared with a strange man behind her and I remember yelling at them to stay where they were and then starting to float again, back in bed, at peace and painless, while the stranger told Mad I should be in hospital and in the morning he would have to see.

Not more than twenty-six or –seven, with light sandy hair and a trim, conformist crew-cut, shrewd blue eyes and a professional, master-of-the-situation way of pulling in the corners of his mouth. His neck was thick and white, with pale yellow freckles. Another five years, I decided, he would be fat.

This was in the morning. The next morning, or the morning after. For there was another blur. I may have lost a day.

"Coming along fine. Better than I expected."

A dry, grudging voice, as if speech of any kind were a concession, professionally not quite ethical; but watching him as he palped my foot and calf, the quick flick of his eyes towards Mad, who was standing respectfully a few feet away, I understood it was costing him an effort. He would have liked to drop the front, to ask questions. Probably a well brought-up young man from a proper home who hadn't seen much of this. The room, the blonde, the bullet—LIFE in block letters.

The resolutely blank look as he kept taking it in gave him away.

So far as the wound was concerned—that only a bullet could have made—I trusted him. Instantly: it was a decent face, an honorable crew-cut. Not the hounding kind. *Give the poor bastard a break*—it hung from him like a price tag. Broad-minded, tolerant—and yet I scented danger. Impressed by what he saw—by *us*—suppose he talked? Added touches? It was a set-up, an event, that you didn't run into every day. And supposing someone listening had a sterner sense of social responsibility?

"Yours?"

The voice was quick and crisp, carefully impersonal, and I looked at him stupidly, not having followed his glance.

"The clarinet? You play?"

Worse: bullet, blonde, and clarinet—by tomorrow he would have told a dozen. And panicking again, all my own fronts down, I licked for silence and a getaway. My foot was coming along; I still had a sick mind.

"It's mine—I don't know for how long. Or at least I don't know how long I'll be playing it." A little hitch to one shoulder; a mock-rueful pull to my mouth. "Even if they let me take it with me—some of my cellmates might object, to say nothing of the guards. Unless, of course, I land in a progressive place where they let me start a band. Maybe you could recommend me."

Right down to his boots. A good job, too: he caught it and responded.

"No use looking on the black side." A vague, slightly embarrassed smile; an aimless hand. "How about the other fellow? What shape's his foot in?"

"Fine—at least when I got outside he wasn't far behind. Lungs in pretty fair shape too—judging by the yells."

He glanced cautiously at Mad, then busied himself with tape and scissors. "Nobody got hurt then except you?"

"His feelings maybe. I seem to remember a reproachful look."

"Then just take it easy for a day or two .... I'll look in again in the morning."

"You mean it's all right to take it easy? Nothing to worry about?" I wanted it explicit. I was afraid of the day and night ahead when I would lie wondering.

"You've been lucky." He smiled again, probably amused to see me scared of being turned in when he himself hadn't thought of it. "Practically back where you started. In the old days there'd have been all kinds of complications."

Then with a glance at his watch he snapped open his case and began putting things away. "Better keep off your feet .... Milk and fruit juice—"

And to Mad, abruptly, over his shoulder, "You heard? See he stays quiet, lots of sleep. Two of these pills at noon and another two at bedtime—"

It was a perfunctory instruction, hardly calling for a reply, but the lack of acknowledgement, the complete silence, made us both turn to look at her. And we were just in time to see face curl and wrinkle like a bit of paper that you've put a match to, then collapse into sobs and streaming tears.

"I was so scared, Sonny—thought I was going to lose you sure—" She put a hand to her mouth and stood staring at us a moment with brimming eyes, then slumped onto a chair.

"Well, try and keep it to yourself for a while. I want him quiet ... and don't forget the pills."

Impatience, embarrassment: he made a feint of looking at my foot again, then dropped the sheet back over it and strode to the door. "Nothing to worry about." Another smile, another vague movement of his hand—assurance and good fellowship and bewilderment all mingled—and then he vanished.

"So scared, Sonny—if you knew the way you were yelling and trying to crawl down the stairs." As soon as he was gone she dropped to her knees beside the bed and clutched my hand. The terrible time she'd had finding him—Cora scared of getting mixed up in something and clamming up on her— trust Cape Breton at a time like this to play it safe!—everybody saying why don't you send for an ambulance. "And then this one when I did find him not being sure he'd mind his own business like I promised .... Leaving you alone so long and wondering what you might do—"

I shut my eyes and turned away. Kneading and worrying my hand, sniffling tears—didn't she know I'd been scared too? A hundred times scareder? And that the one thing now I needed was to be alone? For suddenly released from the fear I was like a deep-sea fish that has been hauled too quickly to the surface. Soft, broken, blubbery—didn't she know she wasn't supposed to see?

Perhaps: for after a minute or two, as if reconnoitring, suspecting she was out of bounds, she withdrew and straightened, gave a self-conscious hitch to her dress and brought a glass of milk. "Milk and juice he said but he didn't look how skinny you are. So tonight it's going to be the thickest steak you ever saw—with mushrooms."

But too late. She had been there, had caught and seen me—been in on it—and I lay back sicking the dogs on her.

32

"NOBODY LOOKING AFTER YOU this morning? Lost your nurse?"

More curious than concerned, even though he said it while examining my foot. I was coming along; a nurse now didn't matter. When he looked up he had the expression of a fourteen-year-old outside a movie-house with an "Adults Only" sign.

"You mean Mad? She's gone to work—leaves about half-past eight. The last few days she's been here on account of me."

"Oh." His face fell slightly—a short-changed look. He had succeeded in getting into the movie only to discover the girls all wore brassieres. "A nice head of hair and it looks natural. German maybe? Swede?"

"She's from Nova Scotia—I don't think they have Swedes or Germans there. She's never said."

"You're from Nova Scotia too?"

"The other way—Saskatchewan."

There was a satisfaction in sidestepping his curiosity, making him work for it, but there was also an impulse, almost an anxiety, to disassociate myself, make clear the extent of our relationship.

"I don't know much about her. We met in a club—over a beer. We were both broke, but I had a couple of beers up here so she came along .... That was three weeks ago—been looking after me ever since."

"Some people are born lucky." He clucked, tilted his head appreciatively and made a slight movement with his hands, as if he saw her spread before him on a table, waiting for an examination. "Nobody like that ever wants to come home and look after me."

"You could find worse." He gave me a cigarette and I drew on it a few times in silence. Man to man now, members of the same fraternity, faintly and companionably competitive. "Big-hearted and a lot to give."

And then, a little shamefacedly, wiping the leer off my voice, "Too much, in fact. Too big-hearted. She was supposed to stay for just one night."

"And you're complaining?"

"Meals, cigarettes, pocket money—what does it make me? Taking it easy while she's out working—"

He pursed his lips and watched me clinically. "I imagine it would take more than three weeks to make you anything very different from what you are."

"Right—but this way you start to see yourself—"

"And the damage to the image was enough to make you step out on a little shooting-match?" The eyes were cold now, speculative, as if I too were a patient brought in for an examination. "I'm just assuming of course that there was a shooting-match and that she had something to do with it."

"Something. I remember thinking I'd give her a couple of hundred and that would be the end of it. But of course I wanted a couple of hundred or so for myself too. One stone for several birds."

"And the score?"

"Not a feather. There were two of us—partners. I haven't seen him since and it's not likely now I ever will."

A brief smile, faintly scornful. Would it have been different, I wondered, if the score had been good? "And the lady—was she in on your little adventure?"

"If she'd known she'd have made sure I wasn't in on it either. It's hard to explain but she's got her own ideas—very definite—and sometimes she can be very firm."

"Incidentally, I'm not the right doctor." Now it was his turn to disassociate himself. Interrupting curtly, standing up, he drew a bit of paper from his pocket and studied it a moment. No need to explain. Our sleazy little world was no concern of his. Not in the least interested in my bed-mate's moral standards. "The *SOS* was relayed. She'd got a name somewhere, but he'd been called on an emergency and the man *he* suggested had the 'flu. I must have been five or six on the list and just having got over the 'flu myself I didn't have much resistance."

"I owe you my life then. Thanks."

"Better thank the lady. As you say, she can be very determined. Usually we send an ambulance."

He glanced around the room, self-conscious, on the point of going, then nodded towards the clarinet. "Getting in your practice? This ought to be good weather for it."

"An hour yesterday. Fifteen minutes before you came. I miss the applause."

"I used to play the clarinet too—at least make noises." Interested: trying to make it up to me. "Mostly the sax, though. Weekends—the first two years in Montreal it kept me eating."

He picked up the clarinet and held it reminiscently a moment, then handed it to me and sat down again. "I've a few minutes before I go back to the hospital. Let's hear something now."

Friendly again—sorry. Tell the poor bastard he's good—help him keep his illusions. Till he's out of this mess, anyway.

It stung a little and I rose to it—played well. Defiant, cool. A feeling of rivalry, a spurt of will.

First a bit of slow Bach—just in case he understood such things. Then—not too much of that, in case he didn't—all the easy, showy things that might impress him if he were the naïve type, trills and fluttery arpeggios; and finally, after a modest meditative little meander, just to show I could be introspective, too, a popular blues tune, competent and smooth.

"I don't understand." His forehead wrinkled. His tongue wet his lips.

"Living like this—no work—" In the spread of his hands he catalogued it all, Mad, the holdup, the room. "Something go wrong? Don't you *want* to play?"

I shrugged, rubbed my knuckles in my eyes and began to like him. "I don't understand either. I said to myself it's time Montreal had a good clarinetist so why not be big-hearted. But they're a funny lot—shy about accepting favours."

"Seriously—"

"Usually I blame my feet. Too big: always a spectacle, not an audition. Maybe I ought to go out and find somebody to take a shot at the other one .... But only in Montreal. At home, where I had my own little band, they were nice neat feet. A fairly respectable size and only two of them."

"Once they hear you, though—nerves or not, some of it must come through."

"Let's blame Main Street—it's got pretty broad shoulders. Wanting to make it in the big time and scared I'm not good enough, don't belong. And that goddammed little band of my own—used to giving the orders—snotty. I had a couple of fair breaks in Toronto and walked out on them. They let me go .... Montreal's been rough—no breaks at all—"

"It shouldn't be that rough." He stood up and scratched his head and then sat down again. "There aren't that many clarinets around—good ones."

"Good or bad doesn't seem to make much difference. Most of the time it seems they want a guitar. Or if they're interested in the clarinet it's got to be saxophone too— both—"

"That's right—you usually double."

"And after being turned down, of course, there's nothing like a good shot of something to set you up again. Two or three shots—the habit grows. Until you haven't got the price of another and just curl up and take it .... There's a week back somewhere in October, just after I got here, that's a blank. And my last hundred dollars and most of my clothes went with it."

He hesitated a moment, circled back tactfully to the saxophone. "It wouldn't take you long—a month, six weeks. At least well enough to get by on, pick up a job—"

"Six weeks and a saxophone."

"I know somebody in Montreal who has his own band too—and I don't think he'd ask for a guitar." He fidgeted a moment, went to the window and stood looking out. "I never played with him but he used to put in a good word for me—introductions along with what you might call his blessing. Without him, I probably wouldn't have eaten."

"The musicians I've known never went in much for blessings. Handier with the knife."

"He can use it too when it suits him .... Just happened to take an interest because I had some problems and was working my way through medical school. I suppose you'd call it a sentimental streak. He'd had his own problems—"

"And you think he might be touched by the story of a raw youth from the prairie practising his clarinet among the cows and chickens and then going wrong in the big city?"

"No predictions—I'd just like him to hear you. And the sentimental streak, incidentally, doesn't go all the way round. When it's somebody for his own band he's one hundred per cent professional .... Besides, who says you've gone wrong?"

I sat back, biting my lip. He said quickly, "Is there a phone downstairs? Give me the number and I'll call you when I get in touch with him. Or maybe drop over. I can't say when, but I won't forget."

At the door he turned. "And about the saxophone—you might as well get started on mine—it hasn't been out of its case for the last three or four years. This weekend, maybe .... And then I'll make a deal—sell it to you for twice what I paid."

The door closed on him and because I didn't dare believe a word of it I took up the clarinet. Didn't dare, didn't deign. To believe would be to hope again, and all at once I was too big a coward. Waiting for the telephone and a call from Mrs.

Painter—hovering in the hall so as not to miss her, afraid to step outside—the knots in my belly every day a little tighter .... No—as I played I made a leap and soared over him, straight to the big-time Sonny, the lights and the applause. An old trick—an escape hatch I had discovered riding Isabel. The long empty hours and the long empty miles—you soared in desperation, dreamed in defiance of the monotony. And if you were going to soar, why not do it right, with style, a flourish? Why hedgehop over ways and means?

In the old days, of course, it had been a different kind of applause, for a different kind of performance; and now, even as I played and soared, there was a taste of bitterness and guilt to remind me.

33

TWO OR THREE MORE DAYS; then it was Saturday night again and we went to a movie.

Mad insisted. My foot was coming along fine and it was only a step down to St. Catherine Street and after everything that had happened I needed something to make me forget.

"Forget? There'd be a couple of cops come in to see the show too—take seats right behind us."

"Just a couple? Big-time gangster like you? Five thousand dollar reward—"

"Give me another week—you and Cora go."

"Who wants to go with Cora? Besides, you *will* forget— it's a funny movie. Shutting yourself up here alone all day like you'd done something—first thing you know you'll end up sick."

"Done something?" I thrust out my foot. "I didn't get this, you know, stepping on a tack."

"Doesn't matter—you were just doing what he told you. Say in a restaurant every so often they slip in a couple of cats instead of chickens—does it make *me* a criminal if I bring the customer a plate of poor-old-Tommy-in-a-basket?"

Deadly serious; voice ringing as if she were counsel for the defense. "And slipping a few things into Charlie's sack doesn't make you one either. Didn't even split with you. Stealing *and* not paying his help."

"Maybe we'd better go to the movie."

"Sure we'd better go to the movie. That's what's wrong with the people in this town—never laugh, just go nosing round for chances. Fast buck, easy lay. Back home now—"

Into her coat—a flourish of lipstick as she turned to the mirror—"Back home now we were laughing all the time. Lots of trouble—lots of fun. Whooping it up—that's Nova Scotia. I've seen it when we couldn't find anything else to do we'd throw potatoes."

"Raw ones?"

"You think we'd take time to peel and boil them?"

"Remember I've never been to Nova Scotia .... About the movie, though—since the cat didn't make me laugh—"

"The cat wasn't supposed to make you laugh. It was just to show you why you don't need to feel in the same class as a lowdown heel like Charlie."

"Thanks for the clean sheet. I feel a lot better."

"Just listen to you: Sour like that all the time first thing you'll be playing sour too. And then it'll take a lot more than a movie."

On the street there was another explanation. "This movie's been on a couple of weeks now and it's better you see it for yourself. Me telling you wouldn't be the same. They might trip you. Just in case."

"Just in case what?"

"In case they catch Charlie and he squeals. You weren't out with him that night. You were with me—at a movie—and then I went back with you and stayed all night."

She gripped my arm hard and strode a little faster. "I'll swear it and you'll swear it and our word's as good as his any day. What movie, they'll say, and you'll be able to tell them all about it—so it sounds natural."

"And my foot—we're going to swear that away too?"

"Never mind—we'll come up with something. It's healing fast anyway. A few more days you can say you had a boil."

"Not on the *heel*, Mad—they're for the neck."

"Lots of places you can have them. What you need's a good laugh anyway."

It wasn't a very funny movie. She laughed for both of us, and after rustling her way through a bag of popcorn took my hand and cuddled it possessively against her thigh. Possessively, contented, as if things were all settled between us, as if she had the right.

Twice, with careful nonchalance, I withdrew my hand, first to bring out my handkerchief, then to scratch my neck, and both times she reached for it again, absently, without taking her eyes off the screen, as you would reach to catch a blanket slipping off the bed.

The picture was no help. It had a band with a bright, sleek young band leader; gleaming sets of clubs and pools and beaches; a cast of sport cars and expensive girls. Morosely I matched myself against it—seedy, outcast, broke.

"I'll bet you'll be in a movie too someday," she said stoutly as we reached the street, "and I'll go round saying sure I used to know him way back when. That fellow in there tonight—who'd lie awake at night thinking about having a time with him?"

On the way home she drew me into a snackbar for coffee and hamburgers. There was a faint saucer-ring on the counter—so faint I didn't see it—and when the girl came for our orders she put her finger on it reprovingly.

A cloth slithered in front of us.

"That's help for you—moving like she had a hangover. Look at the place—half empty and right down town with the street full of hungry people. Just makes me itch."

"Your place it would be different?"

"I'd be talking to people, seeing to it everything was quick and clean. Just look at the face on her—like she wished we'd drop dead."

"That's what I'd wish if I had her job."

"No, Sonny—when you're running a restaurant the customers come first—"

"Who'd want to run one? People like us coming in and telling you to wipe the counter—"

"I only say if you do it right there's money to be made—"

"What's my job to be? Mopping the floor? Making french fries?"

Immobile a second or two as she bit into her hamburger, fingers contracted, head forward—and then she met it with a head-on laugh. "Fine french fries you'd make—we'd lose business fast. No—maybe stand you on the counter with your tooter—find somebody for the french fries that's got a drum—"

Still holding the hamburger, she took a small sip of coffee. "Sure, Sonny—all kinds of things if things were different .... You know something? I wouldn't be surprised by the taste of it if there was cat in *this* hamburger."

Curling her nose, she pushed away her plate and then with a toss of her hair began to laugh. "How'd you like that for a job? Catching cats? Sure—you and your tooter walking along the street with a dozen or so trailing after. Back in school we had a story about a fellow catching rats that way."

The voice went out abruptly in another sip of coffee, like a match dropped into water. For a moment I thought she was going to cry but instead, rallying, laughing again, she swung round on the stool and slapped my knee. "You know Sonny what we need tonight's a drink. A good stiff one to start ringing bells. We've got it coming."

"Some other time." I took her hand and then, self-consciously, let it go. She held it suspended in front of her a moment as if it had been taken with a sudden cramp. "I think I see a plainclothes dick outside right now—and if we go to a bar there'll be a dozen. Trailing along like the cats."

"That's right—no sense pushing your luck. Me, I'm not what you'd call a very good drinker anyway. Never a nice high feeling—just a big head."

"One of these nights just the same we'll tie on a real one. The doctor you brought—he used to play in a band himself and he knows somebody. Maybe things are picking up."

"See what I mean!" Her voice shot up and she clapped her hands. "Somebody like you they just *can't* keep down. Come on—we got to celebrate. Tonight—and we don't need drinks to help us either."

34

It wasn't a very good celebration—one time a little liquor might have helped—and when it was over, turning away from her, I let my indifference show. Why spin things out? Trying not to hurt her now in the long run only meant hurting her that much more. No use telling her I was a wrong "right one." Time to play a little rough—let her see.

I woke through the night and she was standing at the window.

"A pack of drunks," she explained when she heard me stir. "Running and yelling like somebody was getting killed. You didn't hear them?"

"Just woke up. Sounds quiet enough now."

"There was a car. I think they all got in and drove away."

She spoke without turning, her forehead pressed against the window as if she was still trying to see what was happening in the street. Her hair was shining in the light from the street lamp; her profile—chin and nose, with bruises of black for eyes and nostrils—had a waxy, pallid look again, as if an old mannequin had been touched up and given a new wig.

"You know I was just standing here looking at the tree and thinking what a shame. Such a nice big one and they'll have to cut it down."

She paused a moment, seeming to wait for me. "Ever look how it goes right across the street and the one on the other side comes over here? Right now they're rubbing away in the wind, giving each other a nice little scratch."

She came back to bed and slipped under the covers carefully, as if I were asleep and she was afraid of waking me. Her feet were cold. I shivered at their touch and jerked mine away. "What's the idea of standing on the bare floor? You feel like you've been there half an hour. First thing you'll be coming down with the 'flu."

"Takes a lot to bring me down, Sonny. All that fish when I was little. Herring choker—same as my old man. Used to make his own home-brew—strong enough to take the paint off, just like turpentine—and lots of times I've seen him down a whole jug of it and never turn a hair."

35

THE NEXT DAY—Sunday; she was home—I stayed in bed
till noon, keeping my back turned as she puttered round the
room on tiptoe, muttering and burrowing my face into the
pillow each time she asked if I wouldn't like a cup of coffee.
The day was going to be long enough. Too long—too many
irritations, too many moments when I would want to snarl,
let fly. I didn't trust myself and it wasn't coming to her.

One of the best—big-hearted, warm. Even tactful, careful
never to remind me she went out to work and buy the steaks
while I slept late and played the clarinet; everything on the
credit side but her headful of damfool ideas about a right one
some day who would last. And at that, not able to tell the
difference: a real right one or a real rat. Not able to understand
that for someone like her there are only rats, just as for a hen
that goes walking across the prairie, there are only hawks
and coyotes.

"No, Mad—just a cup of coffee." I was out of bed finally,
and springing to her feet as if my yawn had touched a spring,
she was telling me what we were going to have for breakfast.
"I don't *want* bacon and eggs. Please—I'm not hungry. Just a
cup of coffee."

"Funny man! Nothing since that hamburger last night
and now he doesn't want his breakfast! Away to the bathroom with you and we'll see."

Good bacon and eggs; a good cup of coffee. Always good; never a word about the old frying pan and coffee pot, how much better she could do if she had a kitchen and a proper stove. Just good bacon and eggs. Just a good cup of coffee.

And of course I ate everything she put in front of me. After twelve hours, of course I was hungry. Of course she was right. Of course she knew me better than I knew myself.

So quiet and steady behind the big bouncy laugh. Patient: a forbearing, almost indulgent look. Just like Charlie—so goddammed *sure* of me. Play him a while. Take it easy and give him a little line. He'll tire.

He'll tire and he'll eat the bacon and eggs and after a while he'll realize that that's what he needs: a good hot breakfast on a cold winter morning and somebody to cook it for him. Oh yes, he's got his fine ideas about himself and the fine things he's going to do with his little tooter, but easy does it. He'll come round. He'll grow up. He's got the makings.

And yet for all that, it somehow wasn't quite the same as other times. A familiar room with something missing; one of the pictures at a tilt. Watching me as I ate, a hand to her hair each time I caught her. Sentences broken and lost, thin chips of laughter. Up and down, forgetting and fetching. Nervous—something on her mind. Or was I just imagining it?

"I'm going to run over to see Cora now .... You'll be all right till suppertime and it'll be a good chance while I'm away to practise."

A difference, too, in the voice: bright, quick, thin. Not quite sure of herself. Uneasily polite. Something different, something wrong.

She reached for a cigarette and struck a match, smiling as if posing for a picture. False. False and guilty. Something up her sleeve.

"A little job she's doing for me—can't put it off any longer. I was planning to go *last* Sunday."

Patting the front of her dress, then her hair again. Still posing. The smile now a curtain: something going on I wasn't supposed to see.

Or maybe just pretending there was something. The eyes shifty—coming back to see how I was taking it.

Well, I was taking it fine. "Good," I said, "don't hurry back on account of me. I always work better when I'm alone."

I yawned and pushed away my cup. Not hostile or ungrateful, just up to my eyes in my own problems, intent on a future in which she couldn't possibly be involved. A hint that she wasn't winning and never would. The best way: a flat voice and a listless glance, as if it had never crossed my mind she didn't know. Best and kindest; a chance for her to save face, withdraw while the withdrawing was good.

For half a minute I held it, time to light a cigarette, tilt back my head and send a puff of smoke towards the ceiling; and then, shrinking from the slapped look, I mumbled it looked like a pretty cold morning and better not go out unless she had to. Maybe I wasn't in the mood for the clarinet anyway.

"No—I've got to pick up some things and pay my rent— she's keeping my room for me—and I know all about practising. Far better when you're alone."

She relaxed a little, smiling knowledgeably. "Back home when I was fifteen or so they put me in a play once—same crazy preacher that had us in the choir so we wouldn't run round getting into trouble with the boys. As if choir practice and an hour in church on Sunday took up *all* our spare time. Bright fellow him."

She liked reminiscing about Nova Scotia and the story took off on its own. This girl who started having a time with the fellow who played the organ—right in the church at that and him married. Sure in the church—caught them in the basement on one of the tables they'd set up for the Thanksgiving supper—"That's right, on the *table*—"

On and on, yet not quite like her other stories. Still something on her mind. Hand cutting through the smoke with an airy little wave, her eyes just touching mine, then slipping past. Something not quite right—not quite Mad—as if she were trying to make an impression.

"Anyway, this play they put on, I had the third biggest part—a couple of real speeches—and it was a case, naturally, of learning them with expression. So away up the shore I'd go and stand on a big flat rock and sort of have a time—you know, let go and work it out, how it sounded best—and I figure that's the way you like it too."

I nodded politely. "What was your play about?"

"Jesus. Of course he wasn't actually *there*—the preacher said it wouldn't be right—but you kept hearing every so often how he was making out."

"And you—how did you make out?"

"Not too bad. Some people even said I was the best."

She fluttered a little, a hand to her hair again, another flourish of her cigarette; nothing to do, though, with her memories of the play. Something up her sleeve—something in the wind. Ready to leave, maybe? Beating me to the draw?

"A lot of things went wrong, of course, and a lot of people went home. Too long and too deep—the preacher wrote it himself and that's what everybody said who sat straight through—too deep for Nova Scotia." She paused a moment, her head to one side, as if considering whether the judgement had been fair. "What made it worse was the supper going on in the basement—in shifts, on account of the crowd. One shift coming up to listen and another going down to eat—"

"And the girl and the organist—this was the same supper?"

"Same *table*—not the same supper."

"Sounds like a lively little place—away ahead of Saskatchewan."

"In a way—looking back." She drew a deep breath, stubbing her cigarette as if poking among the ashes of the town. "Me, of course, I made a mess of things, but before that—when I first started going to dances and away back when I was little and my old man used to take me in the boat—"

She hesitated, looked up. "You'd like it. Only the other day I was saying to myself it would be just the place for Sonny. Everybody so crazy about dancing—you'd have a band going in no time. Right on top—king."

Herself again. Eyes shining, voice firm and warm. Her queen to my king as arm in arm we walked up Main Street, burning off the hurt of the past like the sun burning off an early mist.

"I had that, Mad—more than enough." I tried to speak quietly, gently; not to hurt her, just for the last time to make things clear. "A little town like you're talking about—maybe it's where I belong—my size—but I'm not ready yet to admit it. Maybe in a few years—maybe I'll have learned by then."

"You're the worst one for picking things up wrong. Wasn't talking about your *size*. I just mean for a year or two—time to save a little money, so when you come back you can take your time and look around."

Wide-eyed a moment with appeal, exasperation. Why couldn't I see it too? "Besides, you never know. Just up the shore about twenty miles from home there's one of those big summer hotels. Nice smart band, people coming from the States and everywhere. Chances are you'd get started there."

I hardened again. Not just small-town size—*her* size. All her plans made—all the strings tied on. "In the meantime," I said abruptly, "I'd better do some work right here. Planning to stay away all afternoon?"

"See you about five." The voice wrong again, the smile too bright and big. "We'll have supper and then maybe I'll have to go back. A dress Cora's fixing for me—doesn't fit right around the arms."

She dropped in to see Cora nearly every day, to pick up things she needed and take others back, but usually it was an aside, a word or two to explain why she had to hurry. Why all the sudden fuss about a dress? Had enough? Slipping out?

"Five for sure—have a nice long play." She turned at the door and gave a little wave. Jerky, quick, without smile or eyes, a screen to cover her retreat—almost as if she were afraid I might follow her, were shooing me back.

And then the stairs. Usually she slipped down quietly, close to the wall so the steps wouldn't creak; but this time, even with the door closed behind her, I could hear the reckless clatter of her heels. The last of the house—the last of me! Perhaps she was tired too. Perhaps last night, over the coffee and hamburger, I had finally made it clear that I wasn't interested in her friendly little restaurant. The bit about her home town and the resort hotel—just a final sputter of hope that things might work out after all.

Fine—let her go. Although instead of walking out she might have told me, talked straight. She owed me that much. She was the one who had moved in.

Wrong—not yet. Nylons on a chair, brush and comb and make-up things on the dresser. More likely out scouting, not breaking with me till she was sure. I picked up the clarinet, played a few notes and went back to the window. One of her truck drivers maybe; or somebody Cora had found. Workout, trial run. But if not this one, then another. For along with all the fuss and flutter there had been something steady, firm. Mind made up. The lady knew what she was doing.

I played and sulked, worried and lay staring at the ceiling: the afternoon wore on slowly. Whoever it was, supposing they went to a bar. And talked. Two or three drinks and a slip—something to set him wondering .... For the fear as yet had barely gone under the skin. The slightest touch and it was raw again.

She was late: just a few minutes off six. Up the stairs as noisy and fast as down, bursting with something to tell but holding it in, the smile even brighter than at noon. "Did you think I was never coming? Ran every step of the way—up the stairs too. Cora still hasn't got it right."

"Got what right?" I glanced at her without taking my lips from the clarinet. "The dress—how do you like it?" She flung off her coat and spun round like a little girl ready for a party. "Still not right under the arms but I said I'll let him see it anyway and then come back after supper. What do you think? Maybe too dark?"

"Just fine—suits you. New?"

I put the clarinet down and tried to look interested, half-glad she was back, half-disappointed. The dress was right for her—exactly right. It subdued and contained her and at the same time set off her hair and skin. The dim, ugly room seemed suddenly alight and blazing.

But *back!* Right where we had left off. She not only lit the room, she overwhelmed and scattered it. "Half price, just the other day. Not such a good fit but a real bargain. What do you think? Maybe too plain?"

Plain dark blue with white collar and cuffs. Prim, almost severe, older than old-fashioned—and smiling and starry-eyed again, cheeks flushed from running, yellow hair shining, she had a theatrically virginal look, like a prima donna costumed and made up for the role of an evangelist.

"Fine—doesn't look to me as if it needs fixing."

"It still pulls here, and if I don't get it right it's going to rip .... Way too old for me, Cora says, something you'd put your grandmother in—but I'm not so sure—"

"Just fine—go back and tell Cora she's crazy."

"I thought you'd like it. Plain and good, I said—that's the dress for Sonny." She dropped her eyes again and for a moment stood looking down at herself, shy and demure and at the same time pleased, as if she had been paid a compliment. Then, with another flash of smile—the wrong one again, false, too bright—she whirled round to some packages she had brought with her and tossed onto the table.

"Ham, rolls, salad! Just something quick because I've got to be back at Cora's at half-past six. Lots, though, so you won't be hungry."

Quick, nervous hands, pointless little laugh. "Cora's maybe leaving town for a few days or I could go back tomorrow. Tea or coffee? At least you got to have a good hot drink."

Something in the wind all right—something from which Sonny was being carefully excluded.

"Come along now—ham's nice and lean the way you like it .... Don't mind me—I had coffee and cake with Cora and pretty soon if I don't watch out I'll have to come sideways through the door."

Somehow, though, she seemed small today—small and slim and wary—and her glance went round the room, touching me and away again, with birdlike urgency, as if she were afraid I might spring to the door when she wasn't looking and cut off her escape.

"If you're in a hurry, don't worry about me."

"It's all right—I'm watching the time." She re-arranged the rolls on the plate, put sugar in my tea. "Matter of fact, while you're eating I think I'll wash out a pair of stockings, have them ready for the morning. And while I'm at it I might as well do your socks."

Not because she needed the stockings for the morning; just to keep out of my way. Uneasy, on guard. Trying to keep something from me, afraid to catch my eye. She made a show of examining my socks for holes, then without speaking again slipped out.

Nearly fifteen minutes. When she returned she hung the stockings and socks on the bit of clothesline, carefully straightening heels and toes, then stood still a moment, slowly looking round the room. Missing me again: just the furniture, the walls, the window. As if she were trying to impress them on her memory.

"Well, I'd better be off." She broke the silence finally and bundled up the collar of her coat as if preparing to step into a blizzard. "I won't be late, and we'll go out for coffee and a sandwich .... Maybe I'll even risk a sundae. Maybe I'll *feel* like risking it."

"Take your time. Don't spoil anything on account of me."

But the curtness and shrug were wasted, for at the moment, just as she was about to go, she wheeled suddenly and kissed me on the forehead. A quick, hard, stamped-on kiss—branding a calf on the run; and then, even while the sensation was still there—the spot of puckered warmth—the door closed on her, and I heard the hard, quick click of her heels again on the stairs.

What was *that* for? Poor old Sonny and his big ideas, a drop of pity, the least she could do? Running out and ashamed to look me in the eye? Where? Who? Why couldn't she have told me?

But there wasn't time to think things through. She had barely gone when I had a visitor.

36

"HERE'S THE SAXOPHONE, and tomorrow I'm picking you up at five. Still no promises but he's interested. And even if you're not right for him he knows some other spots .... In the meantime, you might as well see what you can do with this—"

All in a breath and then he, too, was gone. Someone was waiting for him downstairs.

A single breath and a single glance: the food and dishes crowded onto the little table, the milk bottle on the window, her nylons sharing the clothesline with my socks—and as his eyes slipped past me I heard the camera click again.

Before, they had been curious, slightly startled eyes—a clean-cut, crew-cut, decent young fellow stumbling onto a bit of life in the raw—but tonight they had matured a little, moved from surprise and bewilderment to judgement. *So that was the way the other half lived: well, even making allowances, even with a clarinet thrown in, it was a pretty scruffy way ....*

I reached out and yanked down the clothesline, then shamefacedly put it up again. What if he had noticed? Whose life was I living anyway? All the way from Saskatchewan to make the big-time—no puffed up frog in a little Main Street puddle for Sonny—and still hitched to a horse-and-buggy mind.

Fine—only there they were, my socks and her nylons: a fact, on record; and here I stood, framed in them.

Three hours: the saxophone, the clarinet, a dance band on the radio, another cup of coffee—at half-past nine when she burst in again with her big cheery laugh I was still framed in them. Her nylons and my socks: the camera had clicked and that was the picture.

"Those stairs—takes the puff right out of me. Scared you'd be thinking I was lost this time for sure."

I repeated a few notes, corrected a mistake. "Why, is it late?"

"Way after nine. Cora's such a talker—troubles and advice. Once she gets you cornered—"

A little laugh trailed the words. Uneasy and thin, still false. I looked at her again and saw the colour: more than a five-minute walk in the cold could account for. Mouth vivid and hard with lipstick; a touch of greenish shadow round the eyes. Made up as she hadn't been even the night I met her in the club. She took a step towards me, noticing it was a saxophone I was holding, her hand out to touch it, and there was a whiff of beer.

Right the first time. Cora had been fixing more than dress for her.

"Oh Sonny—somebody's been here! You've got a job! *Already!*"

I stood up, and laying the saxophone carefully on the table asked her if Cora had had many visitors. I must have also gone around the table because now there was distance between us. We seemed to have taken up positions, on opposite sides of the room.

"Just me. There was the dress to fix and then she said let's have a cup of coffee."

"Good coffee? Special brand?"

My voice changed, went sour—started grinding forward on its own. There was no calculation, but it seemed that in the same instant I flared and saw my chance.

"Just like I say—we fixed the dress and then she made coffee."

Caught. A slight, glassy rounding of the eyes. A tip of tongue out, wetting nervously, pink-white and clean against the dark red of the lipstick.

Then with a little jerk of the neck, as if she were straightening out a crick, she slipped out of her coat, walked to the closet and put it on a hanger, came back to the exact spot where she had been standing.

Leaning forward slightly. Tongue out again. Hands picking at her skirt as if she were about to give a recitation. Waiting. Next move mine .... Plain blue dress—white collar and cuffs—

It was the dress that put the thud in my forehead. Because it made her intact, gave her identity. Until now she had been just a sprawl of a woman—wanton, overwhelming, all impulse and devotion; but now, encased not so much in the dress as in its simplicity, she seemed suddenly to have gathered herself together, to have withdrawn, taken shape. Different—something that hadn't been there before, a new dimension. Just when she was walking out on me.

"Who was it this time?" I wanted to explode and shake her—goddammed tramp jilting *me*—but my voice came out small and dry. "Another right one? Or a paying customer?" (Did I really believe it? Probably yes—for a second or two—and anger provided the momentum. Then, true or not, it was a chance. Still grinding away behind me were the socks and nylons.)

"*Sonny!*" Her voice, too, was small—alarm-small, as if it were the middle of the night and she had heard the doorknob turn. "You don't mean that—oh no, Sonny—you don't *mean* it!"

"Cora and a dress! Coffee!" By this time, just because I no longer believed it, there was nothing for it but to go on. The accusation had to be justified. I had to build things up, make a case for myself. "The bloody nerve—to stand there and tell me you got painted up like that for Cora!"

"No, Sonny—no!" She teetered a moment, her face sucked away behind the make-up, only the eyes peering out, frantic, twitching, and then sprang and seized my wrists. "You've got it all wrong—there was nobody but Cora—*nobody*. Don't

look at me like that. I can explain. I can, Sonny—everything—
but not yet. Not for a little while—you mustn't ask me—"

"Who's asking?" Jerking my wrists free, I stepped back.
"What you drink and how many beds you climb into's your
business, not mine, but don't come back here afterwards.
This isn't your headquarters."

She crouched a moment, eyes pinned back, knuckles to
her mouth, then sprang again. "Don't Sonny—not now. Don't
spoil it."

The impact of her body staggered me. I felt her nails
through my shirt. "You know there's nobody else. Sure I was
out doing things tonight but not what you're saying. You're
the right one—the only right one. Look at me—you know
I'm not lying. What I was doing tonight was for *us*—getting
things all set—"

"Not for me—I don't want that kind of money. I'll get
along."

Shake her off—once and for all get the door closed on her;
appeal like that what else was there to do? "When I want
you to go whoring for me I'll let you know."

"No, Sonny—*no!*" Scream curdling the sob. Fists hammering
me back flat against the wall. "It's not true—you're the one.
Cora fixed my face tonight but it was on account of you—
because I told her I was slipping and she said going around
looking so miserable like a beat old bag what did I expect.
But it was for you—you—*you*—"

And then silence, abrupt, total, as when the door is slammed
on the howl and batter of a storm. The frantic look flattened
out, went dead and cold. Her eyes held mine a moment,
sucking at them like lips on a wound, then flickered, lost
their focus. I was no longer there. She let go of me as the
jaws of a dog that has been shot let go, then fell back a few
steps, knuckles to her mouth again.

"I'll tell you what I was doing. I'm going now so it doesn't
matter any more but at least I'll tell you. I went to church
tonight—because I didn't know what else to do."

Her voice dropped for a few words, scarcely a whisper,
then came back clear and firm. "I'd tried everything and

everything was wrong, so I thought maybe it would help if I got round to praying. I tried a few times here but it wouldn't go right, and I said to myself it's because I'm not doing it in the right place."

Her eyes shifted back to me a moment, not to see my response, but as eyes might look at a room or street they were seeing for the last time.

"Last night—when you woke up and I was standing at the window—that's what I was doing. But it wouldn't come, I couldn't explain—and because I'd just got out of bed where we'd been having a time together I was sort of ashamed. There was such a lot to explain—about us—about me, and how I got this way—and all at once it came to me that the right place would be church .... I'd tried everything—I didn't know what else to do. I wanted you so much, Sonny, and every day I could feel you slipping farther. No—"

I made a slight movement towards her and she raised a hand, warding me off. "It's over now—I just want to tell you."

Stone eyes, gentle and unrelenting, completely without illusion; and the voice, extinct and white, went on quietly to explain about the dress. She had bought it a week ago—for me, because it was dark and plain—but just as she said it hadn't fitted properly and now she had to have it in a hurry for tonight. So she had spent the afternoon with Cora—that part was true—but the second time she went out she had gone to church.

"There's one up a piece on Sherbrooke—all lights and yellow flowers and a big organ. I was scared when I got to the door and saw everything so fine and a man taking you to your seat just like it was a movie and then I said to myself why not? The best's none too good for Sonny."

Her voice glowed briefly. She still believed it. "But I couldn't pray there either. Just like here—couldn't explain. Nothing but remember—things I didn't want to remember—they just kept pouring in. How I cut them up at home so bad and everything that's happened since—everything right up to you—trying to pray and instead just remembering. And crying—crying my crazy eyes out like I was never going to get stopped—and people round me pretending not to see and giving me hymn books open at the right place when it was time to sing and standing up like I was supposed to and all the time just crying ...."

She broke off a few moments and as if alone in the room went to the table and picked up the clarinet. Then, head up again, "But when it was over, out on the street, I started feeling fine and I said to myself well anyway you've been there. Maybe that'll do for now—and then next Sunday you can try again. Maybe that's what you've got to do—get it all out first and then start over. And first thing I was laughing, right in the street, walking along and thinking if he only knew what's been going on behind his back. That's what I meant when I said I was getting things fixed—a job with a big band and nice clothes and a car—everything."

Her voice glowed again. She held the clarinet against her cheek a moment, then gently laid it down.

"But I had to talk about it to somebody and it wasn't time yet to talk about it to you, so that's why I went back to see Cora. And she said sure everything's going to work out fine, just like you want, only right now you're a terrible sight from all that crying so first thing go dab your eyes and then I'll fix your face for you. Because if you go back looking like that you're going to keep on slipping sure .... And then she said maybe it would pick me up a little if I had a beer."

She shook her head helplessly, contritely. "Why I lied about the beer and said coffee instead I just don't know. I just don't know. Thinking I suppose it didn't sound right after church."

Again I took a step, tried to say something, and again she put up her hand. "No, Sonny—it didn't work and it never will. What you said just now wasn't because you thought I'd been with somebody, but because you've had enough—because it's over."

She reached for her purse and brought out a handkerchief; then, as if telling herself that that couldn't help now either, put it away again. "I knew I wasn't right for you. I knew it would never work out and I shouldn't have tried holding on.

But I couldn't help trying. We kept having such good times together—I thought maybe I could find other ways to make it up to you. And you and Charlie—in a way I was glad that night you went out and got shot, because I thought he'll understand now you can do low and terrible things sometimes and yet not be low and terrible yourself .... But it didn't make any difference because the way we are it couldn't, and praying didn't help because it couldn't either, and I know now and I'll go."

As she finished she was already starting to gather her things together, the nylons and a pair of old slippers she kept on the closet shelf and put on in the evening when her feet were tired, a few jars and bottles on the dresser, a scarf, a sweater, gathering them together and cramming them into the big purse she always carried, her hands quick and resolute as if, suddenly aware of herself and ashamed, she were gathering together the remnants of her pride; and because everything was finished now, not room between us for a syllable, I picked up the clarinet and put it to my lips silently a moment, then went to the window and stood looking out until I heard her open and close the door.

She went quietly this time—no sound at all except the faint slam of the street door—but for a long time, streets and days, I heard the footsteps. "Sonny and Mad—they got a nice swing. Listen now—sort of go together. Sonny and Mad—Sonny and Mad—just like it was intended."